At one time he thought of him that's the only word anyone him. First Father, then that horrible hunchback he was forced to hang from the rafters of his cell, then that wicked old man in the lab coat, then the heartless undead woman who was to be his, then....

Then Ygor.

When the sister asked him for a name, he chose "Ygor." It was the only name he knew. Old Ygor had claimed to be his friend. But he knew that wasn't true now. The man with the broken neck had just wanted to use him, like all the others had wanted to use him....

He had done such horrible things for Ygor. Yes, he understood that now. The victims still haunted him, their lifeless faces, the crimes he had committed with his own hands.

Not *these* hands—the old ones.

BELA LUGOSI'S DEAD

BY ROBERT GUFFEY

To Alan,

Robert Guffey

3-18-21

MACABRE Ink

Dedicated To
Forgotten Films & Forgotten People

His only 2
last friends in life, this impossibly
hard life no matter under what
conditions it appears, were Bela
Lugosi & Boris Karloff, who visited
him annually in his room on 3rd Street
& cut thru the fogs of evening with
their heads bent as the bells of St Simon
tolled a heartbroken "Kathleen" across
the rooftops of old hotels where similar old
men like Doctor Sax sat bent headed
on beds of woe with prayerbeads between
their feet, Oh moaning, homes for
lost pigeons or time's immemorial
white dove
of the roses
of the unborn
astonished bliss

—Jack Kerouac, "Pome on Doctor Sax," 1961

I.

He met her at the grave.

A last-minute detour before surrendering to the inevitable—at least that's how he'd seen it at the time. The cemetery was not far from the LAX airport, so Mike decided to stop off there before boarding the plane back to his little bedroom in his mother's house in Snoqualmie, Washington. Where all his old friends would laugh at him for failing to live up to his prideful boasts.

The cemetery was one of the first places he visited upon arriving in L.A. two years earlier in 1984. He'd read about it his whole life. It was the final resting place of the man who had started him on his path of wanting—somehow, some way—to be a filmmaker. Lot number 120, Space number 1 contained the grave of Béla Ferenc Dezsö Blaskó, otherwise known as Bela Lugosi.

Count Dracula, Chandu the Magician, Armand Tesla, Dr. Varnoff, on and on. He had memorized the names of Bela's various characters over the years, back when he used to stay up well past midnight to watch the latest creepshow re-run of scratchy old black and white films made long before Mike had even been conceived.

He took a taxi from his apartment building on Yucca and Wilcox in Los Angeles to Holy Cross Cemetery in Culver City, walked up the small hill toward The Grotto, a beatific area framed by eucalyptus trees located just beyond the front gates. He set down his battered, overstuffed suitcase (which was held together with frayed twine because the locks had broken off long ago) and approached grave #120. He stood over the tombstone on that overcast morning, staring down at the little trinkets that fans had left behind for their undead hero: a black cigar, a rubber bat attached to a string, a chocolate donut with orange sprinkles, a little raven and a little black cat carved out of wood, a book of metaphysical poetry by Manly P. Hall, even a hand-scrawled note on blue lined paper addressed to Bela personally. Mike knelt down beside the grave, opened the note, and read it.

Dear Mr. Lugosi,

Though you were dead long before I was born, you are not forgotten. I know you suffered so much tragedy and hardship in your life; however, a man should be judged not by the pain he experienced in his lifetime, but by the effect he had on others. I've watched all your movies since I was a kid. I spent so much of my childhood stuck in bed watching your shadow creep across my television screen. Your films helped me make friends with the darkness. I learned from you not to fear nightmares. I learned that while humans are often something to loathe, monsters rarely are. And that death is impermanent.

You made a career playing so many different forms of the Devil, but I trust your spirit is now hovering with the angels. Good night, Prince of Darkness. Good night, Count. Good night, Bela. Have a cigar on me...your loyal friend....

The note was unsigned.

Mike wished he knew where he could find this person. A kindred soul somewhere out there in L.A. But making such a meaningful contact at this point would be almost impossible. The cliché was true and inescapable: This town could kill you. Look what it did to Bela. But at least Bela had a chance to leave his mark on the world. Mike hadn't even gotten started, and it was already over.

He felt another migraine coming on. For once, he'd forgotten to bring Tylenol with him when leaving his apartment. He wished he could just ignore the mounting pain.

Old Ygor awoke in a prison cell. It wasn't the first time.

Pain wracked his entire body. It felt as if he'd survived

beating upon shooting upon hanging upon torture upon beating. His whole life had been spent in this way: surviving what others could not.

He moaned as he forced himself to sit up on the splintered wooden bench beneath him. His head…swimming….

He planted his boots on the cobblestone floor, but still the blurriness plagued his vision. Panic swept through him. Was he going blind again?

The thought struck him as odd.

Blind? When the hell had he ever been…?

Mike glanced up, suddenly aware of someone else's presence. About fifty feet away. A young woman. Her profile faced him. Quite attractive, in a unique way. She didn't look like she was from Southern California at all. He couldn't quite pin her down. Caucasian? Italian? Persian? She was probably in her early twenties. She had straight black hair that hung down to the middle of her back. A long, smooth neck; naturally dark skin; a petite, ballerina's body. She was dressed in a flowing black gown, black fishnet stockings, and bright blue combat boots.

The wind was quite strong now and blew her hair across her face. She clutched a bouquet of yellow flowers in her hands. Black-eyed susans.

He had the urge to talk to her.

She was probably having a quiet moment with a dead relative—perhaps her father, her mother—and here he was ogling her. Certainly not the best time to approach a girl with a pick-up line. Besides, Mike didn't have any pick-up lines. He hadn't had sex with anyone since arriving in Los Angeles. On those rare occasions when he spoke on the phone with old friends back in Snoqualmie, they didn't believe him at all when he told them this. They didn't think it was possible. They thought Hollywood was some city-wide bordello of sin where you could pluck women out of a crowd and have sex with them on the street corner. He just gave up trying to convince them otherwise. Besides, it was sort of fun having them believe he was getting action every weekend with something other than his defective electric typewriter.

There were moments in Mike's life when he managed to shake off the psychic leash that prevented most human beings from taking a chance and being impulsive. Every time he ignored that little voice that told him, "Don't do it, you'll look like a fool," he never regretted it. One of those times was when he hitchhiked to Los Angeles. Another was when he started talking to Cynthia in his journalism class in high school. And Cynthia soon became his first (and only) girlfriend.

Why not? he thought. What did he have to lose? He was leaving town soon anyway. It's not like this could go anywhere.

He rose to his feet, the anonymous note still in his grip, and walked over to the girl. He glanced around. There seemed to be no one else in the entire graveyard. It was so peaceful and silent here.

From a few feet away, he was able to see the name on the gravestone in front of which the girl stood so respectfully. It was a name one didn't forget: SHARON TATE.

And her unborn child.

Was this person somehow related to Tate? For a moment Mike considered backing away, but then she turned and saw him. Her brown eyes widened, as if startled by his presence. The wind blew her hair in front of her face again. She brushed away the strands of hair and said, "Am I...am I in the way?"

"In the way?" Mike was suddenly confused and wished he had not approached her. "What do you mean?"

"Of the grave," the woman clarified, pointing downward. "I mean, are you here to see...the grave?"

"Oh, no," Mike said. "I came to...." He jerked his thumb over his shoulder. He felt embarrassed. What the fuck was he doing here? Was this the last desperate gesture of an obsessed fan?

"I came to see Bela Lugosi's grave," Mike said. "I guess for...inspiration. Apparently other people had the same idea. Someone even left a note for him." He realized he still held the note in his hand. He lifted it up and showed it to her.

One of her eyebrows arched upward in curiosity. "Do you often steal notes off people's graves?"

Mike laughed. "No, not often. I'm not keeping it. I was planning on putting it back."

"Bela Lugosi's grave, did you say?"

Mike nodded.

"I didn't realize he was buried here."

"Right over there," Mike said, pointing at the only grave that boasted such colorful gifts.

The woman laughed slightly. "I should've known. The bats. It's funny how close the two graves are. Not that they had anything to do with each other. Sharon Tate and Bela Lugosi, I mean. Except for the fact that they were both actors who came to tragic ends."

"They both played vampires," Mike added.

"Really?" the woman said. "Sharon played a vampire?"

"Oh, sure," Mike said, moving closer to her. A car drove past on the nearby street that wound its way deep into the graveyard. For some reason Mike grew nervous the second he saw it. Just before entering the gate he thought, *What if I pick the exact day that one of Lugosi's relatives drops in for a visit?* It would be embarrassing somehow if Bela Lugosi Jr. happened to see this film geek kneeling in front of his father's grave. How could he not come off as a freak?

Is that how he came off to this woman? He hoped not. After all, was she not doing the same thing as him? "Sharon played a vampire in *The Fearless Vampire Killers*," he said, "which was directed by Roman Polanski—you know, Sharon's husband." Mike called her "Sharon" only because this woman had done the same.

"Oh, I haven't seen that one," the woman said. "I guess I'll have to now. You recommend it?"

"I mean…it's not exactly my cup of tea, but it's worth watching. Sure. There's a wonderful scene in the film involving a masquerade ball and a wall-length mirror…. I didn't know you hadn't seen it. It's too bad, I guess. I gave away the ending."

The woman laughed. "That's okay. I wouldn't be watching it for *fun*."

Mike was puzzled. He drew closer to her. "Who doesn't watch movies for fun?"

She laughed again. It was a beautiful laugh. "I need to study her. I'm going to play her."

It took Mike a few seconds to realize what she meant. "Play her? Oh. You're going to *be* Sharon Tate. In a film?"

She shrugged. "Just a student film. Some friends of mine at UCLA are directing this short little thing and want me to play Sharon. They're even *paying* me, which is nice. So, I've been doing research. I decided to come out here. I don't know…I guess it's sort of a pilgrimage?" She laughed. "I'm not very religious, except when it comes to film. I guess that sounds stupid."

"Oh, no, not at all. I understand exactly what you mean. I'm sort of making a pilgrimage myself." He gestured toward Bela's grave once more.

"You're an actor?" the woman asked.

Now it was Mike's turn to laugh. "Not a very good one, I'm afraid. I'm a writer. A *screen*writer."

She grew very excited now and took a few steps down the grassy hill toward where he stood. "Yeah? Have you had them produced? Your scripts, I mean?"

"Well, not yet. I've written three screenplays so far, but I haven't managed to get an agent yet." He thought that sounded rather unimpressive, though he couldn't tell by the woman's impassive expression, so he added quickly, "But I *am* a published writer. I've published a few short stories here and there. Just in little literary journals, you know. They didn't pay much. But the exposure's important." He'd only sold two short stories, one during his last year in high school, the other just after he arrived in L.A. For one story he received about twenty bucks' worth of contributor's copies, and for the other he got a check for sixty dollars. That last one hadn't even been published yet. They were horror stories.

"Well, you have to start somewhere," the woman said. She shrugged. A simple gesture, and yet this woman pulled it off with such grace. "Like me. I've only done a couple of commercials, but I keep plugging away at it. I'm not going to give up."

"You shouldn't. No one should ever give up on a dream." God, he thought, that must've sounded lame.

"I'm hoping this little film leads to something better," she said. "Chad's really talented. The director. He's a friend of an ex-boyfriend. That's how I know him. Do you think I look like her?"

At that exact moment, Mike had been thinking about how little this woman looked like Sharon Tate. For a moment he considered saying, "Yes, very much! I can see why they picked you." But instead he heard himself saying, "You know, it's funny...forgive me for saying this. I don't mean to be offensive in any way. I mean, you're very beautiful. And, really, in a way, you're *more* beautiful than her, but, um...no. Not at all."

She smiled. "That's what *I* told them! But Chad says I can pull it off. I'm a little worried about it."

"Are they going to give you a wig?" Was that a dumb question?

"Yes. And the film's in black and white, so that helps."

"Ah, that's a totally different story. Orson Welles once said that black and white is an actor's best friend. It *improves* a performance. I think he's right." He stared at her for a second, trying to imagine her wearing '60s clothing, her statuesque features cast in noir lighting. "It's your eyes," he said. "They're wide, like hers. Something haunting about them, perhaps. Yes, I can see where you might be able to pull it off. Perhaps Chad actually knows what he's doing."

"I hope so, 'cause I don't."

"Does anybody? I think I'm as lost as you are. Who the heck visits a cemetery to boost their spirits?" He sighed. "Jesus. Particularly *this* one." He gestured toward the tombstone under which Sharon's unborn child lay.

The woman hugged herself, as if she were cold. "I know. I hadn't thought about that before I came. When I saw the name there...." She closed her eyes for a second, then whispered, "Would you like to get out of here?"

At first, he thought she meant Los Angeles. He was about to say, "No." Then he realized what she really meant.

"Okay," he said. "I mean, I'd love to get out of here. With you."

"Let's go get some coffee."

"That sounds great." He neglected to mention that he didn't like coffee. "Anywhere you want to go?"

"Is your car around here?"

"No. I don't have a car. I took a taxi here."

"Who uses a taxi in L.A.?"

Someone who's about to return home to Washington and doesn't care about blowing his mother's money?

Mike shrugged. "This was an impulsive trip. I felt like I was at the end of my rope."

"Why?"

"I'm just blocked on a script is all."

"What's the script about?"

"Well...Lugosi."

"Is it a comedy?"

"I guess you could say it's a tragedy. A Shakespearean one."

"How far along are you?"

He hadn't even started it. His imagination had been crippled by persistent depression. "I'm almost done. I just need to write one more act."

"Maybe you can write in a part for me."

Mike smiled. "You'd be perfect for Luna."

"Who?"

"Carroll Borland. She played a vampire named Luna in Tod Browning's *Mark of the Vampire*. Lugosi is Count Mora, and Luna is his daughter. In life they had an incestuous relationship. In disgust, Count Mora killed his daughter, then shot himself. They came back as vampires. At least, that was part of the back story. That part never made it into the finished film. Carroll Borland will be a major character in the screenplay. She and Lugosi had some sort of intimate relationship, supposedly a platonic one, but it doesn't seem that way based on the way she talks about him during the interviews I've read. I'm sort of letting my imagination fill in the blanks." Isn't that what he always did? After all, he hadn't even outlined this hypothetical screenplay. It was just something that had always been floating around in the back of his head. Nothing more than a phantom. "*Mark of the Vampire* was a remake of *London After Midnight*, a lost film from 1927. Tod Browning remade it eight years later in 1935 at MGM."

"*London After Midnight*," the woman said, allowing the words to roll off her tongue with tones of melodrama. She laughed at herself, then removed a pack of cigarettes from her coat. "That would be a good band name."

Mike laughed. "Yeah, I guess so."

"That's with Lon Chaney? He's wearing a slouch hat and big fangs?"

"Yes, *exactly.*"

"I've seen stills. Chad claims a friend of his found the original print somewhere."

"Of *London After Midnight*? That's impossible. It's been lost for decades."

"Chad says he knows someone who works in the UCLA film archive who located a print."

"That's big news. How come I haven't heard about it?"

She shrugged again. "I don't know. It just happened, not long ago. So, you really think I could be in your movie?"

Mike put his hand over his heart. "Oh, trust me, you're Luna. That's a promise. Something about your eyes. You're the perfect vampire."

"Thank you." She blew smoke gracefully into the dead, still air. "I'd like to read the screenplay when you're done. You know, I've only seen Lugosi in one movie, *Abbott and Costello Meet Frankenstein*. And that was a long time ago, when I was a kid."

"I can't believe it. I mean, that's a good one, of course, but… you've never seen *Dracula*? *White Zombie*? *Son of Frankenstein*?"

"I don't go for horror movies very much. I like musicals."

"I hate musicals, and I love horror movies. Jesus, I need to see this print of *London After Midnight*. Let's go get coffee and talk about this."

"So you don't want to talk to *me*, eh? You just want to get close to Chad to see this old movie of yours."

"I have an ulterior motive, Luna, I confess."

She took a few more puffs on the cigarette, then nodded her head as if to indicate that he should follow her. But first she gently placed her flowers on Sharon's grave.

Mike returned the folded note to Bela's tombstone, picked up his suitcase, and followed the woman through the thin afternoon mist now crawling over the graveyard. A rare sight in L.A., but not so rare on celluloid.

"Hey, what's with the suitcase?" the woman asked. "Were you planning on moving into a crypt here?"

Mike chuckled nervously. Might as well, he thought. But he didn't want to *say* that; he didn't want her to know the suitcase contained every scrap of his clothes. "This is research material I picked up from the library. You know, for the screenplay."

"You do a hell of a lot of research. It looks like it weighs a ton."

"Well, it's gonna be a long screenplay. A real epic. By the way, what's your name? I can't keep calling you Luna."

She smiled and said, "Luna's not too far off, actually. I'm Lucy." They stopped for a moment to shake hands.

Mike realized that his migraine had vanished before it had even fully formed.

"That's perfect," Mike said. "Just like in *Dracula*."

"I doubt my parents were thinking of that. My mother named me after Lucille Ball."

He reached out to steady himself. His massive fingers clawed into the three-inch-thick wood. To his surprise, the wood split in half. The bench shattered, sending Old Ygor falling to the stone floor with a startled cry, like that of a child who's broken a toy without meaning to.

His eyes focused, his vision regained clarity. He glanced down at his hands. They were a pale, mottled green and crisscrossed with grotesque stitches. Some of the stitches were coming out. He was bleeding. He touched the blood. It was cold, so cold.

The coldness permeated his entire body...a body far more massive than the crippled one he'd been forced to deal with for so long while exiled in the castle on the outskirts of that little village. That hateful, stifling jail of a village.

He'd left it, he knew that now. Yes, he'd left it in the company of his friend. The only real friend Ygor had ever known.

His friend was with him now. Though Ygor was the only person in this tiny cell, Ygor's friend was right here with him. He always would be. Together. *Forever.*

Now Ygor remembered. *Everything.*

He rose to his feet and smashed his giant, bleeding fists into the iron bars that kept him from freedom. He'd had enough.

No more bars. No more cells. No more small-minded villagers keeping him from what was his.

And pretty soon...sooner than anyone expected...no more humans.

That would be such a beautiful day. The day that Ygor *alone* lived and walked and partook of the air of Earth. It was his dream, and someday he would bring it about. He didn't know how...but he would. Oh, yes. And his friend—what was left of his friend—was going to help him.

The iron bars twisted in Ygor's fists like child's taffy.

Lucy slid behind her steering wheel, pushed some cassette tapes off her seat (mostly punk stuff from the '70s—The Stooges, Richard Hell & the Voidoids, The New York Dolls), and gestured for Mike to climb inside. Just as Mike settled into the passenger seat, off in the distance he noticed a new visitor standing over Bela's grave. He seemed to be a priest...or, rather, he was dressed like one. He was staring intently at all the presents on Bela's grave.

"Man, I hope that priest doesn't remove all those gifts," Mike said. "Particularly the note."

Lucy's car was parked about fifty feet from the edge of The Grotto. The priest didn't seem to notice their presence at all. "Well, maybe that's his job," Lucy said. "To keep the graves clear. They can't just let everything pile up."

"Yeah, I know," Mike said. "It's just that—hey, what's he doing?"

The priest crouched down on one knee, glanced from side to side as if checking to see if anyone was around, carefully plucked the sprinkled donut from Bela's grave, checked once more to see if anyone was observing him, then....

"Is he going to...?" Lucy started to say.

The priest took a bite of the donut.

"Is this *real*?" Mike said. "I mean, are we fucking dreaming this?"

Lucy shook her head back and forth, not taking her eyes off the masticating priest. "Can we ever really know the answer to that question?"

"The only way to know is to flap your arms real hard. If you fly, you're dreaming. If not, you're awake."

"Oh my *God*!" Lucy shouted. "Look! He's taking another bite!" Lucy put her hand over her mouth and burst out laughing. "That's the most disgusting thing I've ever seen in my life!"

"Let's get the fuck out of here," Mike said, "before he eats *us*."

Still laughing, Lucy put the car in reverse, then peeled out of that graveyard as fast as she could.

In the rearview mirror, Mike saw the priest stroll away from the grave while still munching on that sprinkled donut.

Suddenly, the sound of gunshots.

It felt like tiny insects biting his skin. It took him a few seconds to realize that those "insects" were a barrage of bullets penetrating his barrel-like chest. Ygor smiled.

Half a dozen gendarmes stood in the narrow hall outside the cell, their useless pistols trained on him. Why did they even bother?

One particular officer pushed his way to the front of the crowd. The hateful and familiar face of Inspector Krogh now stood in front of him, the very man who had arrested him so many years ago. The very man who had escorted him to the gallows.

Krogh raised his right arm—his pitiful, mechanical arm—and aimed at Ygor's forehead. Three bullets slammed into the angry furrows of his monstrous, scar-riddled brow. These tiny lead annoyances pushed Ygor back a few steps, nothing more.

Ygor squinted, smiled. He focused all his hate—oh, there was so much of it, stored away for so long inside a body once far too broken to do anything to rectify it—on Krogh's panic-stricken face.

Ygor opened his mouth: "So...."

The gendarmes ceased their fire, so startled were they to hear the creature speak even a single word.

Ygor had avoided speech for so long. Better to let people think he was dumb. But Ygor's emotions momentarily overwhelmed his reason and the words came spilling out, so clipped and precise and deliberate: "How does it feel to come face to face with your worst nightmare? You tried to kill me once, but you did not succeed. How will you do your job? How will you hang innocent men with *no* arms at all?"

Krogh's eyes widened with startled recognition. "Hang innocent...?" The words trailed off. "Ygor?"

Ygor wished he had said nothing. Now he had no more surprises left. Now Krogh knew the truth: there was more than just one ghost in this cell. There were two.

Angry at himself, angry at Krogh, angry at a world that had tried to assassinate him, Ygor clasped his hands into a single fist and swung it at the cell. The bars shattered into tiny iron slivers. The gendarmes covered their eyes and backed away. Too late.

Ygor reached out for one of these little toy soldiers and clapped his hands together with as much force as he could muster, the gendarme's skull collapsing between mighty, decaying hands. Bits of brain and blood splattered on the stark, gray walls of the tomb-like corridor. Krogh shouted the man's name, but Ygor didn't catch it. He didn't recognize the man. He was young, perhaps new to the little village. So few people ever came to this town from the outside, and yet it was possible. After all, Ygor had been asleep. Who knew for how long?

Krogh ordered his men to retreat. They left their murdered friend behind; still they were too slow. Ygor grabbed one of them by the back of his collar and yanked hard like a fisherman fighting a reluctant catfish. He dashed the man's head into the wall once, twice, three, four times in a row. Ygor liked watching that ornamental policeman's cap go flying into empty space. Watching the flesh underneath split open like a jackfruit.

Ygor's gargantuan right hand enclosed what was left of the head as the screaming gendarme fell to his knees. He was screaming. Still alive. Good. So very good.

Ygor crushed the man's skull, the beautiful sound of ragged bone fragments piercing a man's brain echoing endlessly between the dungeon-like walls. Eyeballs slithered down the man's bleeding cheeks and plopped onto the floor. They ended up smeared on the stone floor like fried eggs beneath Ygor's hobnailed boots. The blood smelled like rust. Ygor liked rust.

The rest of the crew had fled behind a five-inch-thick wooden door that now shut with a loud clang. One of them stared at him through a tiny barred window. Ygor's fist split the bars in two, as if they were made of nothing more substantial than liquid, then smashed into the gendarme's face. Bone fragments from the poor man's nose speared the inside of his brain, felled by his own weak skeleton. He toppled backwards, his frightened face and useless uniform no longer an impediment to Ygor's path.

Ygor reached down through the small hole and found the metal bar that kept the portal shut. He'd had experience finding what he needed through touch alone during that horrible time when he had been lost in perpetual darkness, his eyes as ineffectual as the future corpses who stood before him.

Three more bullets nipped at his arm. He ignored their bite and lifted the bar from its metal clasps. He let it go. It hit the floor with the angry shriek of metal scraping against stone. Then he kicked the door open and found himself in familiar surroundings: Yes, the lobby of police headquarters in the small mountain village that had persecuted him for so long. He thought he'd left it behind for good.

Krogh stood in front of the double doors that led outside, his impotent pistol somehow steady in his black gloved fist. Despite his unaffected exterior, beads of sweat poured down his upper lip and into his gray-streaked black moustache.

"No further," Krogh said. Ygor tried to hear the slightest tremor in his voice, but…no. There wasn't a trace. The rest of Krogh's men had backed up against the north and south wall, blood and viscera staining their terrified faces, their shaking fists grasped around guns that could do them no good. They knew this, of course, but what else could they do? There was nowhere to run…unless Krogh decided to open the doors and flee.

But that wasn't going to happen.

This pleased Ygor very much.

He said, "Now I'm going to take your other arm, Krogh, right before you *die*."

He took two steps into the room. The gendarmes flinched, their trigger fingers tightening. But then Ygor paused in his tracks and whispered, "Or maybe I'll just rip it out by its roots and let you live."

Ygor rushed the Inspector, far faster than the fools expected, his dead eyes fixated on Krogh's gun and the fist that gripped it and the warm, blood-filled arm…an arm that would soon be reduced to a phantom…a phantom that would make its presence known only when it caused its sad owner extreme pain.

Such was the price of having only half a body.

Of being half-alive.

"Unbelievable," Lucy said. "So, do you think he was a real priest?"

"What else *could* he be?" Mike said while buttering a dinner roll.

Lucy shrugged. "It's L.A. No one is what he seems. Besides, Halloween's only next month, right? Maybe it was a costume."

"I suppose it's possible. All I know is that it was real fuckin' weird, man."

They were having lunch over at Du-Par's on the corner of West 3rd Street and Fairfax. They spoke for hours about the history of film and little else. Their personal stories became relevant only when they intersected with whatever film was under discussion at that moment. Mike insisted on paying for dinner, even though it meant sacrificing the rest of the money his mother had sent him to leave town. While telling her the general outline of the screenplay he was working on, he realized that his plane had departed twenty minutes earlier. He had no idea what he was going to do once this conversation was over, but for once he didn't care about the future. He just cared about talking to *her*.

After three hours had passed, and Lucy had gone through several cups of coffee, she told him that she had to get back home to study for her part. She asked if there was any place she could drop him off. He told him his address. This was the last day of the month. Technically, he had his studio apartment—and all the garbage he had planned to leave behind—for one more night. So, he told her to drop him off there: 6434 Yucca Street.

As he was getting out of her car, she wrote her phone number and name (Lucy Szilagyi) on the back of his hand. He asked to use the pen for a moment and did the same for her; his full name (Michael A. Fenton) decorated her Mount of Venus like a tattoo. He acted cool, or tried to, and told her he might call her in a couple of days if he could steal some time away from the screenplay-in-progress. She said she'd like that, then grinned and added, "Man, I'll never forget that priest." And drove away. Poof. Gone. Back into the mist, like a Universal Studio vampire.

The second he returned to his room Mike opened his suitcase, grabbed a pen, and jotted the phone number down in his notebook. He didn't want to lose it. It was his only escape route now.

He collapsed onto the bed, smoked about three cigarettes in a row while staring at the cracked ceiling, then sat down at his desk in front of his electric typewriter. His beloved typewriter. The one he had been planning on leaving behind forever.

He stroked it for a second, asked its forgiveness, then put a fresh piece of paper in the machine and began Act One of *Bela Lugosi's Dead*.

2.

The rent was due today, but there had been several times when Mike had given the check to the manager five days late and she hadn't complained—not much, at least. That meant he had about five more days before she started in on him. Who knew how long he could stall after that? Hopefully, long enough.

He began writing *Bela Lugosi's Dead* at about nine o'clock at night, not long after Lucy dropped him off. By the time the sun rose over North Hollywood he had written almost twenty pages, an unprecedented number for him. Usually the research bogged him down, but not this time. This time he was writing about something he had been researching all along, ever since he was ten years old when he saw his very first Lugosi movie on the late-night show. It was *Son of Frankenstein* in which Lugosi played the vengeful, broken-necked grave robber named Ygor. It remained one of his favorite films to this very day. Mike thought Bela should have received a Best Supporting Actor award from the Academy in 1939 for his role as Ygor. But, of course, the only actor to ever receive an Academy Award for a horror film was Fredric March for his portrayal of Dr. Jekyll and Mr. Hyde in 1931, a complete anomaly. Mainstream Hollywood had always thumbed their noses at the horror genre, and Mike would have it no other way. You could get away with so much more when you flew under the radar, specializing in a genre that no one respected or cared about.

He'd read two complete biographies of Lugosi's life and numerous articles published in fanzines. All these facts had been jumbling around in his head for over ten years. It was now time to put them to work.

Perhaps it was easier writing the screenplay knowing exactly who would play one of the lead roles. He beefed up Carroll Borland's role every chance he could get, hoping Lucy would like it enough to keep talking to him. Enough to give him a place to stay.

The phone rang several times throughout the night. No doubt his mother, worried sick. He ignored it. He just didn't want her tired protests to ruin his flow.

He must have fallen asleep at the typewriter. He awoke at noon with his forehead pressed up against the metal casing. When he looked in the mirror, the words Smith-Corona were imprinted in the middle of his forehead like the mark of some crazed deity who had chosen to visit him in the night. He didn't shave or brush his teeth or take a shower. He ate a quick breakfast (a bowl of Honey Nut Cheerios) and continued typing. When he hit page 33 the phone rang again. He gave in to the inevitable. He picked up and said, "What is it?"

Yes, it was his mother. She wanted to know why the hell he wasn't on the god damn plane. She'd waited there three hours for him. Who the hell did he think he was? He told her he wasn't coming back.

"Well, what did you do with my money?" she asked.

"It's all gone," he said. "I bought dinner."

"It must've been a pretty god damn expensive dinner," she said.

"It was," he said, thinking about the steak dinner Lucy had ordered. "But it was worth it."

"Have you gone mad?" she asked. "Wait, don't answer that. You went mad a long time ago. How could you possibly ever think you could make it out there in Hollywood? You're just not the type. You're not a get-up-and-go person. Neither was your father. You're gonna end up just like him if you keep on like this. How're you going to eat out there? How're you going to live? I thought you needed to be out of that apartment by the end of September. Mikey? Are you listening to me?"

He pulled the cord out of the wall, pushed the phone off the desk and onto the dirty carpet, then spun around in his swivel chair and went back to writing the screenplay.

The story poured out of him. There was no rhyme or reason to the structure. It was unlike any screenplay he'd written before. It was completely non-linear. Somehow, without really even thinking about it, he had chosen a *Citizen-Kane*-like structure for the film. Which was rather appropriate. Mike had always felt there were a lot of similarities between Orson Welles and Bela Lugosi, though few respectable film critics would agree.

Both had begun their careers in Hollywood with promising futures, Bela in *Dracula* and Orson in *Citizen Kane*. Both specialized in playing the "King." (The "King" was not necessarily the star of the film, simply the character you remembered most.) And both men always stood out in their various films, even when they had limited screen time. Dracula and Harry Lime in *The Third Man* probably shared the same amount of screen time, and yet of course they stole the show in both cases. After a great splash they suffered quick declines, though for very different reasons. Within only a few years of their great successes, both ended up making films on poverty row. Most sane film theorists wouldn't dare draw comparisons between Bela's bravura performance in *White Zombie* and Orson's in *Macbeth*, and yet the similarities were there. Both films were made on poverty row, and both had emerged through the mists of time as flawed masterpieces. Though Bela's Murder Legendre in *White Zombie* was one of the great Mephistophelean figures in cinema, in Mike's view Orson's turn as the title character of *Mr. Arkadin* (yet another flawed masterpiece) was a close second. Both men were accused of being communists in the 1950s, and could very well have lost important roles in Hollywood because of the blacklist. It was little known, as well, that both men portrayed Dracula, Bela on the stage and in film, Orson on the radio on the July 11th, 1938 broadcast of *Mercury Theatre on the Air*. Orson's raw, brutal characterization of the character was quite different from Bela's suavity, and yet no less valid.

Perhaps it was appropriate, therefore, that Mike took a cue from *Citizen Kane* and began the film with Bela at the end of his life, dying, hallucinating that a beautiful woman with yellowish eyes (the ghostly form of one of his many lovers back in Europe) was sucking the life out of him while his final wife, Hope, hovered over him, asking him if he was all right.

The audience sees brief snippets of Bela's life in flashback, interwoven with the sad aftermath of his death, his funeral, and his tattered legacy seen through the eyes of a young fan trying to piece together the remnants of the old man's broken life in order to write a biography of the once-great actor. In this way Mike wouldn't have to be bogged down by unnecessary details. He could simply highlight the most interesting aspects of Bela's life. The experience of seeing the film would be like riding around inside the brain of a drowning man. Perhaps this would be disorientating, but after all isn't this the way memory works? Who remembers their lives in a linear fashion? No one. So why present it that way on-screen?

The pieces of Bela's life fell onto the page in the order they wished to do so. Mike had no control over it. He didn't want control. What he wanted most of all was three acts before Saturday. (Jesus, he kept telling himself, why the hell couldn't you say you'd only written *one* god damn act? His lies always had to be grand. He was just lucky his tongue hadn't bragged about the "fact" that the screenplay was done and already in production.) But he also wanted something unique and honest, dramatic, and yet respectful of Bela's memory. Mike figured it was about time that someone in Hollywood gave the actor the respect he had deserved during life and yet had been denied for so long. And it looked like the only guy willing to do it was Mike.

He ignored the knock at the door on the morning of the sixth day. He was only two pages away from the end of Act III and didn't want to be bothered. When he finished, at last, wrapping up an incredible scene for Lucy, he crept towards the door, pressed his ear up against it, and listened for the pitter-patter of shuffling feet outside. The landlady and her tattered slippers had a distinct gait. Unfortunately, this building had been erected way back in the 1920s and the walls and doors were thick. It was hard to hear anything through them. He heard nothing, so he decided to take a chance.

He swung open the door, glanced left and right. The drab

green hallway stretched off in either direction, as desolate as the ancient halls of Dracula's mountaintop castle. He peeked around the edge of the door and sure enough saw a piece of yellow lined paper stuck there with Scotch tape. It was from the landlady all right. A polite but stern warning reminding him when the rent was due.

Shit, he thought to himself. He knew this moment had to come, but hoped to will it away like Jaromir Hladik in Jorge Luis Borges' "The Secret Miracle," a short story his creative writing teacher forced him to read in high school. Since there were no monsters in the story, it didn't interest him too much; however, the idea that someone could stop time simply by wishing it so, well, that did appeal to him. A very great deal. After all, he'd spent so many hours in elementary school wishing he could stop time in order to avoid a fight with the bullies after his final class of the day. It wasn't until high school that he learned how to handle himself.

Mike crumpled the note up into a ball, shut the door, deadbolted it, wandered over to his typewriter and pulled out page 90. He set it down carefully on the pile of pages. He hadn't even had time to re-read it, but that didn't matter. He could tell her it was a rough draft, which of course it was. *Very* rough. As rough as you could possibly get without being non-existent.

He patted the pages for a moment, smiling down at them like a proud father. Then he plugged the phone back into the wall and dialed the number he'd scratched into the wooden writing desk. "How is a raven like a writing desk?" he asked himself, thinking of Bela's Dr. Vollin from *The Raven* sitting at the tea party in *Alice in Wonderland*. He imagined all of Bela's characters sitting at the same table, all sinister variations of the same man. Then he thought about how much Bela had despised Boris Karloff's demands for tea time every day at two, delaying production of whatever film they were working on at the moment. This went against Bela's deeply ingrained work ethic. Bela's Mad Tea Party. What a wonderful image. Perhaps he could work that into the screenplay. Why not?

He heard a soft, lilting voice on the other end of the receiver say, "Hello?" Lucy. He hadn't even realized he'd dialed the number yet. That's how out of it he was. How much had he slept over the past few days?

"How is a raven like a writing desk?" Mike asked. He wasn't even sure why he'd said that. Whatever. Just go with it.

"*What?*" Lucy said.

"How, I said, is a raven like a writing desk?" Mike asked again. He picked up the phone and moved toward the corner of the room where he took a seat on his lumpy bed.

"Who is this?" Lucy asked, sounding very annoyed.

Mike laughed. "This is Mike. From the graveyard. You know, the writer. I guess you're not up on your *Alice in Wonderland* references."

Lucy laughed. "No, I am, I just get creeped out when I hear them drifting through the phone at me at midnight."

"Is that how late it is?" Mike glanced at his clock once more. Yes, it still said eight o'clock. The clock must've stopped hours earlier. He hadn't even noticed. Jesus.

"Sorry for calling you so late," Mike said. "I thought it was eight o'clock. I lost track of the time."

"That's okay. You keep weird, writer's hours. I understand."

"I've been writing up a storm the past few days. You wouldn't believe it. My fingertips have calluses." That was true. He stuck the receiver into the crook of his neck and shoulder and glanced down at the whorls on his fingertips. Like tiny galaxies. Karloff as Dr. Janos Rukh peering through his telescope while explaining the secret of the cosmic rays to his colleague, Dr. Benet (Lugosi, of course).

"I was wondering what you've been doing," Lucy said. "Or if I'd ever hear from you again."

"Really? You were thinking about me?"

"Sure. Off and on. I'm surprised it took you so long to call. So...what've you been working on?"

He remained silent for a moment. Supposedly, he'd already finished the first three acts of *Bela Lugosi's Dead*, so he couldn't say that. "Mostly I've been doing research for the final act. Listen, I was just re-reading the first three acts of the screenplay and I think my initial instincts were right. You'd be perfect for the part of Carroll Borland. Would you like to read the screenplay?"

"Are you kidding? That's why I've been waiting for you to call. I can't wait to read it. In fact, I went over to Eddie Brandt's video store the other day and rented *Mark of the Vampire* just to see who I would be playing."

"I'm amazed you went to all that effort. What did you think of the film?"

"I thought it was the worst piece of shit I've ever seen. That ending blows, man."

Mike laughed. "Well...I guess it's more impressive when you're eight."

"But Carroll Borland is beautiful in it, and the one scene I really loved is the part where she has those giant bat wings and kind of floats down from the ceiling."

"That's the one scene from the movie no one can ever forget."

"And I did like watching Lionel Barrymore and Lionel Atwill try to steal each other's scenes. How wonderful it would be to get into a time machine and interact with those people. Can you imagine?"

"I've thought about that a lot. It's been my dream since I was a kid."

"I was talking to Chad about you."

"Chad?"

"You know, the guy who's making the movie with me. The one who knows all about *London After Midnight*. He was really interested in what I had to say about you. He knows people in the business. Maybe he can introduce you to someone in a production company or an agency or something. Hopefully, he'll do the same thing for me. We're supposed to shoot a scene for his movie tomorrow night."

"Yeah, that's great. I'd love to meet him. So...when would you want to read this screenplay?"

"I don't know, what's a good time for you?"

"Let me see...how about right now?"

"*Now?*"

"Too late?"

She laughed. "I was about to get ready to go to bed."

"Oh, I see. Okay, that's cool."

"But...well, I don't have to go to work tomorrow, and the

shoot's not until nighttime. You want to meet somewhere? There's a coffee shop just around the corner from here."

"I would love to do that, but my car's kind of...well, non-existent. There's a cafe right near here called Port of Saints. Ever been to it?"

"No."

"You'll love it. I'll buy you whatever you want. It's open all night. How about it?"

She hesitated for only a few seconds, then said, "What the hell, why not? I'll see you in about forty minutes, okay? Wait. Make it an hour."

"That's fine with me."

The second he hung up the phone he grabbed the screenplay, stuffed the pages in a manila envelope, and hurried down the back stairs so he would not be seen by roving eyes.

"Hey, Ygor. Time to wake up, old boy. Time to take out the trash."

The funny little man was always bothering him, right when the sun rose. But he didn't mind. He liked the light. Liked being out in the sun. He could remember the first time he ever saw it. That warm glowing presence hovering over him, dispelling the gloom of the death-filled castle like an angel. But back then he didn't even know what an angel was. It all seemed like so long ago. His father had revealed the sun to him, right before turning on him and attacking him. Trying to kill him.

But he didn't like to think about such things.

He didn't like to think—or even dream—about the past.

He liked to sleep through the night as much as possible. The blackness of the night scared him so. The night was filled with unknown things and dead things and worse things: little people with torches who wanted to kill him. Or at least they *used* to. So much had changed since then. Now they just shunned him. And he liked it so much better that way.

But they weren't all monsters. Some of them had gone out of their way to treat him well. Sister Marie, for example, had accepted him into the fold the second she saw him. She helped him so much. Taught him things. Read to him from the Bible

and Milton and Goethe. Introduced him to a world of words
and dreams and poetry.

At one time he thought of himself as a monster, because
that's the only word anyone had ever used to address him. First
Father, then that horrible hunchback he was forced to hang from
the rafters of his cell, then that wicked old man in the lab coat,
then the heartless undead woman who was to be his, then.....

Then Ygor.

When the sister asked him for a name, he chose "Ygor." It
was the only name he knew. Old Ygor had claimed to be his
friend. But he knew that wasn't true now. The man with the
broken neck had just wanted to use him, like all the others had
wanted to use him.....

He had done such horrible things for Ygor. Yes, he understood
that now. The victims still haunted him, their lifeless faces, the
crimes he had committed with his own hands.

Not *these* hands—the old ones.

But the Sister told him that the Father, his *true* Father, would
forgive him in the end as long as he followed a righteous path.

One of the last things Ygor told him was that they could
be together forever, just the two of them. And he accepted the
offer. Why wouldn't he? He could imagine no better future for
himself at the time.

He hadn't really known what Ygor meant until he awoke in
the rubble of the castle and staggered away from the oncoming
mob and caught a glimpse of himself in a clear, placid lake.
Ygor's face stared back at him.

But how could that be?

He didn't care, not really. All he knew was this: When people
saw him now, like those young strangers walking by the lake
that afternoon, they didn't flee in fear. They seemed distrustful,
yes, but not horrified. By and by, he found that he could walk
among these humans without causing a riot. No one seemed to
hate him now. That's all he'd ever wanted.

To be left alone.

To *not* cause pain.

"I *said* wakey-wakey, boy. Rise and shine. The two of us,
we've got us a big job to do."

The funny man with the drooping moustache gripped him by the shoulder and shook him hard.

His reaction was sheer instinct. He grabbed the man by the wrist and squeezed. A low growl rose in his throat.

"Hey," the man said, "that's enough now...don't twist me bloody arm off."

An image rose through the mists in his mind: a young boy standing in his path. Crying. Afraid. He remembered grabbing the boy by the arm and raising him in the air to assuage his fears. He was still young at that point. He didn't know how fragile these beings were. That little white arm came right off. Red liquid sprayed everywhere. The child was crying even more now. So, he panicked and tossed the arm in the street and ran. The villagers came after him. They always came after him.

"I said don't twist the arm off!" the man shouted and tried to wrench it away.

Ygor let go. It had been difficult, adjusting to how different this body was. He was far weaker than he had once been, which he considered to be a blessing. Only the intelligent, the *very* intelligent—great men like Milton—should ever be as strong as that. Such people were the only ones who would know how to wield power as great as that with which *he* had been born. And yet, so rarely did such men seem to possess it. Why?

He didn't know. Another mystery he couldn't solve.

Though he was much weaker than he had once been, when he first entered this world, he was still strong in comparison to other men. Strong *enough*.

The funny man, whose name was something simple like Martin or Mervyn, took a few steps back while rubbing his arm. "I was just trying to get you out of bed. No need to abuse me."

Ygor nodded. "I'm...sorry." Thanks to Sister Marie, it was becoming much easier for him to form words. Though the mouth and tongue and larynx knew what to do perfectly well, *he* did not. "Just sleepy. You...surprised me."

"Well, tell me about it, sir. I was up till three in the morning last night listening to you and your nightmares."

God. Now it all came back to him. Another dream about the windmill. Fire and death and angry, frothing faces staring up at him. The nightmares made him grind his teeth, and the grating sounds disturbed the others in the bunks around him. But there was little he could do about it.

"I'm sorry," he whispered.

"Listen, it's okay, friend. Let's just get this job over with. I want to have breakfast with the others."

Martin or Mervyn was a new addition to the hostel. He had come staggering into the mess hall only a week before in a very bad way, hallucinating, seeing strange crimson ropes flitting through the air. The nuns had explained that he was suffering from "too much drink."

Ygor (yes, he too had come to think of himself by that moniker) did not understand this. He liked wine a little too much himself, but it rarely incapacitated him. He had certainly never hallucinated. In the old days he could drink as much as he wanted and would never even grow light-headed. With this new body that was no longer the case, but still his tolerance was high.

"Breakfast," Ygor said. "Too bad...they don't serve wine for...breakfast." He smiled at the funny man.

The funny man's face grew red with anger. "No need to kick a man when he's down. I know why I'm here. None of us is perfect, otherwise why would we be here? Where do you get off? You think you're perfect, eh?"

Ygor was confused. He just shook his head. He didn't understand why the man was angry with him. "No," he said. "I'm not...perfect."

"Good. Then we're all on the same page. Now get your imperfect butt out of that bed and help me get rid of this stuff."

Ygor threw the blankets aside, pulled on a pair of old but clean pants, gloves, a shirt, a jacket, a cap, and a scarf—all provided for him by the nuns. He followed Marvin or Mervyn into the kitchen and grabbed two bags of garbage from the night before. The kitchen served a lot of needy people, and the nightly meals resulted in piles of mess that needed to be thrown out the next morning before the trash men arrived.

The funny man grabbed two bags of his own and said, "This stuff reeks like the insides of a dead cat...not that I've ever smelled the insides of a dead cat. But if I'd ever smelled the insides of a dead cat, I bet it'd smell like this. At least I'm not peeling potatoes. I can't stand potatoes. Why, I'd rather peel a cat than a potato."

Ygor laughed. He often laughed at the colorful way the man complained about the most minor inconveniences. But for some strange reason the man would grow angry and yell at Ygor for laughing. Ygor thought of him as the funny man because he was such a constant source of amusement and jollity. And yet, for reasons he could not comprehend, Marvin or Mervyn never laughed along with him. Ygor didn't understand how someone so funny could be so unhappy.

"Now what're you laughing at?" the man said, kicking the back door open with his foot. The cold mist of morning blew into the kitchen. Ygor followed him, reluctantly, into the fog. "How many potatoes have *you* ever peeled? Not many, I'd wager. Why, it seems to me you've had a pretty comfy life compared to some. Compared to *me*. The nuns really seem to like you. And that young Sister Marie, she dotes over you like you were her pet or something. I wish she'd look at me the way she looks at you. I'd give up drink forever just to hold her in my arms for a few seconds. No, sir, I've had far too much tragedy in *my* life. Why, you couldn't handle even *half* the tragedy the Good Lord has seen fit to drop in my lap. That's why I had to turn to the grog. Sensitive souls like me, we're not made for this world. We need a little something extra to get us through the day. Did I ever mention I was a poet? You want to hear some of my verse?"

They had reached the end of the alley where a large bin stood waiting for their early morning presents. Ygor had done this every day for months. The routine rarely changed, unless Ygor was sick. Ygor was very rarely sick.

"I like…poetry," Ygor said. Sister Marie had read him enough of it at night for him to know how beautiful poetry could be.

"This one is called 'Unicorns Are Creatures of Shadow.'" The funny man dumped the garbage bags on the ground, cleared his throat, took off his cap, placed one foot on the bag as if it were a stool, then proceeded to recite his poem from memory. "O unicorns made of ice/Swift creatures of lightning and fleeting shadows/Those who imbibe the firewater/Fear the tug of Satan's dire gallows/When men—"

He didn't even finish the first stanza. A gloved fist appeared out of the fog and slammed into the funny man's cheek, toppling him off his impromptu stage composed of discarded potato skins. A second blow laid him flat on the ground. Ygor could no longer see him. The fog was too thick that close to the cobblestones.

Ygor's instincts urged him to flee. Something horrible was about to happen, something that would threaten the perfect little paradise he had carved for himself in this imperfect world. But something else, another part of his nature, told him to remain put. He couldn't just leave the funny man alone, defenseless, in this evil mist.

The sound of low boot heels clicking steadily against the stones…a tall, thin figure emerging from the fog.…

The man withdrew a pistol from inside his overcoat. He aimed it at Ygor's face.

"It's true," the man said, perhaps to himself. "I never would've believed it. How? You're…you're *dead*."

"Dead," Ygor repeated, agreeing. Yes. Hadn't he always been dead?

"Why do the truly evil ones seem to hang on better than anyone else? There's a paper in there somewhere. Perhaps I'll be the one to write it. *You*, Ygor, could be the featured test subject. The whole town hangs you…you come right back. I shoot you, dead in the chest…you come right back. What does it take to keep you down?"

Ygor didn't remember being hanged—this was at least one indignity he had been spared—but he did indeed remember this gentleman. How could he forget?

Baron Wolfgang von Frankenstein, the first son of Frankenstein.

The man he called his.…

"What were you *thinking*?" said Frankenstein, his voice filled with hate. "That you could just kill my only brother and get away with it?"

"No," Ygor said. "*Not* your only brother."

Frankenstein's brow furrowed in confusion. Perhaps he wasn't ready for the voice. The voice...it probably didn't sound like the Ygor he was expecting.

"Wh-what're you *talking* about?" Anger was now giving way to apprehension and fear.

Ygor held out his hand. "I'm your...*brother*...too." He clawed at the air, as if wanting to grab hold of the fog itself.

Wolfgang von Frankenstein cocked his head to one side, eyes filled with confusion, as his finger squeezed down on the trigger of the gun.

Port of Saints was a usual haunt for him. It would've looked exactly like a diner out of an old '30s film if not for the tattooed kids with dyed black hair waiting on tables and the '60s funk playing on the radio. Framed photographs of classic movie stars like Jimmy Cagney and Humphrey Bogart lined the walls. Above the counter hung oversized pictures of root beer floats and strawberry sundaes. An assortment of pies sat displayed beneath glass cases near the counter. On battered metal shelves sat little cereal boxes like Special K, Kellogg's Corn Flakes, and Rice Krispies. Colorful gumball machines flanked the entrance. The waiters and waitresses all wore black t-shirts with white lettering on the back, slogans like, "FUCK THE HEALTH INSPECTOR, I'M DOING THE BEST I CAN," "WE SERVE CRACKERS," and "IT'S NOT MY PROBLEM IF YOU'RE NOT SATISFIED."

One of the waiters, a teenager with a metal stud in his nose, recognized Mike and showed him to a table in the corner right near the entrance. The table top was green and covered in granules of white sugar. Mike settled back against the green and white vinyl seat and checked out the other diners. The place was packed. He actually recognized some of the people from zipping through TV late at night. Character actors. He didn't know their names.

After they'd taken their seats, Lucy began gazing at her menu as if it was the only thing that existed in the world. She brightened and said, "Hey, they have a ham sandwich named after Charles Bukowski."

"It's a heart attack on a plate," Mike said, "but it's good." Just before leaving Snoqualmie, Mike had read Bukowski's most recent book, *Ham on Rye*, an autobiographical novel about growing up in Los Angeles, so he often ordered the sandwich in the man's honor.

"Jesus," Lucy said, "you know you're famous when you've got a sandwich named after you." She went back to staring at the menu.

Mike tossed his menu down and studied Lucy from across the table, trying to find even a hint of imperfection. He found himself lost in the subtle contours of her face. All of a sudden, she glanced up from her menu. His first impulse was to turn away, pretend as if he hadn't been staring at her like one of those undead slaves from *White Zombie*. But instead he simply *continued* staring, masking his face with as casual an expression as possible.

"I can never pass up the Bukowski," he said.

A polite teenager, the same waiter who had greeted them at the door, appeared by their side and said, "Hey, man, how's everything?"

"Moderately adequate," Mike said.

The kid laughed. "Same as usual, eh? Do you need more time?"

"No," said Lucy, "I think I'll take the chicken salad and a glass of the house red."

The kid jotted that down. "Excellent. And you, sir?"

"The Bukowski," said Mike, "always the Bukowski."

"Have you read *Post Office*?" the kid asked.

Mike laughed and nodded. "That was my first."

"I know a lot of people who think it's depressing."

"They're reading a different book than me."

The kid smiled and nodded in agreement, then took their menus and walked away.

"So, you're a Bukowski fan," Lucy said.

"It's not the type of thing I would've normally read back in high school. You couldn't get me to read anything other than books about old movies. But a friend of mine shoved *Post Office* into my hands and forced me to read it. He knew I wanted to move to L.A. I think that's why he gave it to me. I thought it was hilarious. So, then I read *Women* after that. I checked it out from the library. I was sixteen at the time. My mom found it in my backpack and flipped out. She didn't want my mind tarnished by 'pornographic trash.' She tossed it into a dumpster. I couldn't go back to the library because I owed too many fines on that one book. Well, that just made me want to read Bukowski even more."

"You were *sixteen* at the time? Your mom sounds pretty strict."

"She was always…well, over-protective, I guess you could say, if you want to put it nicely. She's been that way since I was seven. That's when Dad died."

"Oh, I'm so sorry."

"My…mom couldn't stand the thought of losing her only son after that, I guess. She hovered over me all the time. Smothered me. That's why I had to get out of there."

"How did your…you know…dad die?"

"It was slow…. I was young at the time, but I still remember him acting so differently all of a sudden. At first no one knew he was dying. My mom just thought he was becoming a real son of a bitch. It turned out it was a brain tumor. It actually *changed* his behavior. After a while, my mom figured he was going crazy or something. Finally, she made him go to a doctor, but by that point it was too late. The doctors couldn't do a damn thing for him."

"That's just horrible."

"Yeah, well…I wish I could say I was over it, but I'm really not. I mean, it made me a little paranoid. I suffer from a lot of migraines. And whenever I get a bad one, I can't help but think of my father. I—I don't mean to bring you down or anything—"

"No, it's okay."

"Anyway, I guess that explains why my mom became the person she is today. She does whatever she can to discourage me. She just wants me to stay home and be *safe*. She doesn't want me to take risks. Well, you can't live in L.A. without taking risks. I'm sure you know that. Reading Bukowski's novel *Factotum* convinced me it was possible to live in this city on practically

nothing." He laughed. "I was wrong about that, of course. So...
what Bukowski have you read?"

"Just a few poems. An ex-boyfriend gave me a book of his
poetry for my birthday, then took it back when I broke up with
him." She shook her head. "What a fucking bastard. Let's forget
Bukowski for the moment, okay? I'm more interested in *your*
writing."

"I was just getting to that," Mike said and pulled out an
overstuffed manila envelope. "Now, I want you to know that
this is just a rough draft."

"That's cool, I understand." She took the screenplay from
him and immediately began reading it.

Once she'd gotten to page three Mike grew rather nervous.
"Wait a minute...you're not going to read the whole thing right
here, are you?"

"I'm a fast reader," Lucy said. Her eyes never left the page
during the entire dinner except to make an occasional comment
about a particular line that she liked. Occasionally she'd laugh
and Mike began to feel sweat trickling down his armpits,
which often happened when he was nervous. Was she laughing
because she thought it was funny or because she thought it was
stupid?

She and Mike ate their entire dinner that way. Lucy even
ordered dessert, but only took one bite of it. Mike ate the rest of
her apple pie as he waited and waited and waited.

The entire process took her about an hour and a half. Then,
without saying anything, she went to page one and began
reading the whole thing all over again, but much faster this
time.

"Wait a minute," Mike said, "what're you doing?"

"Sh," Lucy said, and zoomed through the pages at a rapid
pace. He wasn't quite sure what the hell she was doing. About
fifteen minutes later she reached the last page, then looked up
at him, and said, "I've got fifty-six lines. That's not bad. It's
definitely more than I've ever had before. Jesus, this is great.
How long did it take you to write this?"

Mike shrugged. "I haven't been keeping track."

"Do you mind if I show this to Chad?"

"That's my only copy at the moment."

"We could go photocopy it somewhere. There's this Xerox place right over here on Cahuenga. It's open twenty-four hours."

"Okay, well...okay." He actually didn't have enough money left to pay for the dinner *and* the photocopying costs. He glanced at his watch. It was now 2:30 A.M.

"I'll gladly pay for it if that's gonna be a problem," Lucy said.

"Oh, no, that's okay. That's not the problem." He didn't know quite how to say it.

Lucy just kept staring at him with those wide, innocent, brown eyes. "Yes?" she said. "Are you worried about Chad stealing your idea? Listen, he's not that kinda guy, he's—"

"No, no. The problem is...." Just say it, Mike. "Do you... mind if I live at your place for a while?"

Lucy seemed stunned. Fortunately, the waiter came over with the bill at that moment. "Excuse me?" she said.

"Tomorrow morning, I won't have a place to live, and I definitely need a place if I'm going to finish this screenplay. If there's no screenplay there's no part for you, so I figured it might be in your interest to help me, an almost total stranger completely down on his luck. I was on my way out of Hollywood when I met you that day. I'd lost all hope. I told you I'd written this screenplay. It was all a god damn lie. It was just something I had twirling around in my head. I didn't actually have anything down on paper. I wrote this in the last five days. For you. The truth is I wanted to get to know you better, and I wanted to impress you, and I wanted to write something that would bowl you over, and hopefully convince you to give me a place to stay until I get on my feet again. So, how about it?"

After a few moments of silence Lucy said, "You wrote this in *five* days?"

"Yes."

"Is this the first screenplay you've written?"

"No. I've got three others. They're horror films."

"Are there any good roles for me in them?"

"Only if you like screaming a lot and taking off your nightgown while something big and scary chases you around.

No, the part of Carroll Borland is the best female character I've ever written." He laughed. "It's funny, that was always a weak spot for me, writing about women...until now."

"C'mon." Lucy gathered her purse to get ready to leave.

"Where're we going?"

"To get those other three screenplays. We don't want those thrown out too."

Mike tossed the last remaining bills he had on the table and, in a slight state of shock, followed her out of the restaurant. He really hadn't thought this would work.

3.

He woke up to the sound of football. He was lying on her very uncomfortable sofa (though it was far less uncomfortable than his old mattress) and there was a man sitting at the end of the couch near his feet. The man was reading his screenplay. A football game was also in progress on the TV. Occasionally, the man would glance up from the script to see what was happening on the screen. He was young, in his late teens or early twenties. Asian. Perhaps Japanese? He was decked out in all the necessary punk accoutrements: leather jacket, spiked belt, scuffed Doc Martin boots. None of this hid the fact that he was extremely skinny and effeminate-looking. He wasn't intimidating at all.

"Oh, hey, you're awake," the man said. "Sorry about the football game. I hate football myself. I'm just watching it so I can have something to talk to my dad about. I have to go to this party with him this weekend, very dull, not interesting at all. Just forget I said anything about it."

"Who're you?" Mike said groggily.

"I'm Chad." He held out his hand. "Lucy told me a lot about you."

Mike shook the hand. "Hi."

"This is pretty good," Chad said, hefting the screenplay as if he were weighing a slab of meat at a butcher's shop. "You know who you need to meet?"

"Who?"

"Eric Heidecker. Friend of mine. He's a Lugosi nut too. He runs Tinseltown Book & Poster down on Hollywood Boulevard. Ever been there?"

"No, I don't…oh, wait, yes. I *was* there once, with a friend of mine, just after I got to L.A. I think I bought a cheap lobby card of *Black Dragons* there. That's a Lugosi film from the early '40s. It's all about Japanese secret agents who've had plastic surgery to make them look like white men—the better to infiltrate American society. It went into production a few weeks after Pearl Harbor. I've been thinking about writing an article about that. You know, tie the film into the paranoid milieu of the time. But who has time to write articles?"

Chad laughed. "Not you. Not if you're gettin' booted out of your apartment with only the clothes on your back and three and a half screenplays."

"Well, I hope to go back and salvage some more stuff before I make my final exodus. My landlady's not gonna throw it all out for a few more weeks. I hope to at least retrieve my research materials."

"You might as well get that lobby card while you're at it too."

Mike laughed. "I have to draw the line somewhere."

Chad wagged his finger at him. "Uh uh. Any movie memorabilia you have, just hand it to me. I'll store it at my place for you until you get back on your feet."

"Really? Thanks."

"I'm a movie nut too. I'd hate to think of all that stuff just being tossed into the garbage."

"Well, I don't have a lot. A few—"

"Oh, I see you two have met," Lucy said, striding out of her bedroom wearing a tight-fitting psychedelic mini-skirt from the 1960s with white stockings and go-go boots to match. She looked stunning.

"Jesus, you look like Diana Rigg from that old *Avengers* TV show," Mike said—which, for him, was a high compliment. He'd had a crush on Diana ever since he was ten.

"Who the fuck's Diana Rigg?" Lucy said.

Chad laughed. "You'd have to be a nerd to know. And have a high tolerance for PBS."

"I don't," Lucy said. "I once had a boyfriend who had to watch the *MacNeil/Lehrer Newshour* every day. Thank God he went back to his wife. What a bore." She spun around and admired herself in the mirror. "What do you think? Imagine me with a bouffant blonde wig. *Then* would I look like Sharon?"

Mike gave her the once-over, then smiled and said, "Yeah. I guess you would at that."

Lucy turned to Chad and said, "Mike was questioning your casting choice."

"Well...all I said was that she didn't look like Sharon Tate."

Chad patted Mike on the foot and said, "She will. Talent's more important than looks, that's my philosophy. She exudes Sharon's *spirit*. That's what's most important. You'll see. I've already done some tests of her in her outfit. She looks just like her, in the right lighting. It'll be brilliant."

"Can't wait to see it."

"You want to come along for the shoot?" Lucy asked.

"It's not like I have anything else to do. If Chad doesn't mind...."

"What the hell," Chad said. "Eric mentioned he might drop by, so maybe you can meet him. You can help out. Have you ever built a set before?"

"No."

This time Chad patted him on the thigh. "Here's your chance, sweetheart."

4.

Ygor pulled his fists back just as they were about to shatter Krogh's skull. Krogh hadn't even flinched.

"No," Ygor said, "no, no, no." He laughed and patted the Inspector's epaulettes. "I think you'll be more useful in one piece." He picked up the struggling policeman, kicked the double doors open with his boot, and staggered out into the foggy streets. The Inspector fired one last shot, point blank, right into the Monster's heart, the barrel pressed against the thing's tattered black coat. It didn't even slow him down.

An old man driving a wagon down the middle of the street could only gape in fear as Ygor lumbered across his path. The horses reared and whinnied in terror. Ygor, holding Krogh under his left arm, cocked his right fist back and punched one of the horses in the skull. The thick fog did not dampen the sound of bones cracking. The horse collapsed face first onto the ground, its tight reins preventing the corpse from falling all the way. Its head and neck now rested limply on the ground like a snake while the back of the horse was still raised in the air, as if the corpse was ready to continue its job even in death. Judging by the way the old man still snapped on the reins, perhaps even the driver expected the equine corpse to take off into the night.

The other horse tried to run, as if disgusted by the laziness of its companion, wanting nothing more than to follow the path the driver had planned for it. The wagon traced a swift half-circle in the fog, then tipped over onto its side, right in front of Ygor. The old man stared up at him, his rheumy eyes wide with panic, his frail arms held over his head protectively. The creature that mothers invoked to scare children into drinking their milk had now risen from the collective nightmares of these simple people. Only the boogeyman himself could cause such fear in a grown man. Ygor was more than happy to take up the mantle. His instinct was to smash the weak fool right where he lay, reduce him to fragments as insubstantial as the cosmic rays from which Heinrich von Frankenstein had drawn the power to create life from discarded flesh. But no. No. Ygor just as immediately decided against it. Let the bastard live. Let him live and act as his personal messenger. He would spread the word. He would spread the Fear.

The boogeyman had returned from the grave.

Ygor spun away from the old man and dashed down the street at a speed that seemed impossible for such a bulky body. Sometimes, perhaps, agility was dictated by the swiftness of the mind inside it. And nobody, not even Ygor's worst enemies, had ever doubted his cleverness.

Ygor had learned to be clever.

Like a rat or a cockroach, you had to be clever to survive on the outskirts of society. And Ygor had lived amongst enough insects over the years to know how clever such beings really were. For so very long, they were his only friends. Before he met the son of Heinrich von Frankenstein. The *first* son, that is: the Monster.

But he wasn't a Monster. He was a miracle. A patchwork miracle that Ygor now controlled and intended to put to very good use. For with this body, Ygor would accomplish such miracles that even Satan Himself would shrink back in astonishment and fear. Ygor's hands would be the instrument for undoing the work of God.

Leaving a new God in His place.

Ygor half-dragged, half-carried Krogh through the empty streets, knocking him unconscious in the process. Once the policeman ceased struggling, he became less of a bother. Ygor draped him over his shoulders and made for the woods. He remembered now what had brought him back here to the wretched village of Frankenstein. An old doctor named Franz Heidelmann had rescued him from an underground cave in which he had been trapped for so very long. The doctor had revived him slowly, teasing Ygor with electricity, with the power that was rightfully his, determined not to heal Ygor but to manipulate him for his own purposes. Ygor was less than cooperative. The second the *power* was his, Ygor rose off the poor doctor's surgical table and brought the entire house down on top of him. There were others, too, the doctor's assistants who tried to kill Ygor. But they didn't succeed. Ygor couldn't quite remember what happened after the fire broke out in the lab, but he could guess. Krogh must have stumbled across his body amidst the rubble and taken him into police custody. What a fool. As if Ygor could be subdued by seven gendarmes in a pitiful mountain village like Frankenstein.

By and by, Ygor left behind the empty cobblestone streets and ramshackle houses and lumbered off back into the woods where he could be alone and gather his wits together. He found his way to a pool in a small clearing just as the first rays of dawn began to illuminate the forest. Birds fluttered away in panic when he drew near. Small furry animals scurried away and hid in the trees. Deer loped off into the shadows. It was just as well. He wished to be alone. Just him and Krogh.

He dropped the inspector face-down on the grass. Then he turned him over and shook him by the shoulder. The inspector did not move. He wondered if the bastard was dead.

Ygor sank to one knee, placed his massive index finger against the blue vein in the man's neck. Still it pulsed. Good. Very good. Ygor grabbed Krogh by the collar and dunked his head into the pool. He did this once, twice, three times, and laughed as Krogh sputtered and coughed and spat the water back into the pool.

"Enough dreaming, Herr Krogh," said Ygor. "We have work to do."

Krogh lay on his back, only one knee raised, and touched the wounds on the top of his head. Tiny rivulets of blood trickled down his forehead, the spot where his skull had made contact with the edge of a brick wall. Ygor had failed to protect his captive, had rushed past the rows of little sleeping houses—reluctantly—knowing he could kill any or all of the occupants in seconds if he chose to slow down and reacquaint himself with the always welcoming villagers of Frankenstein. Instead he fled, not caring what happened to the limp body in his arms.

"Work?" Krogh said. "What kind of work?"

Ygor stood over him, his boulder-sized fists clenching and unclenching slowly. "I'm hungry. I intend to do a little hunting now. When I get back, I will wish to cook. I expect a fire to be blazing by the time I get back."

At first it seemed as if Krogh would refuse, then the policeman glanced from side to side, understood fully where he was, nodded and whispered, "Yes. I suppose that would be wise, wouldn't it?"

"Don't even think of running away, Inspector. You would be amazed at what extreme *senses* this body contains. I can smell you from hundreds of feet away. I can hunt you down within minutes."

Krogh nodded slowly. "I believe you could."

"Besides, this mist is getting heavier by the second. I'm sure you must be growing cold." Krogh remained silent, then nodded once more. "Work with me, Krogh, and you might just live."

"I trust you won't be offended if I say I don't believe you."

Ygor laughed. He almost respected the man's boldness. "I'll be back soon."

He turned his back on the Inspector and walked toward the trees.

From behind him he heard, "Why're you keeping me alive?"

Ygor turned. "I was unconscious when Heidelmann brought me to his house. I was just as unconscious when you dragged me out of it. I have no idea where it is. You're going to guide me there."

"Heidelmann? But…why?"

"The good doctor left something behind. We're going to retrieve it."

It was obvious that Krogh wanted to ask more questions, but he resisted the urge. He remained silent.

Ygor nodded his approval, then walked off into the shadows….

Mike found himself in someone's extremely fancy dining room in the Pacific Palisades writing HELTER SKELTER on the walls in fake blood. Apparently, Chad had begged his parents to let him use their mansion for the weekend. According to Chad his parents were vacationing in Spain, so no one would be around to "jinx up the works." That's actually the way Chad spoke. Though he was extremely effeminate, he sometimes loved to speak in 1930s gangster language. He came off as a gay James Cagney. It was like watching Cagney from *White Heat* and *Yankee Doodle Dandy* simultaneously.

A whole mess of people were running around building a makeshift wall of mirrors for the big scene that would be shot in the dining room of the mansion. Mike wondered what Chad's parents would say when they found all this fake blood everywhere. Did this stuff wash out? He hadn't asked anybody. He figured Chad must know what he's doing.

Chad briefly introduced him to Eric Heidecker, an overweight, middle-aged man wearing Coke-bottle-glasses. He was about twenty years older than either Chad or Mike. He was soft-spoken and slightly awkward in his mannerisms. Chad left the two of them alone together so they could get to work ruining his parent's walls. Eric stood on top of a wooden ladder, and appeared to be just about done scrawling the second "G" in the word "PIGGIES" right above the elaborate archway that led out into the foyer.

"So, uh, how long have you known Chad?" Mike asked.

"For years. Ever since he was a teenager. He used to come into the shop all the time and buy the coolest lobby cards. I could tell he was into the same movies I was."

"What movies are those?"

"Oh, you know...psychotronic stuff. The entire spectrum of weird shit. *El Topo*. Coffin Joe. Ed Wood. Anything produced by Val Lewton. You name it. We got to talking, and he started complaining about his parents. His parents hate him, you see. They don't want him to go into film. They want him to go into therapy."

"They want him to be a psychiatrist?"

"No, they want to *treat* him. For his mental problems."

"What mental problems are those?"

"Well, according to them, being gay is a mental problem."

"I was wondering about that."

"You had to wonder?"

Mike laughed. "Well, no...I guess not."

Eric shrugged. "I kind of sympathize with them. I mean, they're assholes, yes, but some people just can't help being assholes."

"Or piggies."

"Yes, or piggies."

Eric climbed down off the ladder and surveyed his work. "Looks pretty good, I think."

He glanced over at Mike. "'HELTER SKELTER.' Yeah. Messy, and yet artistically appealing. They almost look like magical sigils."

"Thanks," Mike said. "You know, it's weird. A week ago, I was at the lowest point I've ever been. I mean, I almost felt like jumping off a bridge. Really. And now here I am reenacting the Manson murders in some chi-chi pad up in the Pacific Palisades."

"Life can be weird that way."

"You know what just struck me? Is this whole movie some kind of passive-aggressive attack against Chad's parents? I mean, does Chad somehow identify with a group of freaks who slaughtered a bunch of aloof rich people?"

"That would be my guess," Eric said.

"Say...does this blood come out?"

Eric nodded for a moment, remaining silent. "I do not know, sir."

For a second the deer was as still as a corpse, then he craned his neck upward. Ygor pounced.

Cold, dead fists sank into warm fur and flesh. The poor thing resisted. Ygor gripped the animal's antlers and twisted. Something snapped. He dropped the carcass to the grassy earth, kneeled down beside it. He began to tear the flesh off the bones.

When he returned to camp Krogh already had quite a nice fire going. He was kneeling on the grass, dropping chunks of wood on the fire. Perhaps he was thinking of using it as a weapon. He could go on thinking exactly that.

Ygor dropped the bloody slabs of meat in front of Krogh. "Cook it, unless you want this to be you."

As always, Krogh showed no fear. He raised one eyebrow and said, "Somehow I don't think even *you* would stoop to cannibalism."

"But it wouldn't be cannibalism. Is it cannibalism when you or your friends in the village hunt and kill a lower life form? No, I think not."

"Is that what you are? A *higher* life form?"

Ygor laughed. "Far more than that. Who but a god can rise from the dead?"

"As far as I know, only two men in history ever rose from the dead."

"But the last I heard, he only did it *once*. I've done it again and again and again. I'm still waiting for your little...second coming. When it finally happens, I don't think it'll be anywhere near as impressive as the escapes I've made from the grave."

Krogh said nothing. What was there to say?

Ygor stood motionless, like a lifeless statue erected to the wretched of the earth, his massive arms crossed over his dirt-encrusted shirt and jacket. Watching Krogh. Waiting for him to get back to work.

Krogh did so, without complaint.

5.

"So...this was once the house of the great Dr. Heidelmann," Ygor said. "Now it's my house, to do with as I please."

It was late in the afternoon by the time the strange pair reached Dr. Heidelmann's ruined estate, a generations-old mansion destroyed not only by fire but by a mixture of happenstance and naiveté and extreme bad luck.

Ygor had known his fair share of bad luck, but Dr. Heidelmann had been brought down by a supernaturally high amount of it in a very short period of time.

Amidst the still-smoking piles of wood and ragged pyramids of shattered brick and stone lay the object of Ygor's quest.

"Tell me why we're here," said Krogh. These words were uttered without a trace of anger or frustration, and yet Ygor could detect the subtle hint of authority in the Inspector's voice. It would not abandon him, even when he knew full well that he had now outlived his usefulness. What would it take to break this man? Everyone has his breaking point. For Ygor it had been a three-inch-thick loop of hemp rope tied around a wooden pole in the middle of the village square so many years before....

"We're looking for the basement," Ygor said. "The entrance must be here somewhere. I never left the laboratory, so I wouldn't know exactly where."

"How do you know it's here at all then?"

"Oh, Dr. Heidelmann told me a great deal while he was poking and prodding me. He was half-talking to himself, only using me as a sounding board. He didn't know I could understand every word that passed through those lips."

"I don't understand. Dr. Heidelmann was a good man. A

man of medicine. I've known him since I was a child. Why would he involve himself in such ghastly business, in resurrecting *monsters*?"

Ygor had the urge to rip Krogh's head from his shoulders, but managed to stay his own hand. Why did he care if this little policeman thought of him as a monster? "He didn't believe he was doing anything wrong. He was just doing his job. He was trying to save lives. Dr. Heidelmann did not distinguish between the lives of men and...and *monsters*." Ygor smiled. "That was his mistake. And my boon."

Ygor pointed at a collapsed spiral staircase. "Start digging."

Krogh just stared at him for a second. "But...why? Surely you could dig through that rubble far faster than I."

Ygor sat down amidst the rubble, drew his knees up to his chest. "Yes, I could. But I want to see *you* do it, Inspector."

Krogh sighed. He spread his hands in the air. "Don't I at least deserve an explanation? I saw the Monster eaten alive inside the sulfur pit beneath Frankenstein's laboratory years ago. Will you at least tell me how you ended up in this... in this...this *shell*? Wolfgang Frankenstein told me he shot you dead in his own laboratory. I remember rumors that your ghost was haunting Frankenstein's castle. All that came to an end when the villagers went mad and burned down the entire structure one night. I was certain your ghost had gone away with it."

"I went away...and came back. You don't need to know anything more than that. Now get to work." Ygor pointed.

Krogh nodded and dug into the piles of dirt and stones with his gloved hands.

The shoot went on well into the wee hours of the morning. Mike ended up playing one of the corpses. He felt as if he had arrived.

He and Lucy went home that night feeling exuberant. They stopped off at a hole-in-the-wall coffee shop on Franklin Avenue, only a few blocks from Lucy's apartment, and just talked for about an hour. She was still wearing her full Sharon Tate outfit, except now it was covered in blood. Mike was covered in blood, too. Everyone kept staring at them. Mike was acutely aware of how many guys were staring at Lucy. The attention made him a little uncomfortable—and proud at the same time. He felt as if they were all thinking, Why the hell is that chick sitting with *him*?

The second the door closed behind them Mike wrapped his arms around Lucy's waist and kissed her on her bloody throat. Lucy laughed and pushed his arms away. "Hey," she said. "Lucy's not that kind of a girl."

Mike felt ashamed. "I'm sorry. I just thought...I don't want to do anything to mess this up."

Lucy leaned against the wall and said, "You're cute." She reached out and ran her fingers through his hair. She leaned toward him and kissed him lightly on the lips. "Blood looks good on you."

"Blood looks fantastic on you."

"Well." She glanced coquettishly at the floor and whispered, "Lucy's not that kind of girl, but... maybe Sharon is." She sank her fingers into his thighs and ran her tongue along his severed carotid artery...kissed him on the lips.

After a few minutes, she took his hand and dragged him into her bedroom.

She didn't take off the wig. When he tried to take it off, she stopped him.

She insisted he call her "Sharon" throughout. When he slipped a couple of times and called her Lucy, she beat him on the back with her fists. Mike made sure he got it right after the third time. He wondered if he would have bruises the next morning. During the peak moment she gasped, "Say 'Sharon.' *Say* it." And he did. He said it three times, quite convincingly.

And then she was done, and so was he.

She didn't call Mike anything at all.

The full moon hung low in the sky. It was so huge one could see the craters marring its pale white surface. Its face was not so different from that of a newly risen corpse. Its rays shone down lovingly on Ygor's still form. It wasn't as comforting as sunlight, but still...what was moonlight but the diffuse, reflected light of a distant sun? Though it did reenergize Ygor's new body, it granted him only a fraction of the power available to him from the blazing, noonday orb.

Ygor still sat with his knees drawn up to his chin. He said nothing, just observed as Krogh almost killed himself with exhaustion.

Ygor was surprised he hadn't yet collapsed. He swore to himself he would snap the policeman in two the second his head hit the dirt.

But that hadn't happened yet.

Krogh's mechanical arm continued digging long after his left hung limp at his side. It almost seemed to be possessed of a tenacity even greater than the rest of his body. At last, the final slab of mortar was pushed aside and the stairway leading down into Dr. Heidelmann's basement lay revealed.

Ygor rose to his feet and lumbered toward the black pit in the ground. He pointed at it and said, "Go."

Krogh was almost out of breath, and yet despite this he managed to say, "For a god, you seem to need a lot of help."

"GO!"

Who could resist a voice like a thousand tomb doors slamming shut at once? Krogh nodded and approached the pit. He whispered, "The canary in the coal mine, eh?" then started down the stairs.

Ygor followed him. It seemed as if the fire had not penetrated this deep. No rubble obstructed their path. A bright shaft of maggot-white moonlight shone down on a dark, seven-foot-long object laying near the bottom of the stairs. This was what Ygor had come for.

He kneeled down beside it and ran his dead palm over an ancient family crest well over five hundred years old.

"Who...*what's* in there?" Krogh said. It was the first time Ygor had detected even a modicum of fear in the man's voice.

"This," Ygor said, "is the coffin of Count Dracula."

6.

He did indeed have bruises the next morning, and yet he'd never felt better. He glanced over at the clock and saw it was almost noon.

Lucy had her face buried in the pillow. She lay on her stomach, her head almost entirely covered by Sharon's mussed wig. He reached out and caressed her shoulder. Then he kissed her soft shoulder blade.

"Mmmm," she whispered. "Feels good."

He planted kisses all the way down her spine.

"What time is it?" she said into the pillow.

"Best day of my life."

"Jesus," Lucy said. "You're so fucking corny. I love it." Just as he lifted his head up, she said, "No, no, don't stop. Keep doing what you're doing. Feels nice."

So, he did. Then he massaged her back. When she finally chose to flip over, she smiled up at him and said, "Where'd you learn to do that?"

"My girlfriend in high school taught me."

"How many girlfriends have you had?"

"Including you? Two."

She laughed, reached up and caressed his cheek. "You're sweet. You really are. But I'm not your girlfriend."

Mike felt a slight sting. After only a second, he shook it off and said, "I understand." He'd fucked up his relationship with Cynthia because he'd been too jealous. Too damn possessive. He didn't want to make that mistake again. So, he decided to say nothing more about it. He leaned down and planted kisses on her flat stomach instead. He worked his way upwards. When he finally reached her lips, he smiled and said, "So, do you mind if I stop calling you Sharon?" He slipped off her wig, too fast for her to stop him this time.

"Feel free," she said. "When you get to know me better, you'll realize I have hundreds of different personalities, so I think I can afford to lose one of them. Well, for now, at least." Lucy gently took the wig out of his hand and tossed it on the nightstand beside the bed.

"*For now*," Mike whispered. "That's all I ask. Just for now." In the warm afternoon sunlight, they made love again. This time he called her "Lucy" throughout. He emerged from the tryst far less battered than the night before.

The entire experience felt different, but no less satisfying.

Wolfgang von Frankenstein stroked the trigger of the gun, wanting so much to kill this man who had brought nothing but chaos and death into his life. But something told him to hold back. The voice...this was not Ygor. And yet, it *was*.

"You're...different somehow," Wolfgang said.

"Your father made you," Ygor said. "Your father made me. The two of us. Brothers."

"In my father's diaries, he said the mon...his *creation* developed the ability to talk, at least to a limited extent. He could communicate complex thoughts sometimes, stated simply, as if a seething intelligence were lurking just beneath that patchwork brow. To his very dying breath my father was convinced that his creation could be salvaged, rehabilitated, made *human*, if only he'd had more time. More than anything, he wanted to remove the tarnish from our family name. He was certain he could do it, but mother forbade him from pursuing his experiments any further. And of course, there were always the authorities breathing down his neck. You want to hear the truth? Part of the reason I returned to my family's ancestral home was to pick up where my father had left off, even though I didn't want to admit it, not to my wife, not even to myself. If my father's creation hadn't survived all those years, by God I think I would've rebuilt him myself out of scratch if I'd had to."

All this time Frankenstein drew closer and closer to Ygor,

studying his eyes, seeing life in them, not evil. Life, like sparks of electricity, like tiny lightning bolts embedded in the pupils and rods and cones of this stranger's dark eyes.

Stranger? Frankenstein knew now that this was no stranger….

"Why," said Ygor, "why, then, did you try to kill me?"

"I wasn't trying to kill you," said Wolfgang, "I was trying to kill *myself*. My ambition. All my secrets. My true desires." Wolfgang had tucked the gun back into his belt, and now placed his gloved hand on Ygor's bulky shoulder. "I'm sorry. Sorry you had to run to my brother for help, and not me. He did this, didn't he? Somehow…somehow he placed your mind in…."

Ygor nodded. "Our brother…is an intelligent man."

Wolfgang nodded. "He was willing to go farther than I ever dreamed. Right after…everything happened…." Wolfgang paused for a moment, casting his gaze toward the ground, feeling genuine shame. "I immediately packed up Father's diary and mailed it to Ludwig. I didn't want to look at it anymore. Please understand, I just wanted peace in my home."

"Yes…peace." Ygor nodded once. "That's all I've ever wanted."

Wolfgang had no response. What could he say? "It seems as if you've found a little bit of it, no thanks to me. Apparently, Ludwig made good use of Father's diary. I'm sure I could have as well, if not for…. Enough of that. Tell me, what happened to… to your body? Your original body?"

Now it was Ygor's turn to cast his gaze downward. "Sometimes…I'm afraid to know."

Wolfgang's brow furrowed in puzzlement. "Surely Ludwig would never have put Ygor's…."

"He didn't know…what he was doing. He was…tricked. And he paid the price…for that mistake."

"Tricked? By *whom*?"

"His former mentor, Dr. Bohmer. Bohmer was secretly working with Ygor. It was Bohmer who placed my brain… in Ygor's body. He wanted…no evidence left behind…of his betrayal. Of course, the best place…to hide my brain…was in Ygor's useless corpse." A slight smile spread across Ygor's face. "From one corpse…to another."

"Bohmer? But why would he do such a thing?"

"Ygor...can weave...a fine spell."

"True enough. I've experienced it firsthand. If only I had burrowed the bullets a bit deeper."

"I'm glad...you didn't. If you had...I wouldn't have this body. I wouldn't have...this place to live...and work...and sleep."

Wolfgang squeezed Ygor's arm. "But you can't stay here."

Ygor pulled away. He stared at his brother suspiciously.

Wolfgang said, "No...I mean, of course, you can come back whenever you want. But we need to run some tests. We need to document your transformation. You're living proof that my father...my brother too...that they weren't *mad*. They were geniuses, capable of feats no doctor living today has even *dreamed* of performing. And yet they both succeeded—both of them! The entire world thinks you're a monster. But you're not a monster. You've proven that." Fire had erupted in the recesses of Wolfgang's eyes. He reached out and brushed Ygor's hair away from his rugged, roadmap of a face. "There was never anything wrong with your brain because there was never anything wrong with your soul. My father didn't slip up in that regard. And we can prove it to the *world*...you and I."

Ygor took two steps backwards. "I...don't...need...to... prove...anything."

"But think, man, think of our name."

"Our...name?"

"Yes, of course. Our *family* name. We owe it to Father, the two of us. Don't we?"

Wolfgang watched Ygor's face as it softened and fell.

For the third time, Wolfgang reached out for Ygor. He placed his hand on his shoulder and squeezed gently. "We're both Frankensteins, you and I. Come back to London with me. Allow me to introduce you to my family, to the world, in a proper way. The way you've always deserved."

Tears began to stream down Ygor's face. His lips trembled. He nodded. "Yes...yes...."

They hugged there in the cold fog, two brothers reunited at last.

Mike soon discovered that Lucy wasn't a fan of cooking. She seemed to eat out all the time; her kitchen was a graveyard of white takeout containers. She told him she'd drive him to Du-Par's and they could share breakfast. As they split a BLT Mike thought back to the first time they'd eaten here, only a few days before, and everything that had happened since then. As he stared at her in the afternoon sunlight that angled in through the shuttered windows, he marveled at how beautiful she was. And how lucky he was to have met her.

"I'm afraid I'm going to have to drop you off right after this," Lucy said. "Do you want to go back home?"

Home. It surprised him how casually she referred to *her* apartment as his "home."

"Do you have plans after this?"

"Sure do. I've got to go to work at the restaurant. How do you think I'm payin' for that BLT in your hand?"

Mike laughed. "I guess...I just thought of you as an actress and that's it."

"As if I'm makin' any money off that? Right."

"Well, you did say you got that one commercial."

"Like that pays much? I think it paid for a couple of bags of groceries."

"Well...you're doin' better than me. I think those two stories I sold paid for *half* a bag of groceries. *If* that."

"Don't be so hard on yourself. You're talented. You're gonna make it."

Mike shrugged and waved away her words. A small part of him thought her prediction was unlikely; an equally small part of him couldn't imagine how he *wouldn't* succeed. The rest of him never knew what the hell to think...about anything. His old girlfriend had once told him that he was a complete paradox. "How can the most arrogant person in the world," she once asked him, "suffer from such an epic inferiority complex?"

Lucy reached out and stroked his stubbled cheek. "I'll make sure it happens for you. It *has* to happen. If you don't succeed, how am *I* going to?"

Mike laughed. "Someone like you doesn't need me to succeed."

"Don't be so sure of that." Her smile had faded. "It's hard to get noticed around here. The most beautiful people in the world come to this place. And they all look exactly like each other. It's hard to stand out."

"You shouldn't have to worry about that. You don't look like anyone I've ever met. You're unique."

"Not unique enough. I need a great role, and you're going to give it to me. I'm going to make *sure* you succeed."

"How?"

"I'll show you. Tonight. I work the two to seven shift. The second I get home, I'm taking you somewhere special."

"Where?"

"It's a mystery. Consider it a religious pilgrimage." She smiled and stuffed the final bite of her sandwich between her red lips. "You'll see," she said with a mouthful of bacon.

"I like your confidence," Mike said. "One of us has to have it, I guess."

"You have confidence in me and I'll have confidence in you. We'll balance each other out."

"So…where the hell do you work?"

"I suppose you could say I'm a singer and a dancer."

What did that mean? Was she a stripper? "Yeah, where?"

"At Chuck's Fish Shanty over on La Cienega. I know you've seen it. The front door looks like the mouth of a huge whale."

"Oh, yeah. Looks like Monstro from *Pinocchio*? I've always wanted to go there."

"Once every other hour the waitresses have to walk out into the middle of the restaurant and do this stupid little dance and sing for all the kiddies. It's pretty fuckin' ridiculous. Everyone hates it. For me, it's my favorite part of the evening. It's the only time of the day I feel like an actress. Well…except when I'm with Chad and his UCLA buddies."

"I'd love to see that," Mike said. "Why don't I come to work with you just long enough to—?"

Lucy held her palm in the air like a stop sign. "No. Never. Let's get this straight: DO NOT EVER drop by the restaurant unannounced. I'd die of embarrassment if anyone I knew ever saw me singing and dancing in that stupid fish costume. If you ever do, I'll kill you and toss you out of my apartment."

"You'll kill me, *then* toss me out of your apartment? C'mon. It sounds cute. You don't have to be—"

Her blue lacquered fingernail hovered only inches from his right eyeball. "I'll cut your fingers off. *Never* drop by."

"Well, I promise not to drop by...today. I just remembered that Eric asked me to come by his store."

Lucy smiled. "Cool. It's not that far from Chuck's. I'll drop you off there. You two should have a lot to discuss. Remember to ask him about *London After Midnight*. He's the one who told me all about it. Him and Chad. I think Chad's the only one who's actually seen it, though."

"Jesus, we were so busy yesterday I completely forgot about that. I still can't believe it. Finding a print of that film would be like...stumbling across the Loch Ness Monster curled up at the bottom of the Holy Grail or something. If I could see that film just once, my life would be complete."

Lucy reached across the table and curled her pinky around his forefinger. "You are such an obsessed little asshole. What about last night? That didn't make you 'complete'?"

He placed his other hand over hers and said, "Two days ago you saved my life. Really. Last night you saved it a second time."

The expression on Lucy's face was a serious one. "Wow," she said. "I don't think I've ever saved anyone's life before."

"Well...I've never been saved before. I hope I can return the favor someday."

"You'd need to save my life *twice* for us to be even. But I'll cut down the obligation to just once as long as you promise *never* to drop by Chuck's Fish Shanty. Not just tonight. *Ever.*"

"I promise," Mike said.

"And while you're at it, promise not to talk to Eric too long," Lucy added. "You've still got a screenplay to finish."

Ygor agreed to leave only if Wolfgang would wait long enough for him to say goodbye to Sister Marie. Wolfgang assented. The two of them kneeled down and awoke Marvin or Mervyn from his induced slumber on the cobblestones. Wolfgang explained to him that he had been attacked by a mugger. Ygor didn't like to lie. It gave him a bad feeling in his stomach. A sick feeling, like when he used to help Ygor in his hateful revenge schemes.

But, of course, this wasn't the same thing at all. Wolfgang had thought he'd tracked down the murderer of his only living brother. He had no way of knowing that Ygor was not Ygor at all. The funny man had simply gotten in the way. It was a mistake.

The Frankensteins, despite their undeniable genius, seemed prone to mistakes.

Wolfgang and Ygor helped the funny man off the ground and led him back down the alley.

"Wh-what happened?" asked the man.

"A simple accident," said Wolfgang. "They can happen to the best of us."

"Who the hell're you?"

"Ygor's brother."

"*Brother*? No one even knew he had a family."

"Oh, neither did he, my friend, neither did he. But we'll remedy that situation right away."

Mervyn or Marvin seemed confused, perhaps even a little envious, but made no further commentary.

The Frankensteins dragged the man back into the warm kitchen, out of the swirling fog, closing the door quietly behind them.

1.

Tinseltown Book and Poster was a mess. Mike couldn't figure out how they made any money. It wouldn't be possible to find anything amidst all this chaos. It was a labyrinth of movie posters, stills, books, VHS tapes, and magazines. Anything in the store not related to cinema seemed to be there by pure accident.

From behind a pile of used books, Eric glanced up and said, "Hey, Mike, glad you could make it!" He put down a pricing gun and waved Mike over.

"Hell of a place you've got here," Mike said. "I'd hate to get lost in here. How do people find their way out?"

"How do people find their way *in*?" Eric said. He pushed aside the pile of books and said, "To tell you the truth, I set the store up this way on purpose. The way the store started is that I just wanted someplace to house my own collection. I'm still really attached to it all. So, I try to discourage people from actually buying anything."

"So how do you make a living?"

"My wife's the real business woman. Her father's rich and so is she. As long as this place doesn't make money, we're fine. It's a tax write-off."

"How is that possible?"

Eric waved the question away. "That's too complicated. Essentially, this is a great place for me and my close friends to hang out and watch all the movies they've always wanted to see. You wouldn't believe the people I've met in this place. It's crazy. Come over here." He led Mike over to a wall decorated with photographs of Eric with his arm around some of Mike's childhood heroes: Adam West, Grandpa Al Lewis, Anne Francis, Fay Wray, Charles Drake, Jeff Morrow, Richard Denning, Vincent Price, even Carroll Borland herself.

"Incredible," Mike said, pointing at the photo of Borland. "She's a character in the screenplay I'm working on! Well, sort of. I mean, I don't call her Carroll Borland, but...."

"I know, Lucy told me all about it. And Chad said the screenplay was dynamite. Listen, I know her. Do you want to meet her? I might even be able to get her to read the screenplay, if you'd like."

"Oh, I don't know. I mean, I've taken certain liberties with her character. I wouldn't want her to think...."

"No, no. She's totally cool. She'll love it. Believe me. Did you know she wrote a sequel to *Dracula*? Lugosi himself read it. That's how they met. She just sent it to him out of the blue."

"I don't think I ever heard about that. I don't know...maybe I have. Maybe I could add that into the screenplay."

"Come over here." Eric wrapped his huge arm around Mike's scrawny shoulders and led him over to the far corner of the store where lay the Bela Lugosi shrine. It really did look like a shrine, with an altar and candles burning and rubber bats hanging from the ceiling and posters from some of his more obscure movies adorning the walls. Atop the altar stood brand new VHS copies of almost all of Lugosi's films, even some Mike himself hadn't gotten around to seeing: *The Death Kiss, Murder by Television, Scared to Death,* and on and on.

Eric said, "Did you know that the Lugosi memorabilia outsells all the Karloff memorabilia ten to one?"

"Really? Well...maybe it's because you've got this huge altar here set up in honor of Lugosi."

"No, no." With a disgusted expression on his face, Eric dismissed the comment with a wave of his hand. "I'm talkin' about *all* the memorabilia shops in Los Angeles. I know all these guys. We get together at all the shows around the country. I'm tellin' you, there's been this recent upsurge in interest in Lugosi. I don't know why. Very few people ever come in asking for Karloff memorabilia. Look, I don't have anything against Karloff, of course. It's just interesting to me, that's all. I opened this shop back in the early '70s. Roundabout 1981 or so I noticed all these weird punk kids comin' in askin' for Lugosi stuff."

"Maybe it has something to do with Bauhaus."

"Bauhaus?"

"You haven't heard that song? I'll play it for you sometime. What the heck is this?" Only a few feet away from the altar stood a film projector. "This thing looks like an antique."

"I've had it since I was a kid and it's still runnin'. Every Saturday night me and my friends have classic movie night here. I own sixteen-millimeter prints of a lot of films, most of the great horror flicks. It just so happens that tonight, lucky you, I'm showing a Lugosi film."

"Which one?"

"*Bowery at Midnight.*"

"Holy shit! That's the only Monogram Lugosi I haven't seen." In the 1940s Lugosi made nine films for Monogram Studios. They were generally considered to be some of the worst films Lugosi ever made. Indeed, some critics considered them among the worst movies ever made, period, but Mike had never been sympathetic to that point of view. He knew full well that they were flawed, but somehow, they still continued to exert some kind of strange, hypnotic fascination for him.

"When're you playing it?"

"At eight o'clock sharp. It's that way every Saturday."

"I can't stay that long. I'm supposed to meet Lucy back at the apartment at seven."

"You're gonna let some girl come between you and Lugosi? Okay, I'm kidding. Of course you are. Here's what we can do. We'll just watch it right now. I don't mind watching it twice. I've seen it a billion times already anyway."

Without waiting for a response, Eric walked over to the front of the store, closed all the blinds, grabbed two metal fold-up chairs from a stack beside the front door, set them up near the Lugosi altar, then pulled a screen down from the ceiling by a flimsy string. The screen covered a huge poster advertising Lugosi in Robert Florey's *Murders in the Rue Morgue.*

As Mike watched Eric spool the film into the projector, Mike said, "So, Lucy demanded I ask you about *London After Midnight.*

She says Chad actually found a copy deep in the UCLA archives. I almost shit my pants when she said that."

Eric laughed. "Well, she's got it half-right. You know, she's not into all this stuff like we are."

"I'm trying to change that."

"I'll be stunned if you succeed. No, what Chad found was a series of still photos that've never been seen before. We're hoping someone can reconstruct the film from just the photos. But that's the best we can hope for at the moment. Who knows? It's possible a print will pop up somewhere, sometime, maybe in some South American country. Stranger things have happened."

"I knew it was too good to be true."

"I hate to disappoint. However, I might still have some good news for you. Our latest project is something very promising. Chad and I might be on the verge of uncovering a copy of the test reel that Lugosi filmed for *Frankenstein*."

Mike could feel himself holding his breath. Every horror fan knew the story by heart. In 1931, at the height of his fame, fresh off the phenomenal success of Tod Browning's *Dracula*, Lugosi was offered the role of the Frankenstein Monster. When he discovered that the Monster would have no dialogue, Lugosi refused to appear in the movie. He felt it was beneath him.

Nonetheless, twenty-one minutes of test footage was indeed shot by director Robert Florey in which Lugosi wore an early version of the Frankenstein make-up. For fifty-five years horror fans had yearned to see this test footage. Many mysteries would be answered: What was Lugosi's portrayal of the Monster like at this early stage? Was it as silly as actor Edward Van Sloan (who portrayed Dr. Waldman in the finished film) had once suggested in an interview? What did the Jack Pierce make-up look like? For years film historians had claimed that Lugosi never removed himself from the project at all—that the head of the studio, Carl Laemmle, was so disappointed in the Florey/Lugosi test reel that he fired both men from the project and gave them the job of adapting Edgar Allan Poe's short story "Murders in the Rue Morgue" as a consolation prize. Since *Murders in the Rue Morgue* ended up being a box office flop, this didn't help either Florey's or Lugosi's careers. Laemmle assigned James Whale to direct *Frankenstein*, and Whale gave the role of the Monster to an unknown actor named Boris Karloff. Karloff went on to fame and fortune, often being cast in roles Lugosi most desired. In a moment of epic hubris, Lugosi had created his own monster.

Die-hard Lugosi fans insisted the Florey/Lugosi *Frankenstein* would have been a good movie—perhaps not the classic film that the Whale/Karloff collaboration came to be, but a credible film nonetheless. Many of them wanted to uncover this test footage merely to prove the critics wrong, to prove that Lugosi could have mastered the greatest role ever essayed in a Golden Age horror film. But for years everyone assumed the test reels had been destroyed way back in the '30s. Back then, at the very beginning of Hollywood, no one could have predicted that these flickering shadow shows would accrue generations of fans who'd gladly pay money to see even the *cast-offs* of these early films. Storage space was at a high premium, and not everything could be saved. Besides, who on earth would hang onto a test reel for a horror film like *Frankenstein*?

"How is that possible?" Mike said. "Unless...I heard a rumor once that Carl Laemmle Junior hung onto a copy of the test reel as a souvenir."

"That's right," Eric said. "And Lugosi's last agent, Don Marlowe, once placed an ad in a trade journal offering the test reel for sale for four thousand dollars. A few days later the ad was removed and Marlowe claimed he'd never owned it in the first place."

"Why would he do that?"

"Chad and I suspect that Marlowe placed the ad in the paper in order to generate some interest from Junior himself. Perhaps the reels had been stolen from Laemmle Senior years before. Now Marlowe has it, offers it for sale, knowing that Junior might offer to buy the damn thing back just to keep it out of circulation."

"But why would Laemmle—or Junior—do that? Why would he care at this point?"

"Well, I've heard that Junior was a bit of an eccentric. A real Howard Hughes type. So, who knows? Perhaps releasing the test reel would tarnish the memory of one of his few great successes. Let's face it, Junior was only the head of the studio for about nine years. He spent the rest of his life as a shut-in. One of the few genuine treasures he gave the world was *Frankenstein*. Why tarnish that with this test reel that Junior considered to be something of a joke?"

"So Junior paid Marlowe to return the test reels and then pretend it never existed?"

"That's the prevailing theory. Well, between me and Chad, at least. You see, we consider ourselves to be detectives at the moment—celluloid gumshoes on the trail of a kidnapped test reel from five decades ago."

"A real cold case. So, what the hell happened? How'd you track it down?"

Eric glanced from side to side, as if afraid of eavesdropping spies. "Chad was putting together a retrospective on the Laemmles for a film festival at UCLA. In the course of putting it together, he happened to meet the husband of Junior's former housekeeper. Well, it just so happened that the housekeeper has sticky fingers, particularly near the end of Junior's life when he was half out of his mind with memory loss. The housekeeper stole a lot of stuff that was in Junior's safe back in '79. One of those items was the test reel. The housekeeper's husband was down on his luck and asked Chad if he wanted to buy any of this stuff. You wouldn't believe what was in there. Sixteen millimeters going back to the 1920s. But Chad's eyes immediately focused on the canister marked *Frankenstein Test Reel*. Well, Chad doesn't have much of a poker face, so the old man knew it was valuable. He's demanding a thousand for it. Chad and me are trying to raise the money now."

"Can't you ask your wife for it?"

Eric laughed. "You don't know my wife. She *hates* movies."

"When's the deal gonna go down?"

"Any day now, my friend, any day now."

"But Chad hasn't actually *seen* the film?"

"No. The old man won't even show it to us until he sees the money."

"What a bastard. Can I come with you when you finally make the drop-off?"

"I don't know. I don't want to scare the guy away. This is a delicate situation. We're buying stolen goods after all. This ain't like walking down to Eddie Brandt's and rentin' *The Ghost of Frankenstein.*"

"I understand. But just think about it, okay? I mean, if this is all true, I'll do anything to be there."

"I'll talk it over with Chad. Now…on with our main creature feature…."

Mike and Eric settled back in their chairs and watched the flickering images unfold before their eyes. From this perspective, behind the piles of celluloid detritus, the two of them couldn't even see the cash register.

"What if someone tries to rip off the store?" Mike whispered during the opening credits.

"They won't," Eric said.

"What if someone wants to buy something?"

"They won't," he said.

Krogh instantly recognized the elaborate Dracula crest painted on the top of the coffin. The Dracula family was infamous all throughout Europe and their reputation for unholy savagery had even penetrated into the isolated village of Frankenstein. A few years ago, rumors had spread around the country that a mysterious nobleman calling himself "Baron Latos" was attacking innocent villagers, draining their blood and leaving them for dead. Some of the villagers were still seen to this day, roaming the forests at night, searching for prey. But apparently Baron Latos had been destroyed, or so they said. Was it all wishful thinking? Was this the same creature? Was Baron Latos actually Count Dracula?

"Good," Ygor said, laughing. "Very good! The cellar must have protected his coffin from the fire." He pointed at the lid and glared at Krogh, saying nothing.

"No," Krogh whispered, "I refuse to have anything more to do with you. I refuse!"

Angered, Ygor lashed out at Krogh. He belted him across the face, grabbed him by the shoulders, then tossed him across the dusty concrete floor. Krogh slammed into a stone pillar. Intense pain stabbed his ribs.

Ygor growled, awkwardly unclasped the mahogany lid with his oversized, pale green fingers, then swung the coffin open. Interspersed with moist black soil was a fine gray ash, the ashes of He Who Could Not Die. "The ashes of the undead," Ygor whispered. Dr. Heidelmann had told Ygor everything he needed to know about this strange and merciless being. He would be a useful tool in the coming days.

Ygor turned toward Krogh and said, "Are you afraid of what's inside that box, Krogh? You should be. When we wake *him* up, it won't be the tiny villages of Frankenstein or Visaria that will have to live in fear. No…no, it will be the entire *world*. Now stop your pitiful whimpering and close the lid, then drag the coffin upstairs. *Get to it*."

Ygor stood motionless in the middle of the dark cellar, his arms folded across his chest, looking more like an unreal statue than something that thought and lived and breathed. Krogh knew he was not whimpering, far from it. But he also knew he was lucky to still be alive at all. He needed to stay that way. Not just for himself. The longer he remained by Ygor's side, the better chance he would have to find some way to defeat the monster.

He wrapped his arms around the stone pillar and pulled himself to his feet. It felt like there were thin, sharp knives penetrating the flesh between his ribs. But nonetheless he managed to stumble over to the coffin, slam it shut, then grab the brass handles on the side. Despite the fact that a body no longer occupied the infernal box, it still seemed heavy.

Krogh briefly planted his palms on top of the coffin, leaned his whole weight against it in order to catch his breath. "Where… where are we taking it?" he asked.

"To someone who *knows*." Ygor's black lips curled upward in a sick, self-satisfied grin.

Krogh knew he was getting nothing more out of the fiend. In silence, he grabbed the handles and began slowly dragging the box across the floor. The sound of wood scraping against concrete, like dead fingernails scratching madly at the inside of a box buried six feet below the earth, echoed between the subterranean walls.

Krogh could feel Ygor's glare against his back as he took the stone steps upward towards the pale moonlight.

Queen Zemba sat in her hut in the middle of the Black Forest. She'd been there for over twenty years, ever since the birth of her last daughter. She had many other daughters, but they had all abandoned her. Not like Aishe.

"Mother, why are you so morose today?" Aishe asked, leaning over her and massaging her bony shoulders. "What's wrong?"

The old woman leaned over a foul-smelling metal pot filled with black liquid. "Wrong?" Tears began to stream down her wrinkled cheeks. "Today is the day I must say goodbye to my favorite daughter."

Aishe took two steps backwards, without even intending to. "Wh-what're you talking about? Are you...are you going to...?"

"The water tells me what is to happen, and there's nothing I can do about it. I am so sorry." The old woman hung her head in grief. All of her power...all of it worthless. She couldn't even look her daughter in the eye. "I'm so sorry."

"Mother, no."

The wooden door to the ramshackle hut burst inward. Queen Zemba glanced up to see what had already been revealed to her in the smoke rising from the brew before her; and yet *seeing* the Monster standing there in person was something for which no one could ever be prepared—seeing that massive form filling her entire doorway, his misshapen features made even more menacing by the only source of light in the room: the fire burning beneath the metal pot.

"Zemba," the Monster growled. "Everyone in these parts knows of your powers. I want you to use them now."

"I'm afraid I can't do that," said the old woman, knowing her protests were useless. But she had to go through with them anyway, like an actor locked down to a script he did not fancy.

The Monster stepped further into the room. Aishe, whose face was paralyzed in fear, erupted into warbling screams.

The Monster's growls grew louder.

Zemba reached out and clutched her daughter's hands. "He will not hurt you," she said. And she wasn't lying.

"Just go and sit down in your bed."

Aishe nodded, then lurched back into the shadows and collapsed onto the makeshift bed laid out on the wooden floor.

"What is the task for which you seek my powers?" said Zemba.

The Monster stepped away from the door, revealing a second figure behind him. Zemba recognized him as the Inspector of the nearby village of Frankenstein. He had chased her and Aishe from the town on several occasions.... "For their own safety," he had said. All they had wanted were medical supplies for their wounded animals, but the villagers were a panicky sort. Who could blame them, what with all the troubles that had been plaguing them for so many generations?

The Inspector dragged a coffin behind him.

Aishe gasped again. "Wh-what's in there?" she asked.

"Not *what*," the Monster said. "*Who*. A *man* lies inside that box, not a monster. I want that man pulled out of the next world and brought back into this one."

"No, think about what you're doing," the old woman said. "The time it would take...."

The Monster smiled and bowed like a landed gentleman. The gesture seemed both menacing and absurd coming from this mockery of human life. "We have plenty of time, my dear woman. Plenty of time."

"And why is George Zucco, of all people, working as a gas station attendant?" Eric asked.

"My favorite line is 'Gosh all fish hooks,'" Mike said. "Did people say that even in the '40s?"

"I doubt it," Eric said, opening another can of Coca-Cola. "Maybe in the Deep South somewhere. Who knows? But you've got to admit, Bela's performance is great in this."

"Oh, absolutely," Mike said. "I mean, the man's sharing the screen with two great hams of cinema history, George Zucco and John Carradine, and both of them come off looking like chumps compared to him. Somehow, in even the worst production, Bela maintains his dignity. Even when surrounded by utter chaos. Like in this."

"Ramboona preserve us," Eric said. "Ramboona" was the name of the ineffectual god Lugosi and his followers worshipped in *Voodoo Man*.

At first Mike said nothing in return. After all, who could argue with such a statement? Then, without even thinking about it, the sentence flew out of his mouth: "That should be the name of the magazine."

"What magazine?"

"The one I'm going to publish about Bela Lugosi: *Ramboona Preserve Us*. What a great name for a 'zine."

"You're going to publish a 'zine?"

"I hadn't really thought about it until now. Someone's got to preserve this treasure trove of Lugosi knowledge. Why not us?"

"Us?"

"Yeah. We could both do it."

Eric remained silent for a second. "We could start out by selling them to my customers."

"You think your wife would like to subsidize a magazine?"

"Well, not about Lugosi. She'd think that was a monumentally stupid idea. She's very business-oriented, my wife, Ramboona bless her. If not for her, I don't know what the hell I'd do."

"Well, we won't tell her it's a Lugosi magazine. Tell her it's a movie magazine. Movie magazines sell."

"Oh, I wouldn't want to lie to her."

"It wouldn't be lying. A magazine about Lugosi *is* a movie magazine, right?"

Eric began chewing on a hangnail. "Yeah, I guess you're right. Technically. We could throw in some articles about other movies—some psychotronic stuff—just to make it true."

"Sure. Sounds reasonable to me."

"I think I'd have to show her a complete issue first, though, otherwise she won't go for it. She'll have to see what she's subsidizing. She's funny that way."

"That sounds easy enough. I could write a couple of articles; you could write a couple of articles—"

"Oh, I'm not a writer."

Mike slapped him against his chubby bicep. "C'mon. Just write it from a fan's perspective. I'll edit the stuff for you.

We could put out a call during your movie night for further submissions. I bet we get some interesting stuff that way."

"But what'll we pay 'em with?"

"Copies of the magazine in which their article appeared." That's what Mike had gotten paid for his first published short story. It seemed like a rip-off at the time. It still seemed like a rip-off. Perhaps it was time to spread the rip-off around a little bit.

"We could sell dubbed copies of rare movies through the magazine to help raise funds to publish more issues. That way your wife's not carrying the entire load. And you could place ads for the store here. At that point the magazine pretty much pays for itself."

Eric slammed his hairy fist on his knee and said, "By Ramboona, I'll do it! Or at least I'll ask my wife if she'll do it. As soon as you write a couple of articles, I'll approach her with the idea. And if she agrees, I'll tell you what…we'll own the thing 50/50. You won't be working for me; I won't be working for you."

"I feel like we should draw up a contract of principles like in *Citizen Kane*."

Eric waved him away. "No need. A simple handshake will do." They did indeed shake on it, the white light of the projector casting the silhouette of their shaking hands on the tattered screen decorating the poster-choked wall.

Only the sound of a phone ringing somewhere broke the moment. "That can't possibly be a customer," Eric said, groaning as he lifted his considerable bulk from the chair. He went into the back office. Mike remained sitting while listening to Eric answer the phone with a very informal, "Yep?" He didn't even bother to identify the name of the store. A few seconds later he called out, "Hey, Mike, for you!"

Mike was puzzled. Who the heck knew he was here? He followed Eric into the little office. "Hello?" Mike said, taking the smudged black receiver from Eric.

"I should've known you'd still be there." Lucy, of course.

"Oh. Hey. Are you on your lunch break?"

"Lunch break?" Lucy laughed. "I've been off for an hour. I'm back at the apartment. I thought we had a date tonight."

"Holy shit." Mike glanced down at his watch. "I had no idea it was so late. Eric and I started watching these Lugosi movies I'd never seen before... well, one of them I hadn't seen before... it was amazing...it's called *Bowery at Midnight*...I have a theory about it...it's an example of what I call 'Weird Noir'—"

"Okay, okay, I can see where this is going. Save the details for when we see each other. We need to get going soon if we're gonna make our appointment. You gonna haul your ass on over here or am I picking you up?"

Mike couldn't remember what the appointment was. Had she said earlier? Sometimes he could be quite forgetful. "Where are we going exactly?"

"You'll see. It's a surprise. I'm gonna make you a rich man. Just stay right where you are. I'll pick you up."

"I'll be waiting."

"Bye," she said softly.

"Bye." He hung up. Eric was staring at him with a concerned look on his face.

"Is she coming over here?" Eric asked.

"Yes. She has a surprise for me."

"Oh, Ramboona help you. Lucy's surprises are never pleasant."

"What do you mean?"

"She's a colorful girl, that's all I'm gonna say. Are you falling in love with her?"

"I—I don't know. Why? Would you...advise against that?"

"Advise against it? She's a beautiful girl who loves Cagney. I mean, Jesus, you don't find girls like that falling from trees. Not even in L.A. Especially not in L.A. A lot of people fall in love with Lucy. Lucy very rarely falls in love with them. You know she and Chad dated for a little while."

"I thought that guy was gay."

"Welllll...." Eric wiggled his hand in the air. "Gay. Bi-sexual. Whatever. It didn't last long."

"Things will be different with me."

"Why not?" Eric patted him on the shoulder. "Just be careful, that's all I'm saying."

"Ramboona preserve me."

"That's the attitude. You'll do fine."

Then they went back out into the store to set up chairs for Movie Night.

Twenty-four hours later the ashes moved at last, only slightly at first, then rose from the candlelit floor, within minutes causing a tiny cyclone that congealed together like a grotesque parody of human life. The Monster, who had been standing motionless over the witch and her daughter this entire time, resembling a lifeless statue, suddenly sparked to life, leaned forward and smiled, his dead eyes alive with anticipation. Inspector Krogh awoke from his place on the floor just as a long, white hand reached out from the storm, snatched the witch's daughter by her throat, and pulled her into the maelstrom of ash. She screamed and struggled. The witch did nothing. She sat cross-legged before the fire in the middle of the room, a fire that gave off no heat. Krogh shot to his feet and tried to approach the struggling girl, but the Monster growled and pushed him back down on the floor.

Krogh, the Monster, and the witch all watched as two pale hands enclosed the girl's throat. Then a face emerged from the swirling ash as well, an impossibly long rat-like face that did not bear any resemblance to a human being. Teeth the size of knives sank into the girl's neck. Her screams increased in intensity. As the blood drained from her throat, the ashes solidified until at last a full human figure stood in the center of the room. The fire paled to an icy blue, then slowly began to die out.

In the cramped darkening hut, a tall, slender figure rose to its full height, well over six feet. It still held the girl's lifeless throat in one squeezing fist; the other it held out toward its awed spectators. The rat-like face was gone. The thing that stood before them, blood pouring down its lips and neck and chest, appeared to be nothing more than an older gentleman with handsome features, well-groomed silver hair, a white moustache, the only discordant detail being its eyes: beady and black like that of a sewer rodent. But even these seemed to change within the space of several heartbeats and the piercing dark eyes that took their place would be capable of fooling almost anyone. Then the fire died out altogether, leaving everyone in the dark.

The thing that looked like a human hissed at them and said, "Who returns me to this realm of flesh?"

The Monster pressed his right fist against his chest. "I did."

The thing cocked its head to one side, closed its eyes in seeming ecstasy, let out a soft exhalation of air, then whispered, "For this I thank you."

He—for in the eyes of those observing him, this being had somehow transformed from an "it" to a "he" within seconds—turned his eyes toward the lifeless body in his grip. His grip relaxed. Holding up her entire body with four fingers hooked under her chin, he probed the girl's soft cheek with his thumb, as if reacquainting himself with sensations that had been lost to him for an eternity. "Soon, my child, I shall know the rest of you." He paused, as if listening to an unspoken response. He shushed thin air, then whispered, "Be patient...be patient." Then released her, allowing her to fall to the floor, a lifeless marionette crumpled at his bare feet.

He returned his gaze to the Monster. He cocked one eyebrow, bowed in an extravagant manner, then said in slow, deliberate tones, "I owe you much." This gesture almost seemed like an elegant repeat of the bow the Monster had performed for the witch the night before. What had seemed perverse and ominous coming from the Monster seemed almost ingratiating from this man, despite the swaths of blood staining his mouth and chest. Even the witch felt at ease, wishing she too was young enough to join her daughter at this man's side. She felt disgusted with herself even as the thought passed through her mind.

She would remain disgusted with herself and the dark gods she once worshipped until the very moment of her death, years after these strange beings had left her all alone in this hut surrounded by nothing but the gaseous stench of the swamp and the mocking cries of the whippoorwills and the fantasy that never left her in peace.

The fantasy in which *she* was the one chosen by the nosferatu, not her undeserving daughter.

8.

"Are you going to kill me?" Mike asked.

Lucy smiled like a mischievous angel. "Why do you say that?"

"Because I have no idea where the hell we are."

A few moments before, Lucy had driven them past the entrance that led up to the Hollywood Bowl where the London Philharmonic were playing the best of Tchaikovsky. You could distantly hear strains from Act II of *Swan Lake* drifting through the warm night air. Appropriate. That was the music that opened *Dracula*, *Murders in the Rue Morgue*, and *The Mummy*. For some reason, in the early '30s Universal didn't think a film was a true horror movie unless it began with those familiar strains from Tchaikovsky.

The two of them were now speeding up a hazardous, curving road that led all the way up into the middle of nowhere. The road was not well-lit at all. Occasionally, Mike could see a private side road winding up toward a dark, gated mansion. There were no other cars out tonight. Except for the faint music, silence reigned up here in the Hollywood Hills.

"We're heading to the very top," Lucy said, "of Mulholland Drive."

"Why, what's up there?"

"You'll see." Her smile hadn't wavered.

When they finally reached the very top, Lucy pulled the car off the side of the road and told Mike to get out.

Mike said, "You *are* going to kill me, aren't you? I just knew it. It was all too good to be true. You're some kind of black widow killer, right? The newspapers are filled with your exploits. How long have you operated without getting caught for your crimes?"

Lucy shook her head and laughed. She was still wearing her tight-fitting Chuck's Fish Shanty t-shirt with the official Fish Shanty tag pinned over her left breast. The tag read, "HI, I'M LUCY!"

"So, does your mind just naturally turn toward the dark side no matter what the circumstances are?"

"Yes."

"It's because of all those horrible movies you watched as a kid."

"I was attracted to those movies *because* my mind naturally turns toward the dark side. It's really hard to gauge which came first. It's a philosophical question. I've thought about it a lot. Maybe my mind's just warped. Maybe something dark and evil is growing inside my brain, just waiting for the right moment to rip its way out."

Lucy reached up and stroked his hair lovingly. "Maybe I can do my best to keep the little beastie stuck inside there." She ran the back of her hand against his temple. Mike closed his eyes. She leaned over and nibbled on his ear lobe. "Listen," she whispered, "this is what you're going to do. This is your payment to me. First and last month's rent, okay? You're going to go outside, stand on the edge of that cliff, look out at all the lights of Hollywood spread out beneath you like an electric spider web, and shout out at the top of your lungs, 'I AM A BESTSELLING WRITER!'" She screamed this last sentence directly into his ear drum. Mike yelped in pain and pushed away from her.

"What? No *way* am I doing that."

"You're then going to write out a check to yourself for three million dollars and pin it to your typewriter at home. If you do that, you can't fail. You'll succeed in this town and I'll be right behind you. Trust me, I know."

"Where'd you get this from, EST? You're not a Scientologist, are you? Is this some kind of recruitment drive?"

Lucy rolled her eyes. "Listen, just shut up for a second and do what your landlord tells you to do."

"You're going to hold that fact over my head forever, aren't you?"

"You *told* me I could. Listen…just last year I dated a very famous Buddhist monk who taught an acting workshop. He told us that he *himself* did this way back in 1969 and it worked for him. He became a very successful stage actor in New York for many, many years."

"What's his name?"

"Kane Jeeves."

"That's the fucking pen name W.C. Fields used on *The Bank Dick* back in 1940. You got taken, dear."

"Why would he lie?"

"Have you looked at yourself in the mirror? Was that the excuse he gave to lure you up here? You know how many women he's probably pulled the same stunt with?"

"Kane's not like that. He's a sweet guy."

"I'll bet. If he's so famous, how come I've never heard of him?"

"Are you an expert on the New York stage?"

"Well…no."

"He's famous, trust me. And this *works*. I did it, and the very next day I met Chad and he offered me the part in his movie. This was last summer. And now I've met *you*. Why did that happen? Because I told the Universe what I wanted and the universe heard what I was saying. But you have to be proactive and tell the gods what you want."

Mike sank down in the passenger seat. He knew she couldn't possibly be as perfect as she looked. New Agers drove Mike up the wall, but what the fuck. She was hot and she was funny and she liked him enough to let him sleep on her couch and in her bed and, oh, what the hell….

"I've always been something of a New Ager," Mike said. "At least open to it."

"But it's *not* New Age philosophy. All you're doing is making your intentions known to yourself and the Universe at the same moment. You *need* to do this. Please trust me. If you do this, I'll give you a present." She leaned over again, and this time kissed him on the lips. He wrapped his arms around her tightly and they kissed for a very long time. Way, way off in the distance, he heard the opening strains of Act III of *Swan Lake*.

Count Dracula's newly formed body stood on top of a small grassy hill, his slender frame silhouetted by the full moon. He stared at the moon longingly, as if wishing to embrace it.

"I have unfinished business at the house of Dr. Heidelmann," said Dracula. "We must go there at once."

"It's no longer Heidelmann's house," said Ygor. "Now it's *mine*, the House of Ygor!"

Ygor and the Count stood by themselves a few feet from the witch's hut. Dracula had wished to speak to Ygor alone.

Dracula turned away from the moon and stared at Ygor directly. He raised one eyebrow. "Indeed? I was under the impression the house was now mine."

"NO!" Ygor slashed his massive arm through the air, as if to underscore the word. "I want to rebuild it, to make it a base from which to stage my attack on everyone who ever hated me! First the village of Frankenstein, then Visaria, then the whole countryside!"

Dracula chuckled. "My dear man, your dreams of conquest are so limited. If you allow me to work *with* you...to be your loyal advisor in order to repay you for all that you have done for me...I will grant you the means by which to destroy all of Europe...perhaps even the entire world."

Ygor tilted his head to one side and squinted at the Count skeptically through the encroaching fog. "The entire world?" His fondest wish was to rule everything and everyone, to make every living creature pay for the intense pain he'd been forced to endure his entire life. But it had always been little more than a dream, destined to remain forever unfulfilled. "How would you grant me this wish?"

"Guide me back to the house of Heidelmann...to *your* house...and I will show you. You can direct your man-servant to perform the real work if you wish. It will require some amount of physical labor."

"What will we be carrying?" Ygor's head was now filled with images of buried treasure. Perhaps the Count knew about a cache of which Ygor was unaware. "Gold? Jewels?"

Again, the dead nobleman chuckled. Ygor didn't know if he

liked the sound of that chuckle, but he did not protest or tell him to stop. He wanted to know everything this Dracula knew. "Oh, nothing as paltry as that, my dear man," said Dracula. "No, we'll be digging up something *far* more valuable."

"But...I don't understand. What could be more valuable than gold?"

"Spores, my dear man. A *tremendous* amount of spores." The chuckle transformed into outright laughter, laughter that seemed to rise and swell in perfect synchrony with the cold wind from the north.

Ygor balled his fist, hoping the laughter was not directed at him.

About ten minutes later, Lucy removed Mike's hands from her body and pointed out the windshield. He had to do it. The gods demanded it.

He took a deep breath, opened the passenger door, and stepped out onto the rocky dirt. A single pebble rolled away from him and skittered over the edge of the cliff. Just that little sound seemed to echo through the canyon. He could see the lights of lavish hilltop houses staring at him expectantly like peeping toms. Mike turned back toward Lucy and said, "Everyone's gonna *hear* me. They'll call the cops. These rich people don't fuck around. I'll be arrested for disturbing the peace or something."

"If it makes you feel any better, I'll keep the engine running. The second you're done, hop in the car and we'll drive off."

Mike sighed again, walked over to the edge, looked out at that sea of artificial lights, opened his mouth wide, balled his fists, and...nothing came out. Just a strained whisper.

He heard Lucy laughing at him from the car. He dashed back over to her. "This is *hard*."

"That's why it's important. How much do you want this? You have to be naked to the Universe."

"Is that what Kane said to you before he slipped off your tube top?"

"Do it, or you'll be homeless."

Fuck it. He ran over to the edge, almost slipped and fell and killed himself, for a second thought of his mother and his last phone conversation with her, and screamed in genuine anger, "I AM A GOD DAMN BESTSELLING WRITER, SO *FUCK YOU*, MOTHER!" Then dived back into Lucy's idling Mustang, strapped himself in with the seatbelt, and latched onto Lucy's shoulder as she laughed and laughed and laughed.

"Holy shit," he said, "that felt *good*!"

"I told you! I didn't think you were gonna be able to do it for a second there. I'm proud of you. That was *great*!"

"Really?"

"Oh, it was fantastic. I liked how you balled your fists at your sides. It was very dramatic."

"I think I saw some lights coming on back there," Mike said, glancing over his shoulder. "Right now, they're all thinkin', 'Jesus Christ, it's that Mahatma Kane Jeeves guy gettin' laid again.'"

Lucy patted him on the knee while laughing. "When we get back down to the bottom of the hill, you have to write the check to yourself. Then you're gonna tape it to your typewriter."

Mike stared at her beautiful profile in the near-darkness. He couldn't believe he was sitting in this car with this woman at this time. "Thank you for doing this for me."

"No problem."

"No, really. I haven't had that much encouragement in life. It's nice to meet people who actually seem to believe in me."

"Me and who else?"

"Eric. Eric seems to believe in me. And he hasn't even read my writing yet."

"Eric's got a good eye."

"You want to join us tomorrow for the Bela Lugosi Tour?"

"What's that?"

"It's never existed until now. We'll be the first recipients of the tour."

"I don't have to work tomorrow, so…sure, why not?"

Ygor strolled into the ballroom wearing a tuxedo.

For a moment he was disoriented. It had been late at night when the coach brought him and Wolfgang Frankenstein into

London. He had stayed on the grounds of Wolfgang's estate the entire week, afraid to wander the streets. He had come to London many decades before in the company of Heinrich Frankenstein and his new bride. Much had happened to turn him off Victorian London completely. A horrible scene.

But all that was in the past, or so Wolfgang assured him. This was a new, modern London, Wolfgang explained. A lot had changed since the late 1880s.

And though the city may have advanced technologically, Ygor feared that the people had not changed at all. What if they sensed somehow that he was not one of them? That he was different? That he was....

"A monster," Elsie Frankenstein whispered to her husband in the corner of the lavish ballroom, away from all the finely dressed dancers in their black tuxedos and colorful dresses. "That...that horrible man tried to kill you only a few years ago. Why, he almost destroyed our lives. I still don't understand why you invited him into our home."

Ygor stood to one side of a large statue of the Egyptian God Anubis. Similar Egyptian statues and frescoes adorned the ornate hall. There were so many impressive busts and vases and tombs that one would think this place was a museum. Only by chance had Ygor detected Elsie's distinctive voice through the milling crowd. Elsie's voice was soft and so musical. She was a beautiful woman. So sweet. He didn't wish to scare her or her son. He had tried to stay out of their way for the past week.

"Please understand, my dear," said Wolfgang, trying to keep his voice down. "I just happened to run into him when I was in Germany. The man was down on his luck. I decided to forgive him and make a better man of him. Isn't that a noble goal? To make better men?"

"Of course, but—"

"What would Jesus have done, my dear?"

"Why, he...." She laughed, almost as if she were embarrassed. "Well, he would do exactly what you're doing."

"Of course. There's my girl. Remember what the pastor tells us every Sunday."

"You're right. I feel awful judging the man by his appearance, but I'm just thinking about Paul. I don't want anything to happen to him, like it did before. He was almost kidnapped, Wolfgang, almost murdered by—"

Wolfgang laughed nervously, in low tones. "No need to go into all that again, my dear. You know I wouldn't let anything like that ever happen again. Everything's under control. He's only staying with us until he can get on his feet. I thought it would be a good idea to show him a good time. To see how such a man reacts around real culture."

"But why?"

"Think about it, Elsie. Haven't you ever wondered what really makes a man? Is it genetics or environment? Can a man change his basic nature? Can a brute become civilized? Can you reform a criminal into a respectable man through acts of kindness? Do our brains dictate who we are, or do the people around us?"

A concerned tone crept back into Elsie's voice as she said, "It sounds like you're conducting one of your experiments."

"Oh, well, who knows? Perhaps there's a paper in it somewhere. I can't help it, thinking about such questions. These are the most cutting-edge questions in both psychology *and* biology. After all, I was thinking of proposing a course in genetics to the Dean. If this case study ties in somehow…well, so be it. Oh, but Elsie, I assure you my motivations are ones of Christian charity, not scientific curiosity."

"I'll take you at your word." From her tone of voice, it sounded as if she meant the exact opposite.

"Do that, dear. Now let's go mingle. We don't want my colleagues thinking we're having a row, do we?"

"No. Shall we dance?"

"Of course."

They emerged from behind the statue. Ygor tried to slip into the shadows, not wanting to be seen by the couple, but he was too slow.

"Ygor, my good man!" said the son of Frankenstein. "We were just talking about you. It's so good to see you…isn't it, dear?"

Elsie merely nodded, trying to smile.

"Are you impressed by the place?"

"It's...beautiful," said Ygor. "Whose...home...is this?"

Wolfgang laughed. "Oh, no no, this isn't anyone's home, per se. This is the Grand Lodge of Freemasonry."

"Free...masonry?"

Wolfgang suddenly realized that Ygor had no idea what he was talking about. "Oh...well, Freemasonry is kind of like a *club*. A club of gentlemen. The most rational and influential men of London are members of this club."

Ygor glanced around at the palatial surroundings. His spirits began to darken. He'd known this was a bad idea, the second Wolfgang suggested it. "Everything...almost...too much...feel...out of place."

"Oh, think nothing of it. He's not out of place, is he, my dear?"

Elsie was looking across the room and had to be prompted to respond with a slight pat on the elbow. "What? Oh, no, of course. You should...feel at home here." She turned to Wolfgang. "Excuse me, dear, but I see Mrs. Garth over there. I want to compliment her on the hors d'oeuvres. We'll dance later, dear."

"Certainly," Wolfgang said. Elsie nodded politely at Ygor before she left.

Ygor whispered, "I don't think...your wife...."

"Oh, think nothing of it. She'll get over it, once she gets to know you. I've been testing and retesting you for a week now. I'm impressed by your level of intelligence, your knowledge of literature and history."

"I had little to do...at Sister Marie's house...except read."

"That's excellent. Do you know what this means? My father wasn't wrong about you. You're not a monster, and neither was he. Pretty soon these men will know that, when it comes time to reveal who you are."

Ygor shrank from him in fear.

Wolfgang said, "No, not tonight, of course. We must wait for the proper psychological moment. We must do more tests. You must prove you're human first, a *rational* human, before we reveal your true nature to the world."

"I don't know...if it's...a good idea...to reveal...anything."

Wolfgang placed a reassuring hand on his shoulder. "You mustn't let the past govern your life. Just because you were hated in the past by ignorant men does not mean that *intelligent* men will act the same way. You're surrounded by the most learned gentlemen in the world here. If anyone can see your true value, your true worth, it will be them."

Ygor looked at all the professorial types milling about among the Egyptian statues. They looked like gods to him. For so long he'd yearned to be among people who read books and thirsted for knowledge just like he did. Sister Marie was the only person who even came close to satisfying this urge. After all, the other people in the house were drunks and drug addicts, few of them interested in little more than satisfying the pleasures of the flesh or perhaps freeing themselves from such desires. Either way, their minds were occupied—distracted, one might say—by far more mundane urges. Even Sister Marie was more interested in reading the Holy Bible than the works of Rousseau or Goethe or Milton. These three represented Ygor's favorites.

This place seemed like a dream come true: a veritable Shangri-La located here in the middle of London. The grand nature of the hall itself merely contributed to this sensation of awe.

Ygor pointed up at the detailed Egyptian hieroglyphics on the ceiling and said, "Why does...everything...seem to be... from Egypt?"

"An excellent question," Wolfgang said. "Have you studied Egypt?"

"Yes. I read...Dr. Banning's book...about the expedition... to uncover...Ananka's tomb. Sister Marie...had it...sitting...on her shelf."

"Very good. Very appropriate. Masons identify heavily with Ancient Egypt. We believe that the history of the Society can be traced all the way back to the hermetic priests of Egypt. The priests, of course, were the scholars of their day. They were the advisors to the Pharaoh. The Pharaoh merely carried out the orders of the magicians who worked behind the scenes. The same is true today with modern Kings and Presidents. I wish I could tell you more, but I'm sworn to secrecy. I hope that you, too, will learn everything I know once you become a member of this Lodge as well."

Ygor stared up at Wolfgang in astonishment. He placed a trembling hand against his chest. "Me?"

"Yes, of course. That's why I wanted you to come here and see your future Lodge for yourself."

Everything was happening too fast. It was too overwhelming. "I'm...scared."

"But there's no reason to be. Don't you see, Ygor? If you're accepted into this Lodge, the most influential Masonic Lodge in the world...if you pass all the rigorous tests that await you... no one can deny you your basic rights as a human being. You will have proven your worth as a rational being before the eyes of the Great Architect of the Universe himself. You will be untouchable. You will have proven that my father...our father... was a maker of men, not monsters."

Tears began to form in Ygor's eyes once more. He tried to hold them back. He wanted to thank Wolfgang for placing so much trust in him. He wanted to express to him how fearful he was that he would fail the labors that lay before him. But before he could get over his momentary shock, Wolfgang raised his hand in the air and said, "Ah, here he is. Remain calm, Ygor. You're about to meet the Master of the Lodge himself. He's an expert in Egyptology. The curator of the Scripps Museum in London. He's an Egyptian himself, you know. His name is Khalid Banoub."

Ygor saw the man approaching them through a throng of laughing, chatting guests. He wore a long ceremonial robe and an Egyptian fez. He walked slowly, proudly, across the long hall. A series of torches that hung on the hieroglyph-laden walls in the ancient grip of dog-headed statues seemed to highlight the harshness of this man's wrinkled face. His dark eyes seemed penetrating and omniscient, even from this far away. Ygor felt as if he were being approached by a man whose knowledge far outstripped every Frankenstein he'd ever known, a man who was used to being in complete control—not only of his own movements, but everyone else's as well.

Wolfgang bowed before Khalid Banoub and whispered, "Worshipful."

Banoub nodded, only slightly. "Brother Frankenstein."

At first Ygor felt jealous and confused. Why was this old man calling Wolfgang *his* brother? Then he realized the truth: "Brother" must be a title within the Society that Masons use only amongst each other.

Banoub turned his penetrating, hypnotic gaze upon Ygor. "And who is this...gentleman?"

"This is a new candidate to the Lodge," Wolfgang said. "I hope to lead him through the first degree next Monday."

For several long seconds Banoub stared at Ygor, as if boring a hole into the center of his very soul—if, indeed, he even possessed a soul. Ygor still wasn't certain about that, despite Sister Marie's continual protests. Ygor felt exposed, as if all his dark secrets were laid bare by those far darker pupils.

"We welcome all men to this house," said Banoub, "no matter their station or background. Whether prince or pauper, *all* men are little more than clay when standing in the shadow of The Great Architect of the Universe, He who made all of us. Even you. Even me." Banoub reached out slowly and touched Ygor on the shoulder with the very tips of his fingers, fingers so bony and frail they seemed as if they might crumble to dust upon even this slight impact.

Ygor was so intimidated by the Master's presence he couldn't even formulate a response. Wolfgang did so for him: "We can all agree on that."

Banoub turned toward Wolfgang and nodded, ever so slightly. "Indeed." Then back toward Ygor: "I look forward to your initiation," Banoub said, "assuming, of course, that you are accepted. You can't imagine how much pleasure I derive from the addition of a new soul to our humble Lodge."

Ygor glanced up at the ornate, high ceilings and compared them in his mind with the ramshackle affair in which Sister Marie toiled every day. "The Lodge isn't so...humble," Ygor said, gesturing upwards.

Wolfgang laughed nervously. "What he means is...."

Banoub waved a hand in the air in slow motion. "I know exactly what your friend means," Banoub said.

"Merely that it's very...*impressive*," Ygor said.

"It needs to be," Banoub said, "in order to have the proper impact upon the candidates during our initiations. Rituals must have the proper setting. They must be *precise*, otherwise they would not be effective. Believe me, I know. I come from a land of rituals."

Ygor nodded. He had learned the importance of rituals from Sister Marie. It was important to have a routine, to do the same thing every day in order to keep one's mind occupied, so as not to think about the horrors of the past. "I agree," Ygor said. "I wish I had been raised...with such rituals. Only now am I... learning...their full importance."

"No doubt you will learn even more over the proper course of time, if you're worthy. One must be patient when one is a Brother. I must now bid you both adieu. I have Lodge business to tend to in my quarters."

Banoub turned and walked away so slowly, with such small, precise steps, that Ygor thought of him as a living embodiment of patience, a ritual given human form.

"A very...intense man," Ygor said. "Very...dedicated."

"Yes, indeed," Wolfgang said. "In fact, he's so dedicated to the cause of the Brotherhood that he lives here in the Temple itself, taking care of Lodge business on a full-time basis."

Ygor liked people who dedicated themselves to a cause fulltime, people like Sister Marie. "He must be...a very...noble man," Ygor said.

"Oh, very much so," Wolfgang said.

"I'd like to be...like him...one day."

Wolfgang clapped him on the back. "I'm sure you will," Wolfgang said, "but first you have to be accepted."

Ygor watched Banoub enter a pair of grand double doors decorated with beautiful Egyptian hieroglyphs on the other side of the temple and disappear into the shadows beyond. He wondered what lay behind those mysterious doors.

"That's all I've ever wanted," Ygor whispered.

9.

Khalid Banoub retreated into his inner Temple and kneeled before the fifteen-foot-high statue of Anubis, God of the Dead. He prayed to the god on a regular basis, asking for his forgiveness, always hoping for a response, never receiving one. He prayed to him to grace his mission on Earth with the fortune that only gods can provide. He surrounded himself with reminders of his home, despite the fact that he had defied almost every single god in the Egyptian pantheon. First Isis, then Anubis.

He had defied Isis by stealing the sacred scrolls of Thoth in an attempt to resurrect his dead princess, Mehet-uret, an act of sacrilege for which he was condemned to death centuries before. But he had returned, and had even tried to bring Princess Mehet-uret along with him into this modern world, but had been foiled once again by the rage of Isis. Imprisoned in the Land of the Dead with all the other souls of the damned, Banoub had spent every second of eternity raging against the gods and their misguided view of justice. Justice, to Banoub, was that which benefited him. Justice was him and Princess Mehet-uret together again on the material plane living the life of pure love for which they had been destined...before the gods intervened. Justice was what Banoub was after now. He would not rest, not even in death, until it was granted to him.

Unlike the other souls in the Land of the Dead, who give up so easily and relent to the will of the gods, who give in to an eternity of pain, Khalid Banoub raged and raged and raged and his rage propelled him through the fires of hell. He walked for what seemed like decades through pits of scorpions and blazing deserts, climbing up hills of rotting corpses composed of dearly departed loved ones, raging at the weakness in his own mind every second he was tempted to stop, and at last made his way across the river of death and to the barren shores that surrounded it, tore out the throat of the guardian of the gates with his bare hands and teeth, and kicked out the gates that kept the dead inside. He turned there in that doorway of bright white light and pounded his chest in triumph and shouted at his fellow lost souls to follow him through into the land of the living, but none of them took advantage of the opportunity. The dead masses stared at him from across the river with not even a hint of hope or desire, as if the open doorway wasn't even real. Oh, but it was real. Banoub felt the warmth of the blood of the guardian bathe his body in power. He turned his back on the pitiful souls and burst out of the pits of Death and back into the Land of the Living.

He emerged out of the sands of the desert like a human flower, bathed under the rejuvenating light of an Egyptian sun, and clawed his way back to civilization. Sometimes he wondered, during that day-long trek through the desert, if he was really still trapped in the Land of the Dead, if this were all an illusion meant to torture him some more. At one point he relented to exhaustion and fainted. But then that caravan led by the grave robber Stephen Banning happened to come across his unconscious body and dropped him off at a hospital in Cairo on their way to their ship that would take them back to America along with the treasures plundered from the bosom of the motherland. Oh, if only they'd known they had left the greatest archaeological treasure behind.

Once he was fully recovered, Banoub didn't lose time in reestablishing himself among the land of the living. His former employees at The Scripps Museum told him they had wondered where he'd disappeared to for the past seven years, but didn't ask too many questions. His knowledge was far too valuable to them and they knew that. He immediately went to work. After five years he was finally able to track her down. Helen—beautiful Helen, the modern reincarnation of Mehet-uret, his eternal lover—lived somewhere in England with her new husband, that simpering Frank Whemple boy. It didn't take Banoub long to convince the museum to sponsor his move to London. There he would finally attain his goal.

The last time, Mehet-uret had been repulsed by Banoub's aged appearance and *rejected* him—rejected him, he knew, for that reason alone. This time he would make certain this *could* not happen. He would not reveal himself to her until he had retained his youthful visage, until he looked exactly as he had when they were lovers, centuries in the past. And the only way he could attain this goal was by draining the life energy of the eager young men who scampered in droves toward the welcoming arms of his inner Temple. All to acquire a higher social standing in their hedonistic metropolis. Each one of them deserved the fate Khalid Banoub would bring about for them. These creatures represented the elite of modern civilization? If so, perhaps modern civilization should be destroyed, only he and Mehet-uret left behind, to demonstrate to the gods that he had not turned his back on them completely. Once he and his lover were reunited, he would heal the rift between them and the gods.

By demonstrating his loyalty to them.

By razing London to the ground and replacing it with a paradise on Earth.

Banoub rose from his kneeling position, enacted the Sign of Anubis, then whispered to the god of the dead, "Soon you shall see my loyalty demonstrated. For every soul I attempted to steal from your breast you shall have ten thousand more to replace them. This I, your loyal servant Khalid Banoub, promise and swear. So mote it be."

Then the living corpse turned on his heel widdershins, like a soldier in the army of the dead, and turned to greet the rest of his honored guests.

Lucy was filled with ideas.

Later that night, while they lay in bed together, she excitedly told him about all these notions she'd come up with about specific locales that could be incorporated into his script. She hoped they would be able to film at the actual location, as she loved the Los Angeles houses in which Bela had lived, particularly the more flamboyant ones located up in the hills just below the Hollywood sign. She particularly wanted to film the scene where Carroll and Bela dance in the lobby of The Roosevelt Hotel, very close, wanting so much to be intimate but being unable to do so due to the fact that Bela was newly married. She wondered what Bela's wife thought about the two of them working so close together during *The Mark of the Vampire*, a film she had watched a second time just to soak up the atmosphere of that era. She appreciated the film on a different level now. She no longer expected the film to be logical; and having given up any hope of rationality, the film could be seen in a new light: a black and white dream about unfulfilled desires, crimes of passion, the unending horrors of guilt and grief, and stories imbedded within stories, à la *Hamlet*. Lucy had ideas. And as she sucked at Mike's neck like a vampire that night, Mike closed his eyes in ecstasy and thanked whatever twisted God (or gods) had sent her into his orbit. She was his muse. With such positive reinforcement, he would never allow himself to give up his dream. When he thought about how close he had been to leaving Los Angeles for good...well, he felt ashamed. Ashamed for being so easily defeated. He didn't want to think about that. So instead he focused on the intense sensation of those ivory white incisors that nipped at his flesh and left behind telltale marks so that everyone would know who had been there and why. Mike was hers now. There was no escaping that, which was fine with him. Mike didn't ever want to escape her.

Lucy had to go to work early the next morning, but before she left, she kissed him gently on the cheek and whispered in his ear, "Write while I'm gone."

He said he would and *almost*, by pure instinct and reflex, said, "I love you," but he had learned enough from his last relationship not to be the first to say such things. It changes women. They know they have something over you. They never let you forget it. So, he held back and said, "I'll have twenty pages done by the time you get home."

She kissed him again and vanished with a feline hiss like Count Mora's daughter and Mike rolled over and closed his eyes for a second because the bed was so warm with her recent presence, and he reached out and draped his arm over the spot where she had been and imagined holding her naked body once more, and fell promptly back to sleep.

When he awoke again, he looked at the clock and saw it was twelve noon. "Holy shit," he said with a start and leaped off the mattress. Then calmed down. After all, he had nowhere he needed to be. Lucy was working a full shift today. She wouldn't be home until five. After all the crap he'd been through lately, he deserved to relax a little bit. He'd written three entire acts of a screenplay in five days. How many other people could say that?

He took a shower, whipped up some scrambled eggs, brewed a hot cup of coffee, then sat down in front of the typewriter. He slipped page ninety into the machine and pondered how he would work in the scene at The Roosevelt Hotel. He wrote exactly one page when he stopped, for he couldn't quite exorcise from his head the conversation he'd had with Eric the other day. All those theories about what Lugosi's little films really meant in a postmodern context. Some of those ideas were pure bullshit, stuff he was spinning out of his mind spontaneously, and yet some of it was new and original. He'd never heard ideas like that before. And yet they had been coming out of his own mouth.

Because of all the time he had been spending with Lucy, he hadn't had a chance to take notes on that five-hour-long bull session with Eric. Perhaps, he thought, he should do it now. Before the fire died down in his mind. It's not like it was unrelated to the screenplay. In a way, it could be seen as *research* for the screenplay.

Mike took page ninety-one out of the typewriter and rolled in a fresh piece of paper. He typed the words "Weird Noir and the Dark Prince: Bela Lugosi and the Emergence of the Postmodern in World War II Cinema." And the words began to flow.

He transcribed his and Eric's conversation in a creative manner, reshaping the dialogue into an academic treatise, weaving together disparate elements such as The Theater of the Absurd, Bertolt Brecht, Orson Welles, Marxism, surrealism, anti-Communism, and of course Bela Lugosi. He finished the article at around 5:30, just as Lucy came striding through the door in her Chuck's Fish Shanty uniform.

"Well, did you make any progress?" she asked.

Mike spun around with the manuscript in his hands. He was still naked in the straight back chair. He had forgotten to put clothes on after the shower.

"I've just finished the inaugural article for *Ramboona.*"

"Who the fuck is Ramboona?"

"*Ramboona* is a magazine. Would you like to be on the cover?"

10.

They arrived in London on the foggiest night of the year. No meteorologist in the world could have predicted this fog. Official projections had seemed certain that tonight would be relatively clear.

The fog swept in off the Thames and seemed to congregate around a particular section of London. It covered the abandoned ruins of Carfax Abbey like an immense spider web. As a result, no passerby noticed the very unusual trio that approached the doorstep of the formerly regal estate.

Count Dracula, dressed in a tuxedo complete with cape and top hat, stroked his long silver moustache as he stared at the boarded-up entrance to what had once been his home. He had been driven away from the modern world a long time ago, condemned to a temporary death in Europe where his skeletal remains were put on display for the amusement of peasants who had once feared him. He had come back to life and died twice over since then, but nothing could keep him from fulfilling his destiny here in the center of the modern world. Death somehow seemed less of an impediment to those already intimately familiar with it.

Dracula touched the smooth hand of his consort, the first of his new concubines, the beautiful girl who had been named Aishe in life. He squeezed her hand and said, "This will be your new home. From here you will watch me lay waste to the modern world that chose to reject me so long ago. From here you will watch me ascend to a position of power undreamed of by mere mortals."

Though Aishe smiled seductively, her eyes contained

nothing more than a limbo as lifeless as that from which Dracula had just been freed.

A grotesque shadow, made even more massive by the gaslight lamps on the sidewalk, loomed over the darkly attired pair. It seemed to cleave between the two, as if separating them.

The thing that cast the shadow spoke in angry, guttural tones: "Power, yes, but nowhere near as great as that which *Ygor* will possess!"

Dracula smiled oh so slightly. "Of course, my friend. Am I not here to serve you? To repay you for your selfless deeds?"

"If so, why did we come all the way here? How can this place possibly help us?"

"As you yourself stated, we require a base of operations. This is far better than any you might find in remote Visaria. This estate is shunned by the civilized mortals who dwell here. Perfect for our purposes."

"You still haven't told me what you plan to do with—"

Dracula responded with a clipped tone. "You shall know within the hour. Now, please...*if you will*...remove the barrier that prevents our entrance."

Reluctantly, Ygor reached out, gripped the thick wooden boards that had been nailed up over the black gate, and ripped them away as if they were made of paper.

Dracula pointed a long, slender finger at the gate. "Excellent. And now *this*."

Ygor shattered the lock with a mere squeeze of his fist, at which point all three entered the ruined estate.

Dracula laughed aloud upon seeing the inside of his former home. The mortals had changed nothing, so frightened were they of anything he and his brides had touched. Four coffins lay scattered around the main hall. He opened them, one by one. They were all empty except for the soil of his homeland still lining the interiors. Now he had more than enough at his disposal, as he had already arranged for further coffins to arrive later this evening.

"Excellent," Dracula whispered.

Ygor swept cobwebs away with his massive hands. "I was expecting something more...*impressive*."

Dracula turned to glare at him, but before he could respond a familiar figure staggered through the entrance from which they had come.

Krogh shuffled into the hall, his mechanical arm dragging a cloth sack across the stone floor behind him. Krogh smiled and hissed, "Have you seen the ratsssssss, master? I saw them scaling the walls of the antechamber just outside. There seemed to be ssssssswarms of them. Sssssso many. Too many from which to choose." He began to pout.

"That's good news, Krogh. But did you do as I requested?"

Krogh lifted the bag into the air with the unusual power of his artificial arm. The bag pulsated with life, as if something was trapped inside. Perhaps several somethings. The sound of crying babies emerged from the bag.

Dracula grinned and held out his hand. "Give them to me."

Krogh hugged the squirming bag to his chest. "May I not have just one, for myself? For being good?"

"Keep to your rats!" Dracula snapped. "Now hand them over!"

Krogh pouted again and tossed the bag toward his master. Dracula snatched the bag out of the air and set it down on top of one of the four coffins. He untied the top of the sack and reached inside, pulling out a wailing infant. Only about four months old.

"What are you going to do with *that*?" Ygor said, almost sounding annoyed. "It seems too small for you."

Dracula held up the pale infant in one hand, his long, clawed fingers closing over the fidgeting creature like a venus flytrap. "This is not for me to eat," Dracula said, almost in disgust. "It's my very first experimental subject. I thought it wiser to start out...*small*." He smiled at Ygor, then turned to stare into the innocent eyes of the infant and burst into a fit of laughter that seemed to go on forever and ever and ever.

II.

The next day Mike and Lucy visited Eric's store. They closed the blinds once more and ran the sixteen-millimeter print of *Voodoo Man* for her. Mike was over brimming with ideas. He talked at them during the film as the scratchy images flicked on the screen. He knew exactly what the cover of the first issue should look like, he said. He wanted Lucy to dress up like Carroll Borland from *Mark of the Vampire*. He knew she would look fantastic, if only they photographed her in the right way, with the proper make-up and lighting. If the magazine sold well, it could be their calling card. Their audition, so to speak. A high-selling magazine would prove to possible investors that there was a genuine interest in this Hollywood star dead for over thirty years now. And when they saw Lucy in her get-up, how could they refuse to give them the money to make their film?

"I think it's a great idea," Lucy said, "but we need a finished screenplay."

Mike spread his hands in the air. "It's almost done. I can finish it like *that*." He snapped his fingers.

"And we need content for the first issue," Eric said.

Mike handed Eric the article he had just completed. "I think you're gonna love it."

"He forced me to read it the second I came home from work," Lucy said.

"Yeah?" Eric said. "And what did you think of it?"

"I have to admit, most of it is way over my head. But I loved it. I love how he ties in all these different things that don't seem to have anything to do with each other."

Eric began reading the manuscript right then and there. Mike watched him almost the entire time, glancing away only when something particularly bizarre was occurring on screen, like John Carradine giving one of the worst performances of his career as a half-wit potential-rapist.

The second he finished it, Eric said with a wide smile on his face, "I'm amazed you were able to tie in everything we were talking about the other day into one coherent whole. If the entire magazine reads like this, I think this might actually be worth doing. Can I keep this?"

"I photocopied that specifically for you."

"I'll show it to my wife when I get home. She doesn't know jack shit about Bela Lugosi, but she knows good writing when she sees it." Eric took off his reading glasses and sucked on the edge. He stared off into space for a second, then said, "Chad will do the photography for us for free. He can transform Lucy into Carroll, I'm sure of it. And I'll ask Carroll if she wants to participate. We can run an interview with her in issue number one. I doubt she'll have anything new to add, but I think her presence in the magazine lends us some credibility with film buffs."

"What about that sequel to *Dracula* she wrote?" Mike said. "Didn't you say it had never been published? We could serialize it in the magazine."

"Yeah, you're right," Eric said. "That could be sort of cool. It's like a piece of history no one's ever seen before. By God, you're a genius." Eric laughed and slapped Mike on the knee.

Mike raised his hands towards the ceiling in supplication. "Ramboona be praised."

At that exact moment, Bela said the same thing on the screen.

Eric scooted his wheeled, straight-back chair toward the front counter. He opened a drawer beneath the cash register and removed a gigantic hardcover book that was contained in a wooden slipcase half the size of a human being.

"What the fuck is that?" Mike asked.

"It's *The Book*," Eric said.

"It's more like a weapon," Lucy said.

"In a way it is a weapon," Eric said, "metaphorically

speaking. This is a very rare item, and I'm entrusting it into your care. It's a first edition, so keep good care of it."

Mike said, "Is that...?"

Eric nodded. *"The Secret Teachings of All Ages* by Manly P. Hall. Its original title was *An Encyclopedic Outline of Masonic, Hermetic, Qabbalistic and Rosicrucian Symbolical Philosophy.* I have a photograph of Hall sitting in his favorite ornate chair—that chair's still there in the Lecture Room at The Philosophical Research Society, by the way—with Bela hovering over his shoulder staring at one of the illustrations. I suggest reading parts of the book—maybe not the whole thing because it's so god damn huge—and then asking Hall if you can interview him. Bela used to attend Hall's lectures on a weekly basis. In fact, Hall wrote several screenplays for Bela, but none of them were ever produced."

Mike said, "Hall's the man who hypnotized Bela on the set of *Black Friday* in 1940, right?"

Eric wiggled his hand in the air. "Well, no one knows if Hall really did hypnotize him or not. Some people think it was just a big publicity stunt. According to Carroll, Bela was terrified of really being hypnotized and told Hall just to *pretend* like he was hypnotizing him. He was afraid that Hall might slip in some post-hypnotic suggestion to stop drinking or something like that. For some reason Bela was panicked by the idea of his mind being messed with in any way, even if it was for the better."

Mike said, "You know, I have some stills from *Black Friday* of Hall putting Bela under—or supposedly putting Bela under. Maybe I can show him the stills, ask him to sign them or something. It'll break the ice, get him talking about Bela."

"I think he'll talk to you. I don't know if he'll sign the stills, but he's very approachable. He's quite elderly, in his eighties, and yet he's still very lucid. I've seen him talk for two hours or more about very esoteric subjects. And with absolutely no notes. It's pretty impressive."

"What does he usually talk about?"

"Metaphysical stuff. Hermetic symbolism in Shakespeare's *The Tempest* and the Lost Word of Freemasonry and reincarnation and the true meaning of Atlantis...on and on. I don't know what I think about any of that, but I know it's really fascinating to hear him talk about it."

More metaphysical woo-woo nonsense, Mike thought. *Well, why should I be surprised? It is L.A. after all.*

"That sounds really interesting," Lucy said. "I've been into all that stuff my whole life. Mind if I go too?"

Before Mike had a chance to respond, Eric said, "That's a good idea. I understand Hall was quite the dashing ladies man back in the day. If he doesn't want to talk to *you*,"—here he pointed at Mike—"I'm sure he'll want to talk to Lucy."

"Well, it looks like we have our first assignment," Mike said. He patted the back of Lucy's hand.

12.

L awrence Gill sat in the massive library of his London home, reading a newspaper by lamplight. He set down his pipe when he saw the headline: SIXTH WOMAN MURDERED IN SPITALFIELDS.

Gill leaned forward, his heart beginning to race. The newspapers reported local rumors that the ghost of Jack the Ripper was responsible. Given the strangeness Gill had experienced during the past few years, he couldn't exactly rule out such a possibility. However, his instinct told him that something far more sinister was at the heart of these disappearances and murders.

Gill's wife, Nina, walked into the library with a copy of the newspaper tucked under her arm. "Did you see—?"

"Yes, I did, dear." Gill stood up and tossed the paper on the chair in which he had been sitting.

"Do you still think it's—?"

"I do." He hugged her to his broad, burly chest. Those were the same words he'd said to her only a few months ago after they had survived the conflagration at Dr. Heidelmann's seaside house in Visaria. Gill had gone to Heidelmann in order to be freed from his unusual condition. To his surprise, Heidelmann had actually managed to *cure* him. Afterwards, however, Heidelmann had gone insane and died in a fire caused by the Monster of Frankenstein. Gill had fled the scene with Heidelmann's nurse, Miliza, but not before finding Nina's unconscious body amidst the wreckage outside. She had been wounded by the flames after nearly being strangled to death by Heidelmann himself. Miliza had wanted to leave Nina there, to bleed to death or die in the fire, but Gill refused. He couldn't believe that Miliza would want to abandon another human being so callously. He ditched Miliza as fast as possible and took Nina to a hospital in Visaria. They refused to help her at all merely because of the hump on her back. The people in Visaria, even those who claimed to be doctors, had a superstitious attitude toward those perceived as "monsters." But Gill knew what it was like to be afflicted with a curse by chance and circumstance, to be unable to do anything about it. So, he stole a horse and carriage and drove her broken body to the nearest town to the West where the doctors were more than willing to help her. After a few weeks she recovered. Gill stood by her side the entire time, and by and by fell in love with the afflicted girl. They were married in Germany, then moved to London where Gill set up his new business.

Gill was insistent that his tragic experience add up to something, have *meaning*. He wished to apply his newfound knowledge of the occult to the real world, to help humanity deal with these unknown forces. Perhaps he could prevent someone from experiencing the nightmare that he had been forced to undergo for five long years during which he had died and risen from the grave twice.

He and Nina had become private investigators specializing in cases of the… unusual. The team of Gill & Gill had established quite a reputation in the past few months. When Scotland Yard found themselves stumped by a case of the paranormal, they often ran right to the doorstep of Gill & Gill.

"Does this mean we're going to work again?" Nina asked.

"I believe so," Gill said. "But this time I think we'll be working freelance." He stroked Nina's cheek, then strolled over to the bookshelves that lined the walls. He pulled out Abraham Van Helsing's leather-bound tome about vampirism. "According to Van Helsing, this recent spate of murders follows all the classic signs. I wouldn't doubt if there were two or more vampires at work."

Despite everything Nina had been through in the past few months, despite learning to be cool and aloof in the face of implacable evil, the mere mention of vampirism still made her cringe, bringing back horrible memories of her near-fatal encounters with Dracula himself and Dr. Heidelmann's vampire-like affliction.

She touched her neck, the spot where Heidelmann's claws had ripped open her throat.

Gill couldn't help but notice the gesture. "Oh, dear, don't worry," he said, setting down the book and walking toward her. He embraced her again. "We've been studying and observing creatures such as this for months. I've had firsthand experience for years. The only way they can instill fear is because people refuse to believe in them. But you and I, we know they exist. We know they can die. Only ignorance allows these things to live. Thank God, we're no longer as ignorant as we once were." Gill took Nina by the hand and led her over to the assortment of crossbows, rifles, and pistols displayed on the ornate walls of the library. (His inheritance from the family estate in Wales had come in handy when attempting to fund this operation.) He pulled a crossbow off the wall and placed it in her hand. "You know how to use it, dear. Go ahead."

Nina loaded the crossbow, aimed it at the target hanging on the other side of the room, and got off a near-bull's-eye.

She raised one eyebrow and blew on the crossbow. "If we're going out hunting vampires, I'm going to need a drink beforehand."

Gill smiled. "Now you're talkin'. Scotch?"

"Better make it rum. It's foggy out there."

"My dear, I always defer to your judgment. Two rums coming right up."

The entire staff of Gill & Gill retired to the bar.

13.

They arrived at The Philosophical Research Society about an hour before the scheduled lecture. Mike had called earlier in the morning inquiring about Manly P. Hall's next talk. He was pleased to hear that Hall was delivering a lecture about alchemy that very night—Wednesday night—on the second floor of the Library. According to Eric, Manly P. Hall possessed the largest collection of rare occult books in the entire world...so rare, in fact, that there had been several attempts in recent years to break into the library. Apparently, these attempts had been unsuccessful due to the fact that Hall kept his most valuable books in his private vault at home.

On one hand Mike didn't understand why anyone would go to such trouble to steal a bunch of old books filled with gobbledygook. It'd be as if, a hundred years from now, someone attempted to steal a first edition of *Lord of the Rings* because they thought the events covered within were actually real. From Mike's perspective, The Bible was the first great sword and sorcery novel. However, he couldn't deny the fact that Bela took Manly Hall very seriously. Bela had helped fund The Philosophical Research Society in its early days. He had given Hall so much help, in fact, that Hall later returned the favor when Bela was down on his luck by buying him groceries and other necessities.

And if Bela took this stuff seriously, perhaps his ascent (or descent) into perpetual typecasting in supernatural thrillers wasn't quite as accidental as it seemed. It appeared as if Bela had a genuine interest in the subject. Perhaps Fate hadn't chosen Dracula's cloak for Bela. Perhaps, ultimately, Bela chose it for himself.

Mike couldn't wait to ask Hall these questions. He was amazed by the fact that no other horror fan had thought to track down the gentleman-scholar and talk with him about any of this before now. Bela's association with Hall had been well-known as far back as the early 1940s. Instead, most of the articles Mike had ever read about Bela were poorly researched rehashes of information that had already appeared a thousand times before.

"Where do we buy the tickets for this gig?" Lucy asked. They were currently standing in the middle of a sprawling alabaster temple located at 3910 Los Feliz Boulevard. Only about two miles away, one could see the imposing structure of The Griffith Observatory staring up into the Heavens. It was an interesting visual metaphor: this monument to ancient superstition built in the shadow of one of the most sophisticated observatories in the world. Mike wondered which structure came first. Which was the shadow of the other?

"I think the guy on the phone said we could buy the tickets at the bookstore," Mike said. He took Lucy's hand and gently led her toward a small building. Above the doorway hung a generic wooden sign that read, simply, in classic Albertus font: GIFT SHOP & OFFICE. For some reason it reminded him of the quaint shops he used to see in that old Patrick McGoohan TV show, *The Prisoner.*

A little bell rang when they entered the store. Standing behind the counter was a short, middle-aged man with a paunch and a ring of gray hair clinging to the back of his head.

"Good day," the man said in a nasally voice, as if trying to seem pleased that they were intruding on his silence. Mike wondered how many people dropped by here on an average day. "May I help you find anything?"

"We're just looking," Mike said and tried to drag Lucy away from the counter.

"I'm very interested in books about reincarnation," Lucy said. (Mike rolled his eyes.) "Do you have any books about that?"

"Oh, yes, indeed," the man said, sounding rather like an imitation of Wally Cox. And not a bad one, either. "Right this way."

The little man came out from behind the counter and guided

them toward a wall of books in the corner. Every single one of the volumes was written by Hall. There had to have been at least a hundred of them, all different titles, some of them only thirty pages long, others well over three hundred pages. All of the titles were certainly evocative: *The Secret Destiny of America*, *Invisible Records of Thought and Action*, *The Lost Keys of Freemasonry*, *Man: The Grand Symbol of the Mysteries*, *The Psychology of Religious Ritual*, *The Space Born*, *Atlantis: An Interpretation*.

"This would be the perfect book for you, miss," the man said and grabbed a two-hundred-page hardcover off the shelf entitled *Reincarnation, the Cycle of Necessity*.

"Oh, thank you," Lucy said, flipping through the pages. "This is exactly the type of thing I've been looking for."

"Indeed, have you been interested in the subject for long?"

Mike couldn't believe this little troglodyte was trying to pick up on his girlfriend right in front of him. Before Lucy could say anything, Mike responded, "Yeah, ever since her last life. She once fixed Theodore Roosevelt's plumbing. Do you know where we can buy tickets for the lecture tonight?"

The little man didn't seem to acknowledge the fact that he had just been insulted. Instead, he said, "Yes. You can purchase a pair of tickets right over here. Please follow me."

Lucy flashed him an annoyed glance. Mike tried to look sheepish, as if he didn't know why she was angry. He had always been pretty good at affecting the innocent routine.

The little man turned back toward them, forcing them to stop in their tracks, and said, "Oh, by the way, sir, is there a particular subject *you're* interested in?"

Mike smirked and said, "No. No, not really. I just came in to buy the tickets." Actually, he had no money, so Lucy was the one buying the tickets, but he didn't feel right mentioning that.

"C'mon," Lucy said, "you should pick up one of his books if you're going to interview him."

"Ah, you wish to interview Mr. Hall?" the little man asked.

Mike hadn't wanted to mention that, at least not to this little man. "Well," Mike said, "I had *hoped* to. Or at least talk to him for a little bit. I'm writing a magazine article about Bela Lugosi, and I understand Mr. Hall was quite close to him."

"Yes, I believe that's true. Of course, that was before my time. I'm afraid I've never seen any of Mr. Lugosi's films. I've never been too interested in horror fiction per se."

"That's funny," Mike said, "because that's *all* I'm interested in." Mike had often believed that fiction that advertised itself as make-believe was much more honest than the kind of claptrap that Mr. Hall seemed to specialize in.

"Indeed," said the little man, "then perhaps you'd be interested in purchasing *this* book." He reached for a slim volume entitled *Shadow Forms*. "This is a collection of twelve supernatural short stories Mr. Hall wrote for the pulp magazines back in the 1920s. It was his way of trying to slip esoteric, philosophical knowledge into the mainstream. Eventually, however, he concluded it was better simply to speak to people about such things as directly as possible."

The little man thrust the book into Mike's hand.

"Well, I don't know...," Mike began to say.

Lucy interrupted him. "Go ahead and buy it," she said. "It may help you with your project."

Mike felt chagrined. "Well, I don't really have...." He let the sentence trail off.

Lucy snatched the book out of his hands, sighing. "Jesus, I'll buy it for you. I better get half of your proceeds from this entire project."

"It's a deal. Half of everything I am is yours. Forever." Of course, half of nothing wasn't really worth very much, but Mike didn't want to mention that in front of the little man.

As the man rang up their purchases with a slight, satisfied smile on his wrinkled face, Mike realized that he detected an odor in the cramped store. It smelled like rancid yogurt.

The little man gave them their books in a plain brown paper bag, then ripped off two red tickets from a spool beneath the cash register. After Lucy paid for the books as well as the tickets, she told the little man that she hoped to see him again soon.

Mike almost mumbled, "Yeah, maybe in your next life," but then held himself back. The fact is, he knew he just didn't like to see her being friendly at all with another man. He had to get his jealousy under control one of these days.

"By the way, young sir," said the little man, "what is the name of the magazine you write for?"

"Magazine? Oh, yeah...it's called *Ramboona*."

The little man stroked his smooth, jutting chin. It just occurred to him that the little man sort of reminded him of those Punch dolls so popular in England. "Hm, I'm not sure I've ever heard of that."

"Well, it's a new magazine."

"But that word does sound sort of familiar. Is it from Mabinogion mythology, perhaps?"

"Ramboona is an African voodoo spirit. Very powerful. In 1944, Ramboona was worshipped by a man named Dr. Richard Marlowe who lived just outside Twin Falls. Dr. Marlowe committed several kidnappings and murders in Ramboona's name. It was very tragic."

"It certainly sounds like it," said the little man, "but I don't like to dwell on negative things." Once again, Mike caught a whiff of rancid yogurt.

"Yes, indeed," Mike said, imitating the man's nasal whine.

As they left the store Lucy said, "Why the fuck did you have to be so rude in there?"

"*I'm* rude? Are you kidding? Did you catch a whiff of that guy's farts? It smelled like rotting acidophilus! It smelled like what would happen if *yogurt* could somehow grow a brain and figure out how to fart."

Lucy tried to remain angry while smiling in spite of herself. "You don't have to make fun of the man. He was nice. That book might actually help."

"I guess. I just wish these New Age types would eat something other than granola and prune juice."

"You told me you considered *yourself* to be a New Ager."

Mike remained silent for a second. Why, yes, he *had* said that. He had to cover for the mistake. "I'm the kind of New Ager who eats *meat*." He flipped through *Shadow Forms*, hoping to change the subject. "You know, it just occurred to me that maybe these were some of the stories Bela was interested in making into films back in the thirties."

"You can ask Hall yourself soon enough. I guess that's the room we want." Lucy pointed at a stairway that led up to the second floor of a two-story building. A dim light could be seen on the second floor. Sure enough, another generic sign read, LECTURE ROOM.

"Jesus!" Mike stopped in his tracks and massaged his temples.

"What's wrong?"

Mike remained silent for a moment, trying to rub out the pain with his fingertips. "Wait…it'll pass."

"Another one of your migraines?" Lucy sounded so worried.

Unbidden, the thought entered Mike's head: *I don't deserve her.*

"How long must these experiments continue?" Ygor asked. He was sitting in the corner of the main hall at Carfax Abbey, his arms wrapped around his knees. "I'm getting bored."

Thanks to Krogh's unerring ability to get his hands on every piece of equipment they needed, Dracula had been able to set up a decent facsimile of Dr. Heidelmann's laboratory here in his crypt. Crackling Tesla coils and bubbling beakers threatened to crowd even the extra coffins out of the expansive hall.

"We're nearly done, my good man," said Dracula. "I studied Dr. Heidelmann closely during my time as his patient. His mind was an open book to me." He gestured toward Aishe with a slight wiggle of his fingers. She placed in his hands a glass vial filled with a noxious black substance.

"I don't understand," said Ygor. "Why did you seek out Heidelmann's medical advice? What could someone like that possibly do for you?"

Dracula grinned as he continued mixing and matching the contents of various multicolored vials and beakers. "Why, he managed to do a great deal for me—me and every other member of the living dead on this planet. You see, I went to Dr. Heidelmann under the pretense that I wished to be cured of my vampirism. But that was just a cover story, and yet Heidelmann— fool that he was—actually believed me! I had been studying the scientific progress human beings had made these past decades, and I'd grown worried. Eventually, I have no doubt, these humans will attain the facility for advanced biological warfare. It is only a matter of time until they decide to devote their efforts to creating a virus in their secret laboratories for the specific purpose of attacking and killing vampires. I wished to develop such a virus *first*. And I knew Heidelmann had the expertise to do it. I willingly gave him samples of my own blood, encouraged him to develop a vaccine against vampirism."

Ygor just shook his head. "But *why*?"

"I had him create an antitoxin so I could create a cure *against* it." Dracula burst into laughter.

Ygor rose to his feet. "Is that what you're doing now? How does that help *me*?"

"Steady," Dracula said. "That is not what I'm working on now, though I intend to begin doing so very soon indeed. No, what I'm working on now has a far more *destructive* intent. Krogh!"

Krogh shambled out of the shadows. "Yes, master?"

"Bring me the first subject."

Krogh stepped out of the shadows, a squirming baby in his arms. Krogh had a look of intense sadness in his eyes.

"Hand me the creature," said Dracula.

Krogh glanced down at the infant. Somewhere deep in the recesses of his mind he no doubt remembered his own son when he was just an infant. Only a few months old, innocent, fragile. Dracula himself had a daughter and a son, both of whom he'd murdered and brought over to his side, the realm of the dead. He, too, could remember when they were infants, but that seemed like part of another life. When he thought about infants now, he grew disgusted. At one time, hundreds of years before, he felt the same way about insects. Cockroaches. Flies.

He hadn't seen his children in years.

"Krogh!" Dracula shouted.

Krogh seemed to snap out of it. "Yes...yes, master...I'm sorry. I don't know what got into me." He handed the infant over to Dracula.

"Make sure it doesn't happen again," said Dracula, holding the infant out in front of him at arm's length. The thing was squirming quite spastically now. It didn't want to be here at all. Good. Dracula knew exactly how to get rid of it.

Without prompting, Aishe placed a hypodermic syringe into Dracula's hand. "This," said Dracula to Ygor, "is the liquefied essence of the spores we brought with us from Visaria. The plants that produce these spores are very rare, but Dr. Heidelmann had managed to grow an entire greenhouse full of them in the caverns underneath his estate. For this reason, they're far more valuable than all the gold in the world."

Ygor rose to his feet and lumbered toward Dracula. "But why?" Ygor said. "What do they *do*?"

"These spores have the capability of softening human flesh and bone. When applied in the manner preferred by Dr. Heidelmann, it can be used in surgery instead of intrusive scalpels. But when given to a warm-blooded animal such as this thing, in a concentrated dose, it can have a far less benevolent effect. Observe, friend Ygor, *observe*!"

Dracula slipped the needle into a bulging blue vein in the infant's neck. The baby screamed in pain and terror. Within seconds its flesh began to bubble and hiss and boil. The infant's screams rose like invisible bats into the upper reaches of Dracula's crypt. Then the squirming beast literally melted into a puddle of amorphous flesh that spilled over the edges of Dracula's clawed hands. Dracula cocked his head back and laughed, then snapped his neck downwards and sank his fangs into the shapeless mass of protoplasm. The sound of blood being sucked through virginal arteries filled all the hollow spaces of Carfax Abbey.

"I think so," Mike whispered, massaging his temples.

"Is there anything I can do?" Lucy asked. "I hate to see you like this."

"I'll be okay."

"Maybe you should go to a doctor and see if—"

"No, no doctors. There's nothing they can do for me. I've had these things all my life. Let's just go, forget it happened."

"I'm sorry, I didn't mean to—"

"I'm just so used to it by now, the pain sort of fades into the background after a while." He reached out and squeezed her hand. "Thank you."

"For what?"

"Just for caring about me. That's something I'm not at *all* used to. Having someone *genuinely* care about me, not just themselves? Does that sound...stupid? Cheesy?"

"No," Lucy said. She kissed both his temples, as if to make the pain go away magically, then kissed him on the lips. Mike believed the gesture truly did help.

When they entered the room on the second floor, Mike was surprised to see that there were only about twenty people gathered there. Most of them were older, probably in their fifties or sixties. Mike and Lucy were the youngest people in the room. A series of classroom desks, looking like the sort Mike hadn't seen since elementary school, filled the room. Lining the room stood a series of immense bookshelves that went all the way up to the ceiling. The books seemed very old. Mike glanced at some of the titles very quickly, most of which he'd never heard of: *Lilith, A Voyage to Arcturus, Undine, The Coming Race, Zanoni, A Strange Story.* A copy of *Dracula* stood out from them all. Mike pulled it off the shelf, opened the brittle cover, and was shocked to see that it was a first edition.

"Hey, check this out," Mike said, showing the novel to Lucy. He pointed at the date of publication. "It looks like this thing has been here forever. I wouldn't doubt if Bela himself touched this book."

"Wow," Lucy whispered. "Are all the books in this room that old?"

"I think so." The musty odor that permeated the room seemed to suggest so. He carefully put the book back in its place. All the books in this room appeared to be fiction.

An ornate chair, looking like the one in which Hall had been sitting in the photo Eric had shown him, stood at the front of the room. Hall, however, was nowhere to be seen.

Mike tugged on Lucy's sleeve and gestured toward the row in the back. He preferred observing a crowd from the shadows. His writer's instincts. Lucy sighed, shook her head, and gestured toward the opposite direction: the front row.

"I want to be able to *hear* him," Lucy said.

Mike decided not to argue the point. Maybe Lucy's instinct was the correct one.

Lucy smiled politely at the men and women in the room as they passed by them. All of them smiled back, particularly the men. They seemed pleased to spot a fresh face in the crowd.

As they took their seats, Mike flashed back to grade school when he could never find a desk made for a left-hander. He glanced behind him and noticed that almost everyone had notebooks laid out in front of them. Were they supposed to take notes?

Hanging on the wall was an original watercolor painting of a fat woman with a crazy, faraway look in her bovine eyes. It looked like it had been painted a thousand years ago. Mike leaned forward and saw that the title of the painting read, "MADAME BLAVATSKY." That sounded familiar. Didn't Leo Tolstoy write an eight-hundred-page novel with that name?

Beneath the painting, a door opened. From the doorway emerged a very obese, gray-haired man with a cane. The cane was ornate and old, reminding Mike of the one that Lon Chaney, Jr. used to kill Bela Lugosi in *The Wolf Man*. Mike assumed this old man was Manly Hall, though he looked nothing like the slim, darkly handsome gentleman he had seen in Eric's photo. This man's body had been ravaged by neglect: the ultimate outcome of a life lived entirely in the mind, in the stratosphere of perpetual philosophizing and metaphysics?

And yet, despite his slow movements and uncooperative legs, the man had a twinkle in his eyes that was bright and alive.

Hall lowered himself into his spot with an exhaustive sigh. "Good evening, ladies and gentlemen," he said, then propped the cane beside the arm of the chair.

"Good evening," everyone in the room said at once.

Hall folded his hands in his lap very demurely and said, "Alchemy. Alchemy is the reconciliation of opposites, the transformation of refuse into the purest gold...."

Hall spoke for two hours straight. He never hesitated in his speech, and yet the presentation wasn't overly rehearsed either. It was conversational, very casual. From time to time, Mike glanced at Lucy. She seemed enthralled by what he had to say. About fifteen minutes into the talk, she reached into her purse, pulled out a notepad and a pen, and began taking what seemed to be very extensive notes. Mike didn't understand everything Hall was talking about, but at the same time he didn't think it was a bunch of malarkey either. No doubt about it, this man's knowledge of history and literature and the sciences was erudite and all-encompassing. He could see why Bela had been so enchanted by this gentleman. It was easy to imagine how much more impressive these talks had been back in the '30 and '40s when Hall was still in his prime. Near the end of it all, Mike got the feeling that the man could go on for two hours more if only his body would allow him to do so.

At almost precisely nine o'clock, Hall finished his sentence, then said, "Well, that's it for now. We can continue later." The lecture didn't end. It just paused. Mike suspected that each lecture was a chapter in an on-going oral narrative that would never cease—except, perhaps, when Hall passed away.

When Hall had risen to his feet with the help of his ornate cane, some of the people in the room approached him. They chatted for a while.

"Here's your chance," Lucy said.

Mike nodded, reached into a manila envelope that had been sitting in his lap this entire time, and strolled toward the elderly scholar.

An old married couple—or at least they seemed to be married—were talking to Hall about Voltaire's initial, unsuccessful attempt to join Freemasonry. Mike had no idea what all that was about. When they seemed to be finished, Mike said, "Mr. Hall, sir, may I show you something?"

"Eh?" Hall said and turned toward Mike. He looked directly into his eyes, as if trying to gauge whether or not he had ever met this young man before.

Then his eyes—not bloodshot at all, like so many other old people with whom Mike had interacted in the past—gazed downward and alighted upon the black and white photo of a young Hall hypnotizing a sixty-year-old Bela Lugosi.

Hall stared at the photo for some time, then his eyes

brightened further. He smiled, pointed at the photo, and said, "Why...that's *Bela!*"

"That's right," Mike said. "And that's *you.*"

"Oh." Hall laughed. It was a kindly laugh, like that of the perfect, celluloid grandfather everyone wishes they had. "Yes...I see now."

For some reason, Mike thought it was charming that Hall recognized Bela in the photo long before he recognized himself.

"Let me see this, my boy," Hall said, and took the photo from Mike. He lowered himself back into his chair. He carefully held it by its edges and stared at it with great intensity, as if attempting to reenter that time period through the effort of pure thought alone. "Ah...this is when I hypnotized Bela for that film, *Friday the Thirteenth.*"

"Well, right," Mike said, "but they released it as *Black Friday.*"

Hall laughed again. "I forgot about that. *Friday the Thirteenth* was the working title. The studio changed it because they thought the public would stay away from the film in droves if it was called *Friday the Thirteenth.* You know, bad luck and all."

"I wonder if any of those people were alive when *Friday the Thirteenth* came out...you know, the recent one."

"Oh, I doubt that! These people were old even back then. No, I think the American population was more...well, *superstitious* in those days. Who knows? Maybe that was a good thing. It was a more naïve time, but in some ways people were wiser."

"So...did you really hypnotize Bela?"

Hall looked up from the photo at last and said, "My God, no! He would never allow it. He thought I was going to slip in some post-hypnotic command to make him stop drinking. I was always on him to curb the drinking, but he was absolutely terrified of having his mind changed or distorted to someone else's will. At the time it really frustrated me because so many of his problems could have been taken care of so simply." Hall shrugged, then glanced back down at the fading photo again. "Now I look back on it all and realize that this was an admirable, nonconformist trait in his personality. Even though he flirted with communism as a young man, I think he resented any attempt to control people's lives—even if it was for the better! He hated it when people tried to change his opinion, once he had settled on something. This could lead to some heated arguments between him and me when we hit on a topic we disagreed on. Like the hypnotism stunt, for example. Believe me, I didn't want it to be a stunt. I thought it would be a nice opportunity to show the studio and the public what hypnosis was capable of accomplishing, but Bela would have none of it. But that's a testament to his acting ability. Some of the people on the set were really fooled by it all. I remember. They may have laughed about it afterwards, but at the time they weren't sure what to make of it. Too bad all that effort was wasted on a poor movie. It's a dirty shame."

Mike, still kneeling beside Hall, glanced up at Lucy and laughed. "I wasn't going to ask you for your opinion about the film itself, but...."

Hall spread his hands in the air. "What can you say? The studios wasted Lugosi and his talent while exploiting him for his name."

"I never understood that," Mike said. "If the studio didn't respect him, why would they use his name prominently in the advertising but give him such small roles in their films? You know, like *Night Monster* over at Universal or *The Gorilla* over at Fox or—"

Hall cut off Mike with a wave of a wrinkled, liver spotted hand that was slender and dexterous in the photo, and yet nonetheless still seemed graceful somehow. Even today. "I don't even recognize the titles you're mentioning, my boy. I didn't see most of these films back then. I saw Bela all the time, so I didn't need to see him up on the silver screen. It was too painful for me. I really wanted better for Bela. The studios didn't comprehend his potential at all. I tried to get better movies made for him, but the studios were having none of it." A tired expression washed over Hall's face. He groaned as he planted his hands on the armrests of the ornate chair and tried to lift up his considerable weight. This seemed to require some effort. "Have you ever talked to these executive types at the studios? I doubt much has changed today. They're only interested in numbers, numbers,

numbers, and there I was trying to pitch them on the notion of raising the consciousness of the human race through these little supernatural horror films. All of them ignored us. We got close, Bela and I, quite close. But not close enough to change his career trajectory. Bela should've asked me to hypnotize those studio executives instead of pulling a publicity stunt."

Mike rose along with Hall. "So, the stunt *was* Bela's idea?"

Lucy placed her hand on Mike's shoulder. He glanced up at her. She had a concerned look on her face. Perhaps he was pushing his luck with Hall? Asking him too many questions?

Hall did have a pained expression on his face. And there were still people waiting to talk to him. "You know what," he said, "I'm enjoying talking about my old friend." He shouted over Mike's head: "The rest of you, save your questions for next Wednesday! I'll remember where we left off." Then he turned toward Mike and Lucy and said, "Follow me, you and your lady friend both."

Mike smiled at Lucy. Lucy shrugged, obviously impressed. They followed the old man through a door in the back of the library and into an expansive chamber that was (appropriately enough) lit with candles. There were even more books back here. Most of them seemed much, much older than the books out in the main hall. Were these the rare occult texts Mike had heard so much about?

There were four vintage Saarinen pedestal wingback chairs arranged in a pattern in the middle of the room as if each chair sat at a different point on the compass. Hall waddled over to a mini-bar in the corner of the room and poured himself a drink. "I always drink one glass of red wine after a lecture," Hall said. "Would you like any?"

Mike glanced at Lucy. Lucy nodded yes. "Sure," Mike said. "Why not?"

They watched Hall's hand shake slightly as he poured the three glasses. Lucy leaned into Mike's ear and whispered, "Go help him."

Mike walked over to the bar and said, "Uh, do you need any...help with that?"

"Please carry this to your lady friend over there." Hall

turned toward her. "I'm sorry, what's your name again?"

"Lucy. Lucy Szilagyi."

"Greetings, Lucy. Please sit down." Hall gestured toward the chair that sat in the South position. Hall sat down in the East position. Mike sat down last, in the West. "So, tell me," Hall said in between sips of his wine, "what's your interest in Bela? Just movie fans?"

Before Mike could respond, Lucy said, "We're journalists. Film journalists. We're putting out a magazine, and we want the first issue to focus on Lugosi. Would you mind if we report on what you tell us?"

"Did you bring a tape recorder?"

Mike said, "Uh...."

"No," Lucy said, "but we don't need it." She reached into her purse and pulled out a pen and a small black book that contained all the phone numbers of her many contacts in Hollywood. She flipped to the few blank pages in the back and pressed pen to paper. "I know shorthand." Mike was pretty certain that she didn't.

Hall flashed them a self-satisfied smile. "I knew you two had a higher purpose. I could feel it. Please. Ask your questions. I can't guarantee how long I can stay alert. I have an early day tomorrow."

Mike said, "We could always do this another time if you—"

Hall held up his hand and said, "No, no, this reminds me too much of the conversations I used to have with Bela himself in this very room. In fact, he used to sit right where you're sitting now." He pointed at Lucy's chair. "Some of our finest arguments occurred in this sanctum sanctorum. Please, ask away."

Mike cleared his throat and said, "So, you pitched several different films for Lugosi? What were those projects, and how far did you get with them?"

"Oh, it's been so many years now. Who even remembers for sure? We had high hopes, both of us did. You know, I've read several books written about Bela since his death, and they all portray him as some kind of halfwit just because he turned down the role of the Monster in *Frankenstein*. Perhaps that makes him a bad businessman, but he was not an idiot. You see, I knew both Karloff and Lugosi. Karloff I didn't know very well, but I could tell he was a good businessman. He didn't take his status as a horror star very seriously. Bela *did* take it seriously."

"How did you know Karloff?"

"Well, I pitched a couple of film projects for him when Warner Brothers had signed him to a five-picture deal in the 1930s. One of them was called *The Witches' Sabbath*, all about a German robber baron and his Satanic cult committing various misdeeds in the seventeenth century. I thought I was in a good position to sell the project because I had just written a film for Warner Brothers called *When Were You Born.* It was about a female detective, an Oriental, who uses her knowledge of astrology to solve a murder."

"I didn't know you'd had any screenplays produced," Mike said.

"Oh, yes. The reason I decided to build my Philosophical Research Society in Los Angeles was because I could see what was happening right before my eyes. I could see, even as far back as the '20s, that Hollywood would supplant Madison Avenue as the main shaper of public consciousness. I wanted to try to use that tool for good instead of evil. I wanted to spread certain esoteric truths into the mass media in the form of fiction. I had already done so to some extent with some pulp fiction stories I had published. Those are the stories I collected in *Shadow Forms.* When Bela and Karloff first became famous, I saw a huge potential in their screen personas.

"Keep in mind that *Dracula* was the very first American film to actually depict the supernatural as something that was *real.* Before *Dracula*, all the horror pictures were of the Gothic variety in which the supernatural menace turned out to be a normal human dressing up as some sort of beastie to scare people away from a cache of buried treasure or something along those lines. For years studio executives claimed that *Dracula* couldn't be filmed in Hollywood, that the American audience wouldn't accept a story in which the supernatural was depicted as being real, that it would offend too many religious folks. Well, those executives turned out to be wrong, very wrong. And I saw in the fascination that the public had with such films as *Dracula* and *Frankenstein* a huge opportunity for myself and other metaphysicians. Here was an opportunity to use this magical medium of film to teach the world about real magic and the esoteric secrets that underlay what they perceived to be everyday, mundane reality. I told Bela this on many occasions, and he sympathized with my goals. He was very much in tune with the occult side of life. Unlike Karloff, he had a very specific vision of himself and the importance that his screen persona could have for people.

"We pitched a sequel to *Dracula* for Universal. In my version I went back to the ancient legends upon which Bram Stoker himself had drawn in order to write his original novel. In esoteric lore, the vampire is very much a spiritual being, an astral body that takes over your physical shell and corrupts it from within. Drains it of all its essential essences. The studios saw this approach as being far too strange, too much of a departure from what had been established in the previous film. Bela and I also pitched other projects, one in which Bela would be an old cleric with esoteric knowledge who solves crimes involving the occult. That one would be called *The Mysterious Abbe*. Again, this would have been an opportunity to teach the film-going audience about certain occult secrets that should not be the sole property of fraternal orders. These occult secrets belong to everybody. That's why I wrote my story 'The Emerald Tablet,' which you can see there in that book you have in your hands." Hall gestured toward *Shadow Forms*.

"Because of me Bela accepted the role of Chandu in *The Return of Chandu*. He was a little reluctant because it was a serial and he was trying hard at that point to leave them behind, but I very much encouraged that sort of storytelling because it involved the ancient legends of Lemuria and Atlantis. In the mid-thirties we toyed with the idea of doing our own Atlantis film, *The Emperor of Atlantis*. Bela would have played the Emperor, of course. It was our intent to improve on the Chandu formula, to upgrade the material for serious-thinking adults.

"From behind the scenes I even helped the writers on *The*

Return of Chandu with certain details in the story so that they would be in accord with real history. I suppose you could say I made sure the film was 'esoterically correct,' at least as far as I could without totally rewriting the entire screenplay. I did this for no compensation, mind you. I just did it because Bela requested I do so. My favorites of the many films that Bela made were those that approached this goal of presenting true esotericism to the public."

Mike glanced over at Lucy and saw her scrawling away at her notepad at a rapid pace. Perhaps she did know shorthand? He hoped so. Mike paused, waiting to see if the old man was truly done speaking. He didn't want to interrupt him in mid-thought. All of this material was classic. While listening to Hall's words, Mike couldn't help but think about what Lucy had said as well. A film magazine. As if they were really going to do it. As if it wasn't just a pipe dream. Up to this point, Mike had been very skeptical about Eric's ability to actually launch this thing. After all, what if his wife said no? Eric was a bright guy and all, but he seemed a little too pussywhipped to defy his wife if the answer was negative. But, on the other hand, maybe the idea wasn't so unattainable. Though he hadn't wanted to get his hopes up, Mike realized now that this was just his mom's psychic leash digging into the scruff of his neck again. Why *wasn't* it possible? The centerpiece for the first issue could be an article about Mr. Hall's hitherto unknown influence on the films of Lugosi.

He could even see what future covers might look like....

Then he realized that Hall was just staring at him expectantly while sipping his second glass of wine. Mike cleared his throat and said, "What were some of those films? The ones you felt were...how did you put it? 'Esoterically correct'?"

"*The Return of Chandu* would certainly be one of them. Even the first *Chandu* film, the one in which Bela played the evil magician Roxor. Again, these films were aimed at children, but that didn't matter to me. All that mattered was that the public was finally being inundated with stories in which magic—not Yahweh-induced miracles, but genuine *magic* generated by human beings—was being portrayed as a true possibility. For me, the context didn't matter. Truth is truth, whether in the form of a crude melodrama or from a scholarly old professor standing behind a lectern. Both are equally valid. In that sense, Bela was a teacher. Sort of like I am. We talked about that on many different occasions. Now...what was the question you asked me?" It was obvious that the old man was growing very weary indeed. "Bela's best films, yes? Well, I suppose *White Zombie* would be near the top. A wonderful, new, esoteric twist on the Faust legend. Again, keep in mind that for many Americans that film would have been the very first time they ever heard the word 'zombie' or 'voodoo' or even thought about these African forms of ritual magic. From this cultural perspective alone it's a very significant film, though very few people talk about it in that way. They just think about it (if at all) as a cheap little independent horror film, when it was far more than that.

"What other films? Well, *Dracula*, of course, despite its obvious limitations. I wish they had based the story more on the original novel. Stoker was an Irishman, not British, and was very well aware of the history of esotericism. One need only read his other supernatural tales to see the truth of that. Part of the reason for trying to do the sequel at Universal was to get more of Stoker's original vision out in front of the public. For so many years the public was used to the *stage* version. They would've been very shocked to see the real story unfold before their eyes.

"Bela's first collaboration with Karloff, *The Black Cat*, was a wonderful parody of Aleister Crowley, and somehow stayed true to the decadent spirit of Edgar Allan Poe if not to the original plot of that classic little story of madness and murder.

"You know, some of his films were innovative in a different way, in the sense that they were among the very first American science fiction films. Movie fans don't often think of them that way, but all you have to do is look at *The Island of Lost Souls* and *The Invisible Ray* and *The Phantom Creeps* to see the truth of what I'm saying."

Mike nodded. "You're absolutely right. Let me ask you,

is there anything about Bela that you would like our readers to know about him? Something that's rarely discussed?" *Our readers.* Mike was amazed at how fast he'd slipped into the impromptu role of the journalist.

Hall seemed to think about this question for a second, then said, "Yes. What few people know is that Bela had a hell of a sense of humor. The fact is, young man, you can't have five wives without having a sense of humor. You know, he always wanted to do comedy, but he was never really given a chance. It's unfortunate that he didn't have more screen time in that Greta Garbo film, *Ninotchka*, but that's certainly well worth watching. You can see hints of his comedic skill in *International House*, one of W.C. Fields' first films (which is also science fiction, in a way, since it's all about the invention of television years before its time). Every Lugosi fan should watch that film. And you can even see his comedic skill on full display in something as silly as *Voodoo Man*, which, to be honest with you, I don't think was meant to be entirely serious in the first place. How many films did I just mention?"

Mike shrugged, then glanced over at Lucy. Lucy used the tip of her pen to tabulate it all in her notebook, then said, "Eleven."

"Eleven?" Hall said. "You know what, young lady, please cross out *Voodoo Man*. It's not a very enervating film anyway. Now you have a top ten list. You can run it as a sidebar in the magazine. Manly P. Hall's Top Ten Bela Lugosi List." Hall laughed.

"That's a great idea," Mike said. "I think we'll do that. I can see you're very tired. Do you mind if I ask you just one more question?"

"Certainly."

"I wanted to ask you about the long-lost *Frankenstein* test footage."

Hall cocked his head to one side. He had a quizzical look on his face. "Test footage?"

"Yes, you know, Robert Florey's test footage. Florey was the man who was originally set to direct *Frankenstein*. So Universal got frustrated with the whole situation and replaced Florey and Lugosi with James Whale and Boris Karloff who went on to make movie history with *their* version of *Frankenstein*. Florey and Lugosi were reassigned to *Murders in the Rue Morgue*, an adaptation of the Poe story."

"Yes, yes," Hall said patiently. "Not as good as *The Black Cat*, but it has its moments."

"I think that film has one of Lugosi's best performances. I know it was Ed Wood's favorite Lugosi film."

"You're referring to the test reel that Florey shot of Bela in the Monster makeup?"

"Yes. All we know about it is what Florey once said in an interview. And I think Edward Sloan, who played Dr. Waldman in the James Whale version, was in the test reel as well. He made some comments about the experience later on. He said Bela might have done his own makeup and looked sort of like one of the trolls in that Laurel & Hardy film, *March of the Wooden Soldiers*. Do you remember Lugosi ever referring to it?"

Hall shook his head. "Bela didn't like to talk about *Frankenstein* at all. It was a sore subject with him. And so was Karloff, understandably. But Bela's attitudes toward *Frankenstein* changed over the years. When I first met him, which wasn't long after *Frankenstein* was released, he seemed quite relieved that he had managed to avoid making the film, as if he had narrowly avoided career suicide." Hall smiled at the irony of that thought. "Back then he wished Karloff the best of luck. But that attitude quickly changed when Karloff's star eclipsed him so completely. In the early thirties, Bela was sure he had a future in films outside the horror genre. He never even imagined how it would end up for him. To tell you the truth, I don't think he thought too much about the future. He always lived in the moment. He had survived incredible tragedies in his life, mainly by not caring. And I don't mean in a nihilistic way, but more in a sort of...well, a Zen Buddhist way. Not that Bela was a Buddhist, but you know what I mean. He could...how do you say? *Go with the flow*. He didn't try too hard. He loved good music, good wine. He loved dancing and women. And most of all he loved performing on the stage. He once told me that as long as he had enough money for stage make-up and a loaf of bread and a bottle of wine, he didn't care what happened to him financially. All that changed when his son was born. Becoming a father changes you. Now he began to worry about the future. About not being able to provide for his son. That sort of 'go with the flow' attitude vanished. Now he began to worry, and worry quite often. His health suffered as a result. You can see the change in him. Just look at Bela in, say, *The Raven*, then compare him with the Bela in *The Devil Bat* only a few years later. He went from a handsome leading man to a gray-haired old man in just a few years. This, of course, limited the types of roles he was being offered. And when that happened, suddenly he began claiming he had personally picked Karloff out of a crowd and presented him to James Whale as a replacement. I knew that wasn't true, and yet I heard him tell the story to other people many, many times. I think he told the story so often that he himself believed it. He hypnotized himself, I guess you could say. I always suspected that the story Bela had first told me wasn't even true. I always got the sense that he had been fired from *Frankenstein*. I don't think James Whale liked him. Why that would be, I don't know. I think he just wasn't sympathetic to Bela's acting style. But perhaps the pain of having been fired was somehow easier to deal with as long as Bela told everyone that *he* had made the decision himself. But I do remember Bela saying on several occasions that his version of the Monster's makeup was more along the lines of what you saw in one of the German Expressionist films. Of course, he would've been very familiar with those films, and that style of filmmaking, since he had appeared in several German movies before coming to the United States."

"Was Bela referring to *Der Golem*, the silent film from 1920?"

Hall snapped his fingers, or tried to, and pointed at Mike. "Yes, I think so. And Mary Shelley's story is, of course, merely a variation on the Jewish myth of the Golem. Bela knew that, you see, and understood it. He had read Mary Shelley's novel many years before even coming to the United States. He knew that the Monster in the book was a very loquacious fellow. He wanted the Monster to have that same sort of intellect in the film. He understood that the director, Florey, just wanted to turn the Monster into a mindless machine. Florey was more interested in visuals than ideas. Bela was an intellectual. For some reason most writers don't paint him that way, I don't know why. Perhaps it's because Bela never attended any sort of university. But that didn't matter. He was a very erudite, self-educated man. You'll find that people who don't go to college are often more intelligent than people who do. They feel the need to overcompensate, you see. Bela read about five newspapers a day. He could carry on a conversation about almost any topic, but his main interests were acting and politics and stamp collecting and metaphysics. So, it didn't surprise me at all when he told me he'd read Mary Shelley's *Frankenstein* long before being offered the role. I think the truth is that both versions are true. Bela could be a bit hotheaded and probably did quit—several times. But, ultimately, I think he wanted to be in the film, even if he had to settle for being a mute monster. He would've given the part his all, just like he did with every other part in his life. But studios rarely want to deal with difficult personalities if they don't have to. So, they found a bit actor who was starving and wouldn't put up too much of a fuss with the studio. And Karloff didn't, not until later on when he had more clout. So, it's understandable that Bela didn't like to talk too much about those days. And when he did talk about them, he tended to fabricate, I'm afraid."

"Did you ever meet Ed Wood?" Lucy put her hand on Mike's arm, as if to get him to stop asking questions, but he just flicked her hand away.

Hall smiled, his eyes drooping slightly. "Yes, I met Ed Wood."

"You did?"

"Several times."

"Was he wearing women's underwear at the time?"

Hall laughed—slightly. "Well, I wouldn't know. That aspect of his life didn't come out until later. He just seemed like a normal, handsome young chap, eager to make headway in Hollywood. I think he was just using Bela to try to further his career, what there was of it, but he seemed sincere enough. I think he genuinely liked Bela and wanted to do right by him. The problem was he had no talent...or taste."

"Did you see *Plan 9 from Outer Space* when it came out?"

"No, no, I did see *Bride of the Atom*...isn't that what it was called? I saw it at The Paramount Theatre only about a year before Bela died. I thought it was very sad, given the state that Bela was in at the time. I prefer not to remember him that way. I think he himself would prefer we not remember him that way."

"Do you remember Ed Wood saying anything about the *Frankenstein* test footage?"

"Eddie told me it still existed. I recall that a man named Marlowe, Bela's agent at the time, supposedly told him this. How Marlowe would have gotten a copy, I have no idea. Unfortunately, both Marlowe and Eddie are dead now. The person you need to talk to is Bela's son."

"Did you ever meet him?"

"Oh my, yes, many times. A nice, handsome boy. Looked just like his father. I think Bela shipped him off to a military school because the boy's grandparents were simply fed up with being his de facto mother and father. The fact is that Bela really didn't have time for his son. Oh, he loved him all right, he definitely did, I know that. But I think he loved the stage more. It was in his bones. He had never done anything else. It was his entire purpose for living. And so, he often had to leave L.A. in order to tour in summer stock productions of *Arsenic and Old Lace* or *Dracula* or some kind of midnight variety show that was way, way beneath his talents. Or there were times he and his wife Lily had to leave the country in order to shoot a film in England. And Bela couldn't travel alone. He needed Lily there by his side to be his nurse and chauffeur. He depended on her totally. In many ways she was more of a mother to *him* than to her own son. And she resented it. Resented the months she was forced to spend away from her only son because of Bela and his childlike neediness. It's understandable that she left him eventually. By the time she had the courage to do it, it really didn't surprise me. Bela blamed the Other Man, of course, but it was his own fault. He complained to me about the whole situation, here in this very room. We'd drink wine and I'd listen to all his complaints. I'd try to get him to see how he'd brought this situation on himself, but he was too stubborn and far too fragile to face the truth. Eventually, I gave up. You can't really change anyone, not even with hypnosis. People have to change themselves."

"And this stubbornness," Mike said, "you think that's what led him to lose the part in *Frankenstein*?"

"Yes, of course. That's why Bela's story compels us even to this day." When Hall said the word "us" he gestured toward Mike and Lucy and himself. "It's a classic Greek tragedy. Bela's hubris brought him down in so many ways. But I really think, at the end of the day, his punishment far outweighed the original sin."

Mike wasn't quite sure what to say to that. This conversation was veering into philosophical areas he hadn't anticipated. The article that might result from this encounter would be far better than just a list of factoids about the late actor's career in horror films.

"I guess," Mike said, "we can all learn a lesson from Bela's story."

Hall smiled and spread his hands in the air. "We can *all* learn from a tragedy, particularly a Greek one."

"Even you?"

"Most certainly. Bela taught me a lot, and not just by default. He taught me to live life to the fullest, to keep your head in the clouds as often as possible, to see through the eyes of an enthusiastic and precocious child…but to also know when to come down to earth. Lily was Bela's anchor. But you can't depend on anyone else to keep your feet on the ground. You have to be your own anchor. It's a delicate balance. But we all must do it: keep our spirits attuned to the metaphysical while somehow not neglecting the basic needs of the flesh. The needs of the mundane world. Speaking of which…I better head off to bed now or my wife will be very upset. I'm sure you know how it is. Are you two married?"

Mike glanced over at Lucy. Lucy looked up from her notepad and smiled and said, "No, not quite. I'm afraid I'm not the marrying type."

Mike was a little disappointed to hear that, but he smiled anyway. "Neither am I," he said.

"You never can tell what the future holds," Hall said and rose from the chair.

"But wait," Mike said, "about the test footage. So...you really think it exists?"

Hall nodded. "I think so. But if anyone knows about that, I think it would be Bela Jr. He's a lawyer, you know. He's been fighting the good fight on behalf of his father for many years now. I'm sure you know about the lawsuit he filed against Universal Studios for profiting off his father's image for so many years without paying Bela's estate even a single dime. I think, for Bela Jr., it's a way of trying to right the many wrongs that were committed against his father when he was alive. The boy's still quite devoted to his father. I'm sure he would know how to track down that footage, if he doesn't already know where it is."

"If I find it," Mike said, "would you like to see it?"

Hall stood there in the dim light, an imposing figure suddenly. The misshapen shadow he cast behind him was like something alive, something strange and magical. "Sometimes the past should stay in the past. When you get to be my age, young man, you'll find that the future's more important than ever before. However...." Hall shrugged. "It would be nice to see my old friend one last time, as he was when I first met him, engaged in the art he believed in so deeply. And to see him at such an important crossroads in his life might be illuminating in ways...well, in ways we can't even predict. Certainly, young man, feel free to call on me again if you should discover the footage. I'd be curious to see those moments in time, caught like insects in amber, trapped in a black and white Gothic nightmare. Or perhaps a dream. It depends on the viewer, I suppose. Like all things important. Good night."

Hall retreated from the room quickly and silently, like a shadow. Where did he go? An even deeper sanctum sanctorum? Mike imagined a labyrinth of secret tunnels snaking their way through this alabaster temple in the heart of Los Angeles.

Mike and Lucy were now alone.

They just stared at each for a second. Then Mike whispered, "So, what did you think?"

"Intense," Lucy said. "He gives off this weird, vibrant energy. And my fucking hand hurts."

"Did you get all that down?" Mike meant this sarcastically.

"I think so," Lucy said. Mike glanced at the notes. To his surprise, she really had written it all down.

"Holy Christ, I didn't think you really knew shorthand."

"Sure. I learned it at SCROC."

Mike looked puzzled. "SCROC?"

"Southern California Regional Occupational Center. My mother forced me to take a class when I was eighteen. She wanted me to have something to fall back on in case the acting didn't work out."

"That was smart of her."

"No, it wasn't. That was her way of saying I wouldn't make it. If you want to succeed at anything, you have to have the Eye of the Tiger. You think Muhammad Ali ever said, 'Gee, if I don't make it as a boxer at least I have this dictation job to fall back on?' No, of course not. The secret to acting is to make yourself totally unfit for any other profession. I'll never work a nine-to-five job, never. I'll kill myself first."

Mike smiled. "You know what? I really like you."

Lucy reached out and patted Mike on the hand. "I like you too. I'm famished. Let's go to Du-Par's and get some clam fucking chowder. And an apple pie."

They did just that.

But they made sure to lock up Hall's empty library before they left.

14.

Tonight was the night.

Outside the Temple of Khalid Banoub, Ygor drew his heavy coat close to his breast and said to Wolfgang, "I'm afraid."

Wolfgang patted him on the shoulder. "No need to be afraid. We've all been through this. Having attained the coveted thirty-third degree of Scottish Rite Masonry, I've been through this whole process many times over. And look at me, I'm fine. Nothing bad is going to happen to you."

"No," Ygor said, "you...don't understand. I'm not...afraid... of physical harm. I'm...afraid...I'm not...worthy."

"All men with a soul are worthy of being a brother. That's the point of the Brotherhood, to bring together men of various social stations under one roof in order to erase the invisible lines that separate God's children here on Earth. Come, enter our Temple and see for yourself. No one here will reject you. They're all good men."

"I'm...sure...they are," said Ygor. What worried Ygor, however, was that *he* wasn't a good man.

Benjamin Franklin, Rousseau, William Blake, Voltaire. All had been Masons. How could he hope to be worthy of being included in such company?

The gentlemen milling around the Egyptian artifacts that filled the grand Masonic Temple all wore dapper tuxedos. Their clothes seemed to fit them so well. Wolfgang had a tuxedo tailored especially for Ygor, and yet it still didn't seem to fit quite right. Perhaps he just wasn't used to such things.

Khalid Banoub emerged from within the inner Temple that lay behind the closed double doors Ygor had seen at the party. He seemed to float across the tiled floor while remaining perfectly still, the other Masons moving out of his way one by one. A messianic figure parting a sea of tuxedos.

There was something about the eyes of Khalid Banoub that disturbed Ygor down to the very marrow of his bones, but he could say nothing. He knew this feeling of discomfort was his own fault, his own inherent feelings of worthlessness.

"Greetings," said Khalid Banoub. "Are you ready for your ascension into the ranks of the Brotherhood?"

Ygor remained silent for a moment until Wolfgang prompted him with a nudge in the ribs. "Yes…though I am…a little… nervous."

"All men are. It's no fault of your own." Banoub turned and gestured toward a gentleman appraising a statue of Bast, the goddess of cats in Egyptian mythology. "As you can see, most of the men here are wearing white aprons, the white triangle at the top of the apron turned downwards. After tonight you will be given an apron as well, except your triangle will be facing upwards. Until you've successfully completed the third degree. Then your apron will look like theirs."

Ygor was confused. He wasn't sure if he was supposed to ask questions. "But…what does that mean?" he asked.

"It symbolizes power. All ritual can be described as a ceremonial invocation of power. And that's what you will have once you join our ranks. Not only will you attain valuable amounts of power you never possessed before, a heightened sense of self-worth and personal enlightenment, but you will also share your own unique power with the Brotherhood. We're all about sharing here."

"That's…good to hear," Ygor said. "I…like…to share." An old man in a lonely forest taught him that long ago. He knew that old man was probably long dead, and the thought saddened him.

The gongs of a clock tower rang in the distance. Banoub said, "It's time to begin. You as the candidate shall wait out here in the main hall. We will summon you when it's time for you to enter the inner Temple."

Ygor nodded at both Banoub and Wolfgang and watched the

assembled gentlemen wander off into that sacred inner room. Wolfgang glanced over his shoulder and gave him a reassuring nod.

Ygor was now left alone amidst the valuable artifacts. He felt dwarfed by their presence, insignificant in the shadow of such ancient power. And yet at the same time he felt as if his entire life had led him to this one moment.

Du-Par's was hopping, as usual at this time of night. Mike and Lucy opted to sit on the patio outside. It was a humid Los Angeles night, no need for a jacket. It felt like the middle of the afternoon.

Mike drank an iced tea while eating a bowl of chili with Saltine crackers. Lucy, true to her word, ordered clam chowder. But Mike had barely touched his food because he was too busy reading Lucy's notes on their encounter with Manly P. Hall.

"God, this is great stuff," Mike said.

"I'm surprised you can make out what it says."

"I know a little shorthand—just enough, at least. I had a journalism teacher who taught me. Or tried his best to. Besides, I've always had bad handwriting. If I can make out *my* incomprehensible scrawls, I can definitely make out yours. And I have a good memory. Your notes here bring the conversation back almost verbatim."

"I think you should start writing the article immediately."

"What about the screenplay?"

"There's no reason you can't do both, right?"

"No. No reason at all."

"I think this is something you have to do. It's something *we* have to do."

Mike smiled. "You're really excited about doing this, aren't you?"

"There aren't any magazines around like this. No one remembers these weird, obscure films. *You* do. You've got so much knowledge in your head about this stuff, you could probably fill up forty-one issues with your writing alone. But that won't even be necessary. Once the first issue comes out, we'll get in submissions from all over the world. There's a whole underground network of freaks out there just waiting

for a magazine like this. And you're on the same wavelength as
every fuck-up in this great nation of ours. No one ever went poor
underestimating the perverseness of the American public. You
know who said that?"

Mike shook no.

"I did. Just now."

"But I don't know anything about distribution or printing
or...or typesetting or...."

Lucy reached across the table and patted Mike on the back
of his hand. "But other people, way dumber than you, somehow
managed to figure it all out. I'm sure we can do it too. Sometimes
you just have to make the leap. And the best time is when you
have nothing left to lose. Mike, why sit around waiting for it to
happen?"

"Waiting for what to happen?"

"Life. This isn't a test reel. This is it. Your one shot. My one
shot. Let's forget about 'Making It' for a little while and just do
something fun and stupid. Hell, and maybe other fun, stupid
people will appreciate it. Why not?"

A broad smile broke out across Mike's face. Slowly. He
started laughing.

"What's wrong?" Lucy asked.

"Nothing. It's just that...." He gave her hand a tight squeeze.
"You know, I was on the verge of suicide before I met you."

Lucy glanced to one side, perhaps a little nervous, then her
red lips parted as if she were about to respond with something
terribly profound. She said, "We remember forgotten films."

"Excuse me?"

"That could be our slogan. 'We remember forgotten films.'
Forgotten films. Forgotten people. It's the perfect match. Don't
you think?"

Mike hefted his glass of iced tea in the air. Lucy hefted her
cherry coke. The glasses clinked together under the fluorescent
patio lights. Mike thought of the resultant sound as a bell ringing
in a new future for both of them.

"Happy New Year," Mike said.

It was only the second week of October.

Halloween would be arriving soon.

Ygor knelt blindfolded somewhere within the inner Temple. He didn't know where exactly. He was disoriented. He had been through much in the past twenty minutes. He could feel the presence of others standing around him, behind him. His head was still spinning. Somebody was talking near him, reciting some kind of speech with flowery words that had a medieval quality about them. He heard the clash of metal above him. Chains? Were they going to put him in chains? No, please God, no....

More talking. Then the sound of thin, sharp metal sliding gently against each other. Not chains. Swords.

He was told to put his hand on something...a piece of paper? A book. Something sat on top of the book...metal...he felt it with the tips of his fingers...yes, of course...Wolfgang had hinted about something involving a square and compass. He was told to recite something. Even though he didn't understand the esoteric words, he did as he was told.

He heard the sounds of chairs creaking as dozens of people...men...rose from their seats and surrounded him. For a moment, he felt claustrophobic. On edge. He could fight off all of them if he had to. He'd done it before. But this sounded like a few dozen. Here comes the hanging. Another crucifixion?

"What do you most desire?" a voice asked him. Khalid Banoub's low, steady tones.

He felt like saying, "A...cigar? A...glass...of wine?" But he didn't. A voice beside him (Wolfgang's?) whispered, "Illumination."

So, he repeated the word.

A thin, weak hand grabbed his own. Banoub began talking at him again...more esoteric jabberwocky he didn't understand. Banoub was kneeling in front of him, he could tell. They were facing each other. Banoub was performing his most solemn duty as Master, initiating this poor blind beggar into the Ancient Mysteries. He was explaining what the Great Lights were... the Great Lights of Freemasonry...Ygor comprehended every other word...at least that meant his comprehension was getting better....

Then the blindfold was ripped from his head at the exact moment that he heard the regular and rhythmic clapping of gloved hands. The assembled chanted in tandem, "SO MOTE IT BE." He blinked against the blinding light that now filled the room. Where was that light coming from? His heart was racing. He felt like he might stop breathing at any moment. Silly, silly. He'd been through so much in his life (lives?). This was just a stable of common tricks to alter the consciousness of the gullible...a part of him knew that...the same thing that happened when you went to a faith healer in a revivalist tent...a dog and pony show...an esoteric circus. And yet, nonetheless, his heart raced. The first blurry objects he saw upon opening his eyes: the square and compass laid out on a version of the Holy Bible the size of a manhole cover. At least, it looked like the Bible. Upon closer inspection, he realized it was only the New Testament; the Old Testament had been left out for some reason. This was fine with Ygor. The New Testament had Revelations, the only book of the Bible violent and bizarre enough to match his own experiences in this world. He kept staring at the square and compass as Banoub explained their symbolic significance... followed Banoub's long, magician's finger as he guided Ygor's attention to three flickering blue candles sitting atop a human skull perched on the altar right beside the Bible. Everything was explained to him, and yet none of it was any clearer. Any yet...and yet for some reason he felt as if something quite significant had occurred in his head tonight, something no amount of reading about Masonic ritual could ever have given him. He'd undergone an experience like no other in his life, and wondered why all this affected him on such a deep level. He felt a great wave of emotion rolling over him as he glanced furtively at all the men standing in militaristic rows on either side of him. He felt connected to everyone in that room in a manner he could not define.

The words ceased flowing out of Banoub's mouth. Ygor realized that none of them, at any point, had been reading off cards; they had actually memorized all this. He found it to be an incredible feat, how smooth the ritual was. It went off without the slightest wrinkle, without any of them stumbling over even a single syllable.

Everybody returned to their seats. He found himself being led toward the East where Banoub presented him with his own white apron inscribed with the symbols of Masonry. These symbols and others in the Lodge were explained to him in great detail. He was told the three pillars of Masonry were Wisdom, Strength and Beauty, that no god, no religion, was more valid than another, that the gods of the East can co-exist happily with the gods of the West. The entire experience he'd just undergone was interpreted for him by an old man he'd never seen before. This man presented all the words in a theatrical manner, like a professional actor, but Ygor didn't really understand what he was talking about.

When it was all over, everybody clapped for him and congratulated him and welcomed him into the fold.

He was a brother now.

A man.

He should have been elated.

Why, then, did he feel like collapsing?

15.

On the way home through the snow-covered streets, Wolfgang said, "You did very well. I'm proud of you."

"Thank you," Ygor whispered. Suddenly, he had to lean against Wolfgang for support.

"Is there anything wrong?" Wolfgang asked.

"I just...feel...exhausted."

Wolfgang smiled. "Oh, don't worry about it. I felt tired myself after my first initiation. It's trying. This is one of the most important nights of your life, second only to your third degree. When you'll become a Master Mason. Too bad you don't have time to make it that high before the installation ceremony this weekend."

"What's...the installation...ceremony?" Ygor said.

"It happens once a year during the winter solstice. It's when we install all the officers for a new year. It's the one time of the year when all the families of the Masons are allowed inside the inner Temple to take part in the ritual installation of the officers. Everyone lends their support just by their very presence."

"Will I...have my...energy back...before then?"

"Oh, of course!" Wolfgang said. "You'll feel much better by tomorrow morning. Trust me."

Ygor smiled and followed Wolfgang back home to the estate of Frankenstein.

The next morning Mike woke up at around eight o'clock, well before Lucy. Careful not to disturb her, he climbed out of bed, took his typewriter into the living room, and began working on the article. He didn't put any clothes on, didn't even stop for breakfast. Lucy didn't wake up until noon. By that time, he had written the first twenty pages of the essay. Ready to take a break, he handed Lucy the initial pages and wandered into the kitchen to make both of them some food. About fifteen minutes later he came out with plates of scrambled eggs and toast and coffee and orange juice.

Lucy was just finishing the last page. She set the piles of pages down on the cushion beside her. She looked up at him with her poker face. Sometimes he couldn't read her expression at all. This both unnerved and excited him at the same time.

"Well?" he said, knowing she wanted him to ask the question. "What do you think?"

"I think...." She drew the sentence out on purpose, just to add some suspense to the situation. "I think we need to mug Eric."

They decided to corner Eric in the back of his store at around two in the afternoon. On their way there, Lucy told Mike this would be the perfect time because The Wife was not liable to be hanging around. Lucy knew the woman's schedule pretty well. The Wife, she explained, didn't like Lucy hanging around the store because she was under the impression that Lucy was "an incorrigible slut." Lucy had actually overheard the woman saying these exact words.

"Of course," Lucy said from behind the steering wheel, "she's exactly right. But her charming accusations don't apply in this case. I would fuck my own brother before I fucked Eric. And I don't even *have* a brother. Eric's a sweet guy, but...come on, man. I mean, Jesus."

They parked behind the store only when Lucy concluded that The Wife's white convertible was nowhere to be seen. Then Mike and Lucy crept through the back door and surprised Eric by creeping up on him from the store room. Lucy leaped out from behind a pile of crates and sank her fingernails into Eric's shoulder blades while screaming, "I'm gonna eat chu, motherfucker!"

The Slushee that had been in Eric's beefy hand went flying through the air and landed on a pile of old *Vertex* magazines. Eric spun around and shouted, "Damn it! You almost killed me!" He grabbed at his heart. "I think I just had my first heart attack."

Lucy was now laughing uncontrollably. "I couldn't help it. You're such an easy target. How many times have I told you to lock the back door?"

"I know, I know. What're you two doing here?"

"We wants *money*," Lucy said in a deep voice. "Lots of it!"

"Oh, okay, well, at least that's a new approach. No explanation, no sob story, just leap right to your demands. I'd rather have an addicted gambler or a drug addict as a friend. At least I can wrap my mind around that. But this...I don't even know where it all goes. When am I going to get back all the other hundreds of dollars I've lent you?"

Lucy propped herself up on the counter. "You know the answer to that question."

"I know, I know, when you make it big. Listen, I believe in you, Lucy, I always have, but really, please understand that I'm not denigrating you at all when I say I'm not holding my breath."

"You're gonna want in on our new business venture."

"Our?" Eric glanced at Mike.

"Show him the manuscript," Lucy said. "I'm Mike's agent. You're his publisher. Remember?

"Publisher?" Eric said. "Oh, man, I don't know about that. My wife wasn't enthusiastic when I told her the idea and she—"

Lucy just pointed at the manuscript with one of her blue lacquered fingernails. "Read."

Eric took the manuscript and read the title out loud, "'Life Is Not a Test Reel: An Interview with Manly P. Hall.'" Eric glanced up at Mike. "You actually went ahead and did it?"

Mike said, "We both did. Lucy took the notes. She knows shorthand."

Eric looked at Lucy in surprise. "Really? I thought you told me you had absolutely no marketable skills to put to use in any legitimate job market."

Lucy shrugged. "I lied."

Eric shook his head back and forth and lowered his considerable girth onto a stool that sat behind the counter. "I'd always intended on doing this myself," Eric said, tapping a fingernail against the first page of the manuscript, "interviewing Hall about working with Lugosi. I always knew he lived right around here, and yet it was just something I never quite got around to doing for some reason. But you two did it. That's great." He glanced over select passages, laughing occasionally. "Wow, there are some real gems in here. Is this finished?"

"No, not quite. It's only about halfway done. Lucy wanted to come down and show it to you right away for some reason."

"Because it's still hot off the presses," Lucy said. "Can't you feel it? Feel the narrative traction and nervous excitement rising off the page? Infusing you with the mad desire to inculcate yourself in our profitable new business venture?"

Eric laughed. "What do you mean, '*Our*'?"

"Lucy made herself a partner," Mike said.

Ygor lay in his room on the second floor of the House of Frankenstein, suffering from horrible dreams. This was nothing new. He'd suffered nightmares before. Nightmares of abandonment. Nightmares of hunchbacked dwarves threatening him with fire. Nightmares of a beautiful, scarred woman rejecting him with a hiss of abject disgust. Nightmares in which he ran and ran and ran from hordes of angry villagers, torches held aloft in the fog-laden night.

But not dreams like these.

He dreamed of the eyes of Khalid Banoub, saw those twin slits beckoning him from across a great distance, from the other side of a dark river where skeletal beings crawled along the oddly dry soil searching for something they would never find.

Ygor shot up out of this nightmare, whimpering in fear. He lowered his face into his hands. Something was wrong, he knew it. He could feel his energy draining from him. He realized that he recognized this feeling. It was not new.

In his previous life, when he was still inside the body his father had created for him, he remembered the feeling of electricity being drained from him during his father's numerous experiments. He felt like he was dying. But when his father sent the lightning coursing through his veins, he felt the exact opposite. He felt like a giant among pygmies, like he could do anything.

This sensation of being drained of vital life energies...this is what he experienced during the initiation...this is what he was experiencing now. But how could that be? He was no longer inside the body his father had given him. Unless...unless Khalid Banoub had figured out a way to do the same exact thing to a normal human body.

Ygor rose from his bed, pulled his clothes out of his closet, bundled up warmly, then climbed out the second story window and scaled down the side of the stone walls to the grounds below. He didn't wish to wake up Wolfgang, Elsie or Paul on his way down the hall. This route would be better. He didn't want to say anything to Wolfgang until he had confirmed his suspicions.

He dashed off through the snow, retracing the route they had taken from the temple of Khalid Banoub.

RAMBOONA Magazine #1 hit the stands about three months later. The table of contents page looked like this:

LIFE IS NOT A TEST REEL: AN INTERVIEW WITH MANLY P. HALL

LUGOSI AS SHAMAN: METAPHYSICS & THE HISTORY OF THE HORROR FILM

A GUIDED TOUR OF LUGOSI'S HOLLYWOOD (WITH A MAP OF HIS VARIOUS HOMES)

THE FILMS OF BELA LUGOSI AS BORDERLINE SURREALISM: IN-DEPTH ANALYSES OF *WHITE ZOMBIE* (1932), *THE BLACK CAT* (1934), *SON OF FRANKENSTEIN* (1939), *THE CORPSE VANISHES* (1942), *SCARED TO DEATH* (1947), *GLEN OR GLENDA* (1953), *BRIDE OF THE MONSTER* (1953), and *PLAN 9 FROM OUTER SPACE (1959)*

WEIRD NOIR: BELA LUGOSI & THE BLENDING OF GENRES: *BLACK FRIDAY* (1940), *INVISIBLE GHOST* (1941), and *BOWERY AT MIDNIGHT* (1942)

A CONVERSATION WITH BELA LUGOSI, JR.

COUNTESS DRACULA: CARROLL BORLAND'S SEQUEL TO *DRACULA*

THE UGLY AMERICAN IN EARLY HORROR CINEMA:

DR. X (1932), *MAD LOVE* (1935), and *DARK EYES OF LONDON* (1939)

BLACK DRAGONS: WAR PROPAGANDA & RACISM IN 1940s HOLLYWOOD

A CONVERSATION WITH MAILA NURMI (VAMPIRA) ABOUT ED WOOD, ORSON WELLES & *PLAN 9 FROM OUTER SPACE*

BELA LUGOSI & MARSHALL MCLUHAN: PRECEDENTS OF POSTMODERNISM IN 1930s HOLLYWOOD: *INTERNATIONAL HOUSE* (1933) and *MURDER BY TELEVISION* (1935)

COMPLETE LUGOSI FILM CHECKLIST

Eric threw a launch party at his store. He invited everyone who had been interviewed for the magazine or involved in even the smallest way with putting it together, which included almost all of Eric's regular customers, as well as the panoply of film freaks who wandered into his little store on a weekly basis. A beautiful black and white photo of Lucy (as Luna) adorned the cover. They chose Saturday, January 3rd, 1987, as the launch date: the beginning of a new year, a new chapter. In honor of Bela, Eric ran a pristine print of Ed Wood's 1955 "masterwork," *The Bride of the Monster.*

Draped from the ceiling were elaborate banners depicting Bela in his various filmic guises. Other, smaller banners depicted some of his most infamous and sinister henchman: Dwight Frye as the maniacal, insect-eating Renfield from the 1931 *Dracula*, stuntman Edwin "Bud" Wolfe as the absurd and yet unforgettable iron robot from the Universal serial *The Phantom Creeps,* and pro-wrestler-turned-actor Tor Johnson as the mute giant Lobo from *Bride of the Monster.*

Some of the cast and crew of *Bride of the Monster,* who had been interviewed for the magazine, showed up for the party. All the Ed Wood heads in the room went crazy. And these fringe figures in Hollywood, who had been cast into the dustbin of cinematic history for so long, lapped up the attention. Many of them weren't even aware that there was so much love out there for films they had made over twenty years before.

For Mike, despite yet another migraine blooming behind his temples, seeing the joy in the tired eyes of these people made the entire enterprise worth it.

In the back of the store Mike leaned against the counter, beside a cardboard cutout of Bela as Murder Legendre, watching all of these fellow outcasts and freaks mingling together. What surprised him most when interviewing these people was discovering that actors he had grown up watching on TV, people he'd held in awe and who seemed almost mythological to him, were just normal folks, most of whom now made their livings doing very routine jobs as plumbers and waitresses and welfare beneficiaries. Mike hoped that the added attention of this magazine would push some of them back into the spotlight and get them out of the rut into which they had fallen. It boggled his mind that he, Mike, was now in a position to help *them*, when their twenty-year-old shadows had done so much to help *him* while growing up with a phantom for a father.

At his elbow a familiar, soft voice said, "A penny?"

He glanced over at Lucy. She held a penny in her hand.

"For *my* thoughts?" Mike said. He held out his hand.

She dropped the penny into his palm. "I'd say they're worth at least that much."

"I'm just amazed this is all happening. We pulled it off. I seriously thought Eric was going to lose all that money he gave us, but we might actually be able to pay him back."

"I always knew we'd be able to pay him back. At least that much."

"You always did know, didn't you? How is that?" He reached out and brushed her arm lightly. "Where do you get all your self-confidence from? Where can I get some?"

Lucy smiled sadly. "The ironic thing is that it has nothing to do with *self*-confidence. It was confidence in *you* that kept me going throughout the whole thing. Confidence in your enthusiasm. I knew it would leak over onto the page somehow and just magically draw people to the magazine."

Mike laughed. "How does that work? I inspired your confidence, but I don't have any of my own. It's a paradox."

"It makes no sense at all," she said and kissed him on the

lips. He returned the kiss and thought about the first time he'd ever seen her at the graveyard. After a few minutes, she pulled away and said, "But it doesn't have to, does it?" She slipped her arms through his.

"No. It doesn't."

"You needn't worry about it too much. Remember what Manly told you. Just go with the flow, dude."

"Is that what he said?"

"Pretty much. In different words."

"I wish he'd shown up," Mike said. "It would've been the perfect capper. It really all started with him."

"Oh, he has better things to do than hang out with a bunch of freaks watching *Bride of the Monster.*"

"He's sort of a freak himself."

Lucy smiled. "That's true. But he's a scholarly freak. With a dubious reputation to uphold. We should bring a copy of the magazine to the PRS with us. I wish Bela Jr. had shown up."

"I'm kind of glad he didn't, not after all the horrible things he said about the Ed Wood crowd in that interview. It might've been kind of awkward, particularly since Eric chose to play *Bride of the Monster* throughout the party. I told him to choose one of the earlier pictures, like *The Raven* or *Murders in the Rue Morgue,* but he didn't want to listen."

"I think it was a good choice. It fits the mood better." Lucy glanced over her shoulder at the screen and watched Bela's stunt double being ripped to shreds by a flaccid rubber octopus.

"My only regret is that Bela Jr. wasn't able to put me on the trail of that lost test reel. I was hoping that would be the centerpiece of issue number one."

"I doubt it even exists anymore. That guy who was offering to sell a copy to Eric turned out to be a big no-show, right? Consider it a sign from the universe."

"I don't know, I don't know. Something tells me it *does* exist. Otherwise, why would Marlowe have an ad in the paper selling it? What would be the point?"

"Perhaps to do this. To stir up speculation. Cause a mystery."

Mike shook his head. "In 1970, there wasn't much interest in Lugosi. He couldn't have planted the info in the paper with the hopes that a couple of film freaks in Hollywood would get intrigued by it and waste their time trying to track down non-existent footage. That doesn't make any sense, unless he was the world's most impractical prankster. Which, by all accounts, he wasn't."

Lucy patted him on the arm. "You're too hard on yourself. Just be happy with what you got right with the magazine, not everything you *weren't* able to accomplish."

Mike sighed. "That's always been my problem. It's hard to get out of my own way sometimes. Did I tell you about those copies I stuck in the Tower Records magazine rack? The cashier told me they sold out within a couple of hours. How wild is that? Did I tell you that?"

"*Twice*, before the party started."

"Oh, yeah." He smiled sheepishly.

"Now, c'mon, let's go mingle with the rest of the freaks. Who the fuck knows? It's still early. Maybe Vampira will make a surprise guest appearance."

"Well, I doubt that will happen."

With the curious timing of a badly written film, Vampira (one of the most memorable characters from Bela's last film, *Plan 9 from Outer Space*) showed up only a few minutes later. Mike couldn't believe it. She'd been the most difficult interview subject of them all. Mike had been forced to commit sophisticated acts of espionage-level detective work in order to track down the woman at all. It had taken him at least six weeks of wading through false leads before finally discovering that she lived right in his backyard: only a few blocks from his and Lucy's apartment in a little studio behind a house owned by two people who had never even heard of Vampira. Mike couldn't find Maila's phone number, but had gotten a hold of the landlords' number. These people had absolutely no idea that their tenant had once been a famous TV personality who had dated all the greatest actors in Hollywood including Orson Welles and James Dean. What they *did* know, however, was that their tenant valued her privacy so they gave him the runaround for several days. All Mike's calls went unanswered. Finally, he showed up at their front door. When he explained he was a magazine writer, they relented and directed them to the tiny bungalow in their backyard. Mike knocked on Maila's door only to be told to go the hell away or she'd call the cops on him.

Mike decided not to give up. He and Lucy staked out the place and learned that Maila often strolled over to the park across the street around lunchtime and fed the pigeons. It was Lucy who recognized her. To Mike she looked no different from any other eccentric old woman wandering the boulevards of Los Angeles. Only after Lucy pointed out the distinctive bone structure of the woman's face did Mike finally agree that, indeed, this was Vampira, the proto-Goth sex goddess who had bewitched America briefly via the pointillist dots broadcast through their television screens. It was during this initial excursion that Mike and Lucy confronted Maila. Thankfully, she did not run away. Perhaps it was Lucy's presence that made Maila feel at ease. Mike had noticed on several occasions that Lucy's presence often enabled him to gain access to people and places that would normally be off limits to an awkward single white male with poor social skills. A pretty young woman seemed to trump whatever peculiar albatross lay draped around his neck—an albatross that others could detect, but which was invisible to him.

Maila talked to Mike and Lucy for about twenty minutes, then agreed to a tape-recorded interview to be conducted on that park bench at precisely noon the next day. For some reason she did not want them anywhere near her bungalow. True to her word, she showed up at noon and regaled the two of them with hilarious and tragic stories about 1950s Hollywood including her ascent to fame and her rapid decline due to being blackballed by very powerful people who had taken a dislike to her. The interview was really a series of unresolved tangents, and Mike had had to reconfigure the conversation in order to add some logical continuity to it, but at the end of the day he was very happy with how it emerged. Maila demanded final approval of his manuscript—something no one else did, by the way, not even Bela Jr. who was a god damn lawyer fachrissakes—and Mike agreed, to his regret. He and Maila went back and forth about twenty times over a billion and one little corrections, including the proper placement of a comma. Despite her humbled state, Maila's ego had not abated. She was still the Queen, even if Hollywood had long passed her by. By the time the entire convoluted process was over, Mike was convinced that Maila hated him for some reason. This was the main reason he never expected her to show up for the party.

To his eternal surprise, Maila showed up with three young men who looked like thalidomide babies that had been raised exclusively on The Sex Pistols and The Ramones. Each of them had some severe physical deformity that was somehow made less shocking by their punk rock attire. They announced themselves as The Maila Nurmi Experience and performed an entire set of hardcore punk songs on top of Eric's counter while Maila stood below them and sang the lyrics. They performed six songs, the first of which was called "Vampira's Bacchanal." The other six were all based on 1950s science fiction themes: "The Manster's Mistress," "Mommy Has a Death Ray," "The Tingler Hippie Hit," "Stink Star from Another Dimension," and "The Day My Cunt Caught Fire." (Now *that's* class, Mike thought.)

Mike was a little annoyed that Maila didn't bother to inform either him or Eric that she would be performing music (after all, they could've advertised that in all the flyers he and Lucy had taped on telephone poles all along Melrose and Hollywood Boulevard, or at least gotten the place properly equipped for the performance), but overall Mike was just pleased to see the dear old woman loosening up and having a good time. She seemed to enjoy her return to the spotlight, no matter how meager that spotlight actually was. The counter of Tinseltown Book & Poster was by no means the same as hosting one's own show on nationwide television, but Mike had learned something about actors while on this strange journey: ultimately, actors (good ones) didn't care how many people were in the audience during a performance; they would perform just as well for five as for five thousand. He was surprised by how flattered some of his boyhood heroes had been when he told them a real *magazine* wanted to interview them. Mike had expected a boot in the pants and a door in the face from most of them, but that had not been the case. With the exception of Maila, all of them were more than pleased to talk about their past work. In fact, it was difficult to get some of them to shut up; he wouldn't have had it any other way.

The small crowd went crazy for the impromptu performance of The Maila Nurmi Experience. Some of the audience members hadn't seen Maila since they'd filmed *Plan 9 from Outer Space* with her. Mike knew the photographs taken of this unprecedented Ed Wood reunion would have to be featured on a double page spread in issue number two.

Yes, what began as an uncertain experiment actually seemed to be successful in a big way. Mike had so many ideas, he'd planned out the contents of the magazine going all the way up to issue number twenty-five. *Jesus, I can't wait to begin*, he thought as Maila hit a high note on an encore of "The Day My Cunt Caught Fire."

Khalid Banoub stared into the oval mirror hanging on the wall, then ripped it off and tossed it at the statue of Anubis standing on the other side of the inner Temple.

Immediately, he regretted it. He ran over to the statue and ran his sensitive fingers over the onyx surface. "Please forgive me, great Anubis!" he cried. "I didn't mean to offend you. I was just…so frustrated." He sank to his knees before the statue. "I'm so sorry. I steal as much energy as I can with each initiation and yet it never seems to be enough. I do seem to get younger, but only by a paltry few seconds each time. It's not enough. It's not *enough*! If I'm to present myself to Mehet-uret, I need to look *exactly* as I did when we were in love so many centuries ago.

"These weak fools…they willingly give over their precious life energies to me during their sad little initiations, never knowing they're giving up their ability to perpetuate their race." Banoub chuckled. "And yet *still* it's not enough. This cesspool, this *London*, is populated by shadows that don't deserve to be called 'men.' Why, these creatures are barely discernible from their wives. This is what the passage of so many centuries has done to the human race. If only I were back in Egypt when the true gods, gods such as you, were still recognized for their power. Only there would I find men who could provide the energy I need. But that place, that time, is gone forever."

Banoub clawed at the immobile statue. "I can't wait any longer. I *must* have the energy to make my move. And *you* must give it to me. I will perform an act of devotion to you so unmistakable that my faith will be proven for centuries to come. Soon, the winter solstice will fall upon us, the perfect time in which to conjure up your familiar here upon the wretched earth. Yes, I can draw upon the assembled energy of all my initiates at once, including their wives and children. Your familiar will materialize here in the inner Temple, at which point I will set it loose upon the city. It will take for you a thousand lives for every pitiful soul you now hold in bondage. And then you will see. You will see how much I love you, and you will give me the gift I crave. You'll have to." Banoub shot to his feet and raised his balled fist into the air. "You'll *have* to!"

He reached out, grabbed the fist of Anubis and pulled downward. The statue rotated, disappearing into the stone wall, replaced abruptly with a different idol: an obsidian statue of Anubis' most powerful familiar in the Land of the Dead, a creature that could sometimes act as Anubis' representative on Earth. According to the ancient scrolls, it was known to the High Priest of Karnak only as Onbuljah. It possessed the grotesque body of a scorpion and three huge heads: that of a toad, a bearded human, and a cat as black as the deepest hour of midnight.

Something crashed within the Temple. Banoub turned. "Eh? Who's there?"

Banoub heard the shuffling of feet.

Banoub spotted the shards of an ancient vase lying on the tiled floor near the double doors. They were open a crack. The anger of the gods rose within Banoub's chest. An interloper...a *cowan*...lurking within the sanctuary of the gods?

Banoub rushed toward the entrance of the inner Temple far faster than his skinny, fragile body would seem capable. He burst through the doors to see a hunched figure scampering about amidst the ancient artifacts of his homeland.

He reached out and grabbed the cowan by the back of his

collar. He spun the figure around and wrapped his hands around his throat.

Ygor, the new initiate. The expression on his face was one of utter panic.

"Though you are indeed a Mason," Banoub whispered, "you have not yet attained the right to observe the sacred activities of your Master when the Lodge is dark. You must now pay for your sacrilege…with your *life!*"

Ygor brought his arms up and tried to break Banoub's hold on his throat to no avail. Banoub was far stronger than he seemed.

"Stop struggling!" Banoub commanded. His grip tightened, tightened. "Go to sleep…and when you awaken, you will be in another world…on the other side of the black river with Anubis and his loyal hordes…."

Ygor's eyes widened in fear. He increased his struggle rather than allowing himself to be killed.

Banoub was stunned. "How is this possible? No one mortal has ever been able to resist before, unless…." His gaze dug deeper into Ygor's soul. What he saw there, or rather *didn't* see, confused him. Perhaps frightened him. "You…you're already *dead*." Banoub let go of the man's throat and backed away. "How can this be? Has Anubis sent you to *spy* on me?"

Ygor said nothing. He turned and ran toward the exit. The creature was fast, like a jackrabbit. A dead jackrabbit. Before Banoub could get over his shock, the dead creature was gone.

Banoub ran toward the door and out into the snow-covered streets, but the sidewalks were desolate. There was no sign that Ygor had ever been there.

Banoub staggered back into the inner Temple, pulled a hidden lever on the statue of Onbuljah, and watched as the proud statue of Anubis took its place once more. He stared up at Anubis' implacable face. "I have no idea what you're planning against me, but by the end of the week my loyalty will have been proven. You will have no need to send your minions against me. I will be yours, body and…." He hesitated, wondering if he could legitimately offer such a thing. What if he was like the pathetic creature that just ran out of here? What if he had no soul? How would he ever know? What did it feel like to have no soul? Did it feel like this? He looked down at his hands and touched them, but he felt nothing. They didn't seem cold. They didn't seem warm. They were just...*there*. Could it be? Was he a mere hollow husk operating out of pure instinct alone?

No. Just as soon as the thought entered his head, he rejected it. Could a thing without a soul *love*? Could it love as much as *he* loved Princess Mehet-uret?

Of course not. There was no reason to doubt. Just move forward. Claim the prize. Attain the goal. Never falter.

His hands lowered, resting by his side, as he straightened to his full height and whispered to the statue of Anubis, "Body and soul."

16.

Mike got into a fight with Lucy in the middle of issue number seven. It started out as a normal day, as pleasant and as difficult as any other, the usual responsibilities of the magazine piling in front of them. Since the publication of the first issue, they had received more and more subscribers and submissions that needed to be waded through. Most of the submissions were insane. Some weren't even written in English. Some came written in ink on lined paper. Others were totally inappropriate. Why send porn to a film magazine? Mike tended to trash the real time-wasters, even if the writers included a self-addressed stamped envelope for a reply. When he was a teenager, furiously submitting his stories to magazines all around the country, he was always pissed when the editors took their sweet time getting back to him. Now he understood. Looking back on those early stories he'd written, he felt ashamed he'd ever allowed those atrocities to leave his little typewriter in his little room in the little town of Snoqualmie.

They had just finished eating breakfast. Lucy was sitting at her desk in the corner of the living room, methodically filling envelopes with copies of the latest issue, and Mike was sitting at his desk putting the finishing touches on an article about "Darwinian Cinema" (horror films in which Darwin's Theory of Evolution was the main impetus of the plot) when Lucy turned to him and said, "Mike, do you think you'll ever get around to finishing your screenplay?"

Mike tensed the second he heard the question. It was the mutant elephant in the room; it always had been. He'd written so much in such a short period of time. The screenplay was good. He knew that. It would only take a day or so to bang out the final act. And then Lucy would be happy. They would both be happy. Wouldn't they?

"I don't know," he said, not turning away from the typewriter, "I guess when the grind of putting out the magazine winds down—"

"That's what you've been saying for over a year," Lucy said. "The grind's never going to wind down, not at this pace. The second you finish one issue, you start on another."

Mike tried not to get angry. He didn't want this to turn ugly. He turned around slowly and said, "I thought you would be proud of me. The reason most of these magazines fail is because they're not consistent. They don't stick to a schedule. I've been getting the issues to the printers on time ever since we started this. The readers get the new issue in their home at exactly two-month intervals. The readers are happy. The buzz keeps growing. Neither of us have had to get real jobs. We're just barely skating by, of course, but I think things will get better. They're already getting better."

"Mike, I am proud of you. You work hard on the magazine, I know that. It's just…I don't want to do this forever."

"Do I need to remind you that doing this whole thing was pretty much your idea? You *encouraged* me to do this!" He could feel the anger beginning to burn in his chest, like acid reflux, eating at him from the inside-out.

"Well, it was originally *your* idea, and I *know* I encouraged you. And you ran with it. Your writing, your knowledge, is what's making this thing float. I know that. I'm not taking that away from you. But I'm an actress. Do you know how many auditions I haven't gone to in the past year because you needed help getting the magazine together?"

"You act like you're doing me a favor. This is *your* magazine too. You're listed as an associate editor. We're both living off the proceeds. Thank god Eric isn't demanding more of his share, otherwise we'd be out on the street."

"I'm not getting any younger."

"You're more likely to break into Hollywood through this

magazine than through those god damn useless auditions. How many have you been on? How many parts have you actually gotten? We're meeting real producers and directors all the time because of the magazine. Something will break for you. You'll see."

"Most of the producers and directors we interview for the magazine are near death."

"Well...not all of them."

"Most of them. Mike, I'm not trying to get on your back or insult you. I'm trying to help you. It's a brilliant screenplay. If you'd just finish it, I think so many doors would open for you. For *us*."

"For us?" He rose from the chair. "Is that what this is all about? You want me to finish the screenplay for you, so you can get your claws into your precious part and star in a real honest-to-gosh movie and then everyone will love you and you'll get super famous and what? What, *then*? Leave me for someone else? Then I'm stuck with just this magazine."

"Why would I leave you? I've seen how much energy you've put into this project. I thought you were writing the part for me. Didn't you say that?"

Mike glanced down at the floor. After a while he whispered, "Yes."

"Then why would I leave you for finishing it? I'd be more likely to leave you if you *didn't* finish it."

Mike's head snapped upward. He glared at her. "What the hell is that supposed to mean?"

Lucy seemed genuinely distressed. "That came out totally wrong. I didn't mean it that way."

"What is this, some kind of fucking ultimatum? Write the screenplay now or I dump you?"

"No...I didn't say that at all."

"I always knew you didn't love me. Are you just hanging around for your precious fucking *part*?"

Lucy shot up from the chair and kicked it across the room. It almost hit Mike in the knee. "Is that why I let you live here for free when I barely even knew you? Is that why I've been helping you with the damn trashy magazine for almost a year? Is that why I've practically given up my acting for you? Because I don't love you?"

"Oh, Christ, Lucy, what acting career did you have to give up? You should be lucky you met me, otherwise what the hell would you be doing to fill up the hours in your day?"

Lucy's mouth gaped open. For a second it seemed like tears were beginning to form in her eyes. But that instant vanished very quickly. Only rage filled her eyes now.

She began to walk right past him.

He regretted it. He wanted to take it back. He reached out and grabbed her elbow.

She wrenched it from his grasp. Slowly, in a harsh whisper, she said, "No one talks to me like that." It felt as if she were staring right through him.

"Lucy, I…please don't go. Let's talk about this."

"We just did."

He couldn't contain it. "Well…then *fuck* you!" He pushed her up against the door. The look of shock on her face was palpable. "Don't expect me to come chasing after you like all the other fucking little brainless lapdogs you're used to. I've got work to do. I can't waste time with you right now."

Lucy grabbed the knob and threw the door open. She said nothing. The finality in her eyes was far worse than any words her lips could have formed at that moment.

The door slammed shut. The framed movie posters on the wall jiggled en masse, as if an earthquake had struck the seventy-year-old building. *Black Dragons* (Monogram, 1942), starring Bela Lugosi and The Lone Ranger, Clayton Moore, fell off the wall. Mike spent five minutes finding a hammer to put the poster back in its place, just to be doing something. He took another two minutes to hammer a bent nail into the wall.

Then he sat back down in his chair and tried to continue writing the article. Impossible. He couldn't concentrate. Where the fuck was she going? Was she ever coming back?

Mike slammed his fist into his typewriter three times fast, which accomplished nothing more than making his fist feel like it was on fire. He rose from the desk, grabbed his jacket, and ran out the door. He almost forgot to lock it behind him.

He exited through the back of the building where she usually parked her car. Of course, it was long gone. *Jesus, Mike, you're fucking stupid. Why didn't you go after her? That's what she wanted. It was a test.*

A test. Why do I need to be tested? All women were like this. They played games, even when they didn't know they were playing games.

He stood there on the sidewalk, motionless, trying to figure out what the hell he should do. He couldn't keep working, not while this whole thing remained unresolved. Great. Now he was going to get behind on the magazine. All because of Lucy....

He needed her. He needed to know she would always be there for him. He could take care of the writing, fine, but the business side of things? He was completely unorganized. He wouldn't be able to find the list of subscribers without her.

And he needed her for other reasons. She kept him grounded and focused. He loved her. Of course he'd write the screenplay for her. That was his intention all along. He'd just been so busy. She'd chosen the wrong moment to ask him. He'd been feeling a little stressed anyway, and now....

Now it was too late.

He slammed his fist into his forehead. People were looking at him funny. Even the sick, scraggly, homeless crew who perpetually camped out on the corner were looking at him funny. He needed to do something about this.

Eric. She'd probably go see Eric. She often went to him for advice.

"Babies!" Old Ygor waved a scarred green hand in the air. "I'm not interested in babies! I want the world to bow before Ygor, to worship him!"

"And so they shall," Dracula said in soothing tones, reaching out and stroking Ygor's massive shoulder.

They stood in front of Dracula's makeshift lab within Carfax Abbey surrounded by the rare, spore-bearing plants known to botanists as the *Bavaria Formosa*. Dracula used his other hand to gesture toward the plants. "And this will be the tool, the unstoppable club you will hold in your mighty fist, to force humanity onto its knees."

Ygor seemed confused. "But how will melting babies do that for me?"

In the background, a few feet behind Ygor, Aishe was on her knees sucking blood from a small blob of protoplasm. This, of course, was a mere appetizer for the main course. The sucking sounds reverberated throughout the crypt, the perfect soundtrack for Dracula's conversation with the slow-witted brute about world domination.

Dracula flashed a charming smile and said, "But don't you see?" He reached out and plucked a large leaf from the *Bavaria Formosa*. "Dr. Heidelmann had the wrong idea. Why use these spores to help people when, in concentrated doses, they can *destroy* humanity instead? In this lab we can liquefy these spores and infect the whole city of London."

"But how?"

"By introducing the liquefied concentrate into the water supply." Dracula strolled over to a pit in the middle of the room and glanced over the side. This pit had once been used to torture "heretics" in the Middle Ages. Dracula had removed the iron spikes from the bottom of the pit and was now taking advantage of its ideal, moist environment to grow the plant and its precious spores all along its curved, stone walls. "We'll do it at midnight," Dracula said, "when no one is watching. By morning everyone in London will have been reduced to amorphous protoplasm! The streets will be awash with crawling vestiges of humanity, mere blobs of warm flesh waiting to be relieved of the blood flowing through their useless veins. We won't have to hunt them down anymore like foxes. We'll simply wander through the streets and feast on whatever we need. Imagine it. Streets paved with nothing but living flesh and blood that can neither protest its fate nor run away from it. Oh, but it'll be able to think. It'll be able to think and feel and know the horrible future that lies in wait for it." Dracula turned his back on the pit and faced the Monster once more.

"But how will this give Ygor power and devotion?"

Dracula was growing impatient with the Monster, but his

outward charm never faltered. "Once your power has been demonstrated in this way on the entire city of London, you will be able to make any demands you wish. Remember, this city tried to *destroy* me many decades ago. They *thought* they succeeded. Fools. They would do the same thing to you if they could, if they knew you were here."

Ygor nodded enthusiastically, images of apocalyptic destruction no doubt forming in his mind's eye. "When can we do this thing? When will the plants be ready?"

"Soon," Dracula said. "I hope to strike by the night of the winter solstice." Dracula laughed under his breath. "How appropriate. The time of year when everything *living* runs and hides." Dracula glanced over his shoulder at Aishe. "Are you finished, my dear? Remember, we have a date to go out tonight."

"Where are you going?" Ygor asked, concerned.

"Aishe and I have not been out hunting tonight. We're getting...*impatient*, shall we say? We need to flex our muscles out there in the cold night. Though it will be difficult, I'm certain we'll find something...somebody."

"Let me go with you," the Monster said. "I don't like being cooped up in this place. I need to be outside."

Dracula lay a calming hand on the Monster's shoulder once more. "You can't go outside, not yet. You're far too conspicuous. If somebody saw you and tracked you back here it could jeopardize our plans. You have to be patient. You can do that, can't you?"

Ygor nodded reluctantly.

"Besides, Krogh can go outside and get you anything you need. Isn't that right, Krogh?"

Dracula and Ygor glanced toward the corner of the crypt where Krogh sat crouched amidst a curtain of spider webs feasting on a rat.

"Aishe," Dracula said, "toss the boy a bit of dessert."

Aishe smiled, ripped off a piece of the flesh she had been sucking, and threw it at Krogh. Krogh eagerly snatched it out of the air and began sinking his teeth into it like a dog.

"Be good to Ygor, Krogh. Your master is going outside for a breath of fresh air." Dracula turned to Ygor and said, "Keep each other company."

He snapped his fingers, at which point Aishe stood up and followed him out into the brisk night air. Despite the fact that it was forty below, Aishe was only wearing a thin gown. Neither of them could feel the cold.

Dracula slipped his arm around Aishe's moon-white shoulders and said, "That dumb brute may be of use to us yet, though I fear the level of conversation is not improving. Why can't everyone be like you, dear, hm?"

Aishe lips widened in a bloody smile, nuzzled her head against her master's shoulder, and purred in satisfaction.

She said nothing as they strolled down winter streets covered in ankle-deep snow as pure as the air they need not breathe.

Mike sprinted two blocks to the nearest bus stop, took the 181 bus to the corner of Argyle and Hollywood Boulevard, sprinted toward Hollywood and Vine, and hopped on the 217. This journey took about twenty-five minutes, what with all the damn stops in between. Precious seconds were eaten up by a guy in a wheelchair. Mike thought about Lucy the entire way there, and that fleeting moment when she almost broke down in tears. Even that single second of vulnerability was remarkable for her. She rarely allowed herself to cry. Something inside her prevented her from doing so. Someone rang the bell and the bus stopped near Hollywood and Highland. Mike leaped off the bus the second the doors opened, dodged a cluster of street performers breakdancing for loose change, crossed the street, jogged past the Ripley's Believe It Or Not Museum, past the once-glamorous Egyptian Theatre (now showing signs of unmistakable decay), past the newsstand, past a magic store and Larry Edmunds' Bookshop, and finally arrived at the front door of Tinseltown Book and Poster. Sometimes Eric liked to shut down the store for an hour or two at random moments during the day, whenever the whim struck him. Mike sure hoped this wouldn't be one of those moments.

Eric was just hanging up the "WILL BE BACK IN TEN MINUTES" sign (which really meant an hour) when Mike arrived.

"Thank God I caught you," Mike gasped.

"You look awful," Eric said. Mike planted his hands on his knees and bent over, trying to catch his breath. "What the heck's wrong with you?"

"Is Lucy here?"

"No. No one's here. It's been a slow day. I figured I'd drive over to Golden Apple and pick up the latest batch of comics. You know, the first volume of that new Moebius series that Marvel is publishing is coming out today. I've been looking forward to it. I've never seen any of Moebius' stuff translated into English. I heard Moebius is going to be there for a few hours. I was hoping to get his autograph."

"Moebius?" Mike said. "The artist? Really? That sounds pretty damn cool."

"I know. I mean, how often does Moebius hang around on Melrose? Maybe we can interview him for the magazine. You gonna come along?"

Mike was just about to accept when he stopped himself and said, "No, no. Normally I would want to, but I can't right now. I have to find Lucy."

"Why?"

Mike sighed. "We had a huge argument. It was a misunderstanding."

Eric laughed. "I'm surprised it took you guys this long to get into an argument."

Mike waved his hand in the air. "No, no, we've had arguments before, of course, but nothing like this. She walked out on me. She's not coming back."

"Oh, c'mon, she'll be back. If it was a misunderstanding, then she'll realize that and—"

"I told you, it got out of hand."

"Well, what do you mean?" Eric was listening more carefully now.

"I...I sort of pushed her up against the door. I was just so angry in that moment. I wasn't really thinking. I'd never try to hurt her at all. It was more of an accident. I wanted her to stay, but...it all came out wrong for some reason."

"Well, that *does* sound pretty bad," Eric said. He seemed

uncomfortable even discussing it. Mike doubted if Eric had ever gotten into a fight with his wife during the entire fifteen years they had been married. "You shouldn't have pushed her."

"I know that, Eric. Don't you think I know that?"

"Listen, the entire time I've known her, she's gotten into knockdown fights with every boyfriend she's ever had. The fact that it took so long to happen with you two is sort of a miracle. I think that's love. I'm going to stick to my original position. She'll be back. But you need to apologize."

"I know. That's why I'm trying to find her. Where could she be, if not here?"

Eric laughed. "There's a million places she could be. You know that. I wouldn't start calling her million and one friends, though. That'd make you look like...."

"Like what?"

"Well...like a pussy."

"Christ, Eric, look who's talking. I can admit when I've done something wrong. Does that make me a *pussy*?"

"Well, kind of. Just forget about it and go see Moebius with me."

"Eric—nah, forget about it, man. You go on ahead. Maybe I'll just go back to the apartment and sweat it out there. Fuck. I wish there was some way of getting a hold of her."

"You want me to drop you off?"

Mike just stared off into space for a moment. Then said, "You think...you think this is the end for us?"

Eric sighed and patted Mike on the shoulder. "Oh, c'mon, get off it. She's never been more productive since she's been with you."

"That's not the way she sees it. She thinks I'm holding her back. That I'm preventing her from going on auditions and landing that Big Role."

"Are you sure that's what she said?"

"You couldn't misinterpret it. She was very loud."

"You guys just need to talk this out. Here, let me drive you home."

"I think I'll just take the bus back. I need to think this through. Maybe I *am* holding her back."

"Trust me, man, you're not. I've known her longer than you have. This is the happiest she's ever been."

All Mike had to do was recall the expression on Lucy's face when she was yelling at him to doubt those words. He mumbled his goodbyes to Eric, told him to have fun at the Moebius signing, then wandered away toward the bus stop. He didn't think about much on the way home. Perhaps he didn't think about anything.

She still wasn't there when he returned. Of course she wasn't.

He waited around a little bit longer, staring at the phone. He thought about an old Dorothy Parker story called "A Telephone Call." He'd read it in high school. It made him laugh to think about it. He should write a short story. That would take his mind off it. But he couldn't think about anything to write, except for re-doing "A TelephoneCall." And that seemed sort of pointless. So, he tried to work on the magazine instead. He finished Part One of his article on "Darwinian Cinema." He did it by rote, like a bricklayer putting down the final few bricks in the pattern. He'd reread it later, proofread it. At least it was done. He glanced at the clock. It was not five o'clock yet. He was hungry and there was nothing to eat, but he didn't want to go out and get anything in case she called or came back while he was gone. And if he was gone, she would think he didn't care. So he stayed right there and got hungrier and hungrier until he couldn't stand it anymore and went out to get something to eat from the hamburger joint down the street and when he came back he was certain she'd come back while he was gone because some of her things were missing, but then again he couldn't be sure. Maybe nothing was missing. It's not like he catalogued all her belongings in his head. He wanted to hold her again. He ate half the hamburger, wishing he'd never left to go get it. He threw the other half in the trash.

He turned on the TV and put on a VHS tape of *The Return of the Vampire*, a Bela Lugosi movie he was going to review for the magazine. He liked it better this time around. How come Lugosi fans bashed this movie so much? It wasn't bad. It wasn't bad at all. He jotted down some notes for the review, then drifted off to sleep. He woke up at around three in the morning. She still wasn't home.

He was certain it was over. He'd always known that he couldn't hold onto her. She was just too beautiful for him, too smart and perfect. Why did he ever think he could hold onto someone like that? This was inevitable.

He turned on the radio to a jazz station he'd never heard before and eventually drifted back to sleep to the sounds of a Pharoah Sanders piece called "Balance." He'd never heard a song that sounded more unbalanced. Perhaps that was the irony of it? It matched the chaos in his own mind perfectly.

He dreamed of vampires and Nazis and fog.

He woke with the dawn. He decided not to wait around for her today. It was over.

He got dressed in his best clothes, the ones she liked, and blew a lot of money he couldn't afford to lose. On a cab. The cab took him to Culver City. To a graveyard. To the spot where he met her.

He was there when the gates opened. He strolled up the long, snaking driveway to The Grotto. He found the spot by memory. Lot 120, Space 1. He stood over Lugosi's grave. Someone had left a brand-new cigar on the grave. Did dead people smoke? Perhaps not. But perhaps they did appreciate the gesture. Everyone wants to be loved, even the long dead.

He replayed the scene in his mind. This is where he was standing. This is where she was standing. This is what he said. This is what she said. This is when he first heard her laugh. This is when—

"I'm sorry," he whispered to her, wishing she could hear him.

A voice from behind him: "Are you family...or a fan?"

A man's voice.

Mike turned around slowly. An old man stood behind him. The old man wore a heavy trench coat, like a spy in an espionage film from the 1950s. An unusual sight in Los Angeles. However, it was an overcast day. It could very well rain. Mike hadn't even brought a jacket. He envied the stranger's foresight.

"Excuse me?" Mike said.

"Are you a relative of the deceased?" the old man asked, gesturing toward Lugosi's grave.

Mike was a little annoyed by the question. Did this guy work for the cemetery? What right did this guy have to plow him with questions? "No, I'm not a relative. I'm just...yes, I guess you could say I'm a fan. An admirer." The stranger kept staring at him, as if wanting more. "I've written about him and his films for a magazine I publish. Edit. Me and my girlfriend, Lucy, we've put out six issues so far. We're working on the seventh." The stranger continued to stare at him. "Is that sufficient?"

The stranger barely moved or exhibited any emotion. "You like his films?"

"Yes, of course. Why the hell else would I come all the way out here to visit his grave?" He turned his back on the man.

"What's the name of the magazine?"

"Ramboona."

"I have an issue."

Mike turned around. "Really?"

"Are you Mike Fenton?"

Mike laughed. This was just way too weird. "Yes, I am."

"You published a photo of you and your girlfriend in the back of issue number two, the one with Godzilla on the cover."

Mike laughed again. He couldn't believe it. The guy wasn't just bullshitting. He really had read the magazine. "Who're you? Are you...are you a relative?"

"No. Not a relative. But I once worked with the man many years ago."

Mike turned all the way around now. "How so?"

This was the only time Mike saw the stranger hesitate. "Well, I probably shouldn't say. Not at this point at least. I own a number of sixteen-millimeter films starring our dearly departed friend here. One of them is a test reel of his scenes in *Frankenstein.* I'm sure you've heard of these scenes."

"Yes...of course I've heard of them." Mike wondered if he could keep breathing long enough to hear the man out. Ever since Eric's deal fell through, and the potential seller scurried back into the woodwork, Mike had almost concluded that the test reels really were a myth from the beginning. "Did you try to sell these to Tinseltown Book & Poster in L.A.? I know the owner, and he got this offer about a year or so ago—"

"He was dealing with a prankster," the old man said. "No one has ever had a copy but me. I…." He paused, hesitating. Thinking something through. "I might be willing to sell it. Would you and your magazine…be willing to buy them? Or at least put me in touch with a potential buyer?"

"We'd be very interested," Mike said, thinking if he said "we" it would sound more official. Of course, he knew he didn't have the kind of money this guy would probably want for the film. But at the very least he could wrangle a viewing of the film out of him. If only he could *see* it. Just once would be enough. "What sort of price are we talking here?"

The old man waved his hand in the air. "Maybe it's best if you see the film first, before we start talking about a price. If you're not interested, do you know people who might be?"

"Sure. If all else fails maybe we could run an article in the magazine. That would be sure to generate—"

"No, no, no," the old man said. He seemed to panic. "I'm not interested in bringing that kind of attention to myself. You see, no one must know I have it. And no one must know that the buyer has it. Is that clear?"

"But…what's the point of buying it then? If we can't show it to anybody?"

"You would have the satisfaction of owning a piece of history. Of having seen it yourself. For your *own* enjoyment."

"Is that why you have it?"

The old man glanced down at Bela's grave and said. "The reason I have it, and how I came to own it, is not relevant. It's a curious tale, I admit, but one that I can't share with you at the moment."

"It's all very cloak-and-dagger. I mean, if I—if the *magazine* were to buy it, it's because we would want to build a whole issue around the footage and reproduce it and sell it. There're a lot of film fans and scholars out there who would chew off their own arm to see that footage. Well, okay, maybe they wouldn't chew off their own arm, but they would certainly pay a reasonable price to own a copy for themselves. Perhaps we could build a whole documentary about Bela around the footage. We've been thinking of branching off into that area anyways. You see, we wanted to do a travelogue where we take the viewers on a journey around Hollywood to all of Bela's various homes and studios and other places he used to hang out around here. If you worked with him, if you knew him, maybe you could take part in it."

"I could suggest some sites from behind the scenes. I'd be happy to do that. But I can't appear on camera at all. Or be interviewed. I can't be linked to this footage in any way. Perhaps... perhaps you could conjure up some kind of cover story. You're a writer, are you not?"

Mike nodded.

"Then you wouldn't have any problem coming up with a little fairy tale for your readers about how the footage came into your possession. Something that sounds plausible and titillating. Perhaps an anonymous source mailed it to you. If that's not dramatic enough, perhaps a man called you on the phone and asked to meet you alone in a dark alley off Hollywood Boulevard or something."

Mike laughed slightly. "Maybe *you* should be the writer."

"I thought I was, at one time. But no, that's in the past. Here." The old man reached into his inside coat pocket and removed a small black notebook and a pen. He jotted down something very quickly, then handed a piece of paper to Mike. "You can contact me there. Show up at my door at precisely six o'clock tomorrow night. If you don't show up, I'll assume you're not interested and move on to another potential buyer. Is that fair?"

Mike glanced down at the paper. It was an address up in the Hollywood Hills. He knew that was a ritzy area, though he'd never been up there himself...except for that one time with Lucy.

"Yeah, that's fair."

"My name is Kurt." He reached out and shook Mike's hand vigorously. It was a powerful grip. Kurt was much stronger than he looked. The contact lasted less than two seconds. Then their hands fell away from each other. And Kurt looked down at Bela's grave and said, "Farewell, old friend. I certainly hope you have more peace in death than in life." He began to back away from the grave.

"Wait," Mike said, "what brought you all the way out here today?"

Kurt smiled. "What brought you?"

Mike shrugged. His first instinct was to lie, but why bother? "I got into a fight with my girlfriend."

Kurt spread his hands out before him. A strange October mist appeared out of nowhere and began crawling across the ground like something alive. "The same occurred to me." The old man laughed as the mist began to obscure his figure. He released a gravelly, phlegmatic laugh. "Let's just call it Fate, something Bela knew a great deal about, eh? So many of his films are laden with it, often tragically...but not always. And, in real life, he was guided by it and brought down by it. I believe Bela placed his faith in Fate more than in any other higher power. It's appropriate, therefore, that our transaction unreel in this way. Good day! And good luck with your girlfriend!" The old man continued to talk while backing away down the twisting driveway that led to the front gate.

"Yeah," Mike yelled, "I'll need it! You don't know my girlfriend!"

"Just remember," the old man called out, "never try to reason with a woman. Just let her be angry. If you just let her be angry for a few days, she'll act like it never happened. Never feel the need to resolve a fight. Just follow her lead. Don't try to be right. You'll never be right. Remember that, and you'll do fine."

At last the mist ate him up, and the old man disappeared.

Mike shouted, "Thanks! I'll remember that!"

If the old man responded, Mike didn't hear it. He wrapped his arms around his chest and tried to warm himself from the sudden mist. The graveyard was growing spookier by the second. Mike glanced back down at Bela's grave. He had nothing to leave for him, nothing except his wallet, some small bills, and some loose change.

Hadn't he read somewhere that the Egyptians buried corpses with pennies resting atop their eyes as payment for Kherty, the ferryman who rowed the spirits into the Land of the Dead? And hadn't Bela played an Egyptian in *Chandu the Magician*? Mike reached into his pocket, found two pennies, and set them on the grave. The gesture was about thirty years too late, but nonetheless it was better than nothing.

"Next time," Mike whispered, "perhaps I'll be able to bring something better."

Lawrence Gill couldn't sleep. He rose out of bed, trying not to disturb Nina. They hadn't found a good lead on the vampire murders and the slow progress was killing him. He'd always been impatient. He liked to do things with his hands when something was bothering him. At one time he only believed in things that he could touch and feel. Of course, those days were long behind him.

He slipped on a robe and went downstairs to the library to read. Perhaps the scholarly books of Dr. Istvan Lazlo would give him some sort of clue.

A little over five years ago destiny took a chunk out of his life that could never be replaced. He could never be the same, not now, knowing what he knew. When he thought of how many years he'd been sleepwalking through life, ignorant of the invisible forces that were all around him, waiting to pounce, he grew sorry for all the poor souls out there who had not had the advantage of experiencing a tragedy like his. He'd reached the point in his life when he could appreciate the knowledge all his pain had brought him. Now that the curse was behind him, he could sometimes even look the monster in the face in his mind's eye and be content that he'd confronted the thing and beaten it down. With Dr. Heidelmann's invaluable help, of course. Poor Dr. Heidelmann. If only the old man had lived to see everything he and Nina had accomplished with their second chance at life.

Gill removed the Lazlo book from the shelf, sat in his favorite armchair, then poured himself a glass of Scotch.

From behind him he heard a familiar voice: "You're not going to pour me one too?"

He turned and smiled. "Oh, I didn't want to wake you. You know how hard it is for me to read without Scotch."

"It's hard for you to do anything without Scotch." Nina said it with a mischievous smile.

"Well, we all have our demons. Compared to some, this isn't a bad one."

"I've seen your *worst* demon. I'll take a glass of Scotch over that one any day." She held her hand out.

Lawrence smiled and poured her a glass.

She took a sip, then said, "Lazlo helping you out?"

"Well, I've barely cracked open the book yet. I thought he might mention *something* that could lead us to these monsters."

"All the murders have been committed at night. We should be out patrolling."

"But the police are already doing that," Lawrence said. "We should be concentrating on some other avenue, something they haven't thought of yet."

"You know, all the victims have been…well, women of the streets, shall we say?"

"I know. That's why all these rumors have been floating around about the return of Jack the Ripper."

"I think we need to draw out these fiends. Give them some worthwhile bait." Nina flashed Lawrence her doe eyes.

Lawrence just stared at her for a second. "Are you suggesting that you…? No, absolutely not. I won't allow it."

"Why not? I can wear the costume we used for the masquerade ball. I'll have a wooden stake hidden in my garter belt. You'll be tailing me, just in case something does happen."

"No, that's ridiculous."

"It's better than sitting here moping around with Dr. Lazlo."

Lawrence said nothing and just stared at the carpet.

"Pour yourself another glass," Nina said, "and you'll see I'm right."

When he got home, Lucy was sitting on the living room sofa.

"Hi," he said.

"Hi," she said.

He threw his keys onto the table beside the door. His typewriter still sat on the table. Notes for the new issue lay scattered around it. Unfinished business.

"Where've you been?" he asked.

"Where have *you* been?"

"Bela's grave."

Lucy cocked her head to one side. Her brow furrowed. "Really?" She wasn't expecting that answer. "Why?"

"I wanted to talk to you."

"Why'd you think I'd be there?"

"I didn't think you would. I didn't know where you were, how to get a hold of you. I went and saw Eric and he hadn't seen you. I tried to work on the magazine and couldn't. I wanted to tell you I was sorry. But I couldn't. So, I went to the place where we met...to talk to that beautiful girl I met that day and tell her I was sorry. And I did. I hoped...I hoped you'd hear me somehow."

Lucy's confusion turned to a smile.

"I know it's stupid." He cast his gaze at the beige carpet. Jesus, it needed to be cleaned. Neither of them were good at upkeep. They were always so busy with their next Great Idea.

"No, I don't think it's stupid. I think it's sweet. I'm sorry you had to go all that way to talk to me. I should've called you. But I was just so angry. I don't think I've ever been more angry. When I left here, I'd totally decided to break up with you."

Mike felt a knife twist in his heart. "And now?"

She shook her head. "I thought I was done with you, then when I woke up in the morning...I just...." Tears began to form in her eyes. It was so rare to see her like this. She crossed her arms over her chest. She couldn't look at him. "I love you, that's all."

It was infectious. Mike could feel the tears welling up in his own eyes. "I love you too."

She breathed deeply, shook her head slightly, as if trying to will the tears away. "I'm sorry I brought up the screenplay. I know you're working hard. You don't have to finish it on my schedule. It's up to you. It's your work, not mine."

"No, you're right. I have been procrastinating. I'll finish it. I'll work on the magazine during the day, and at night I'll finish it. I'll just finish it and get it out of the way."

"You don't have to do it for me. I'm not going to leave you because of a stupid screenplay." She laughed at herself. "It's so fucking stupid. I don't know what I was thinking. I'm sorry."

Mike got up and sat down beside her. He wrapped his arms around and drew her close. She hugged him, rested her head on his shoulder. He stroked her long, smooth hair, his cheek resting against her head. Her scent was intoxicating. It was so good to have her back in his arms. He'd convinced himself that he'd never see her again.

"I love you," he whispered and she looked up at him and they kissed and pretty soon they were on the bed and they were showing each other how much they'd missed each other, and the entire time Mike was thinking about nothing but Lucy and her body beneath him and then the second it was over he thought, *Where were you last night?* And he remembered what the old man told him: *If you just let her be angry for a few days, she'll act like it never happened. Never feel the need to resolve a fight. Just follow her lead.* And as they lay there naked under the covers he thought, *Don't ask her, don't ask her, don't ask her.*

Lucy released a satisfied sigh and ran her palm up and down his bare chest, entwining her leg with his. "This is the best part of a fight," she said.

Mike said nothing as he stroked her hair once more. He was staring up at the white, cottage-cheese-ceiling when he heard the words emerge from his mouth: "You never answered my question."

"What question?"

"Where were you last night?"

She pulled away slightly. She hesitated. "I was at Chad's."

Mike sat up, anger coursing through him. "You were at your ex-boyfriend's house?"

"C'mon, Mike. You know he's gay."

"Gay, bi-sexual, whatever."

"I didn't know where else to go. We haven't been like that in a long time." She could see the hurt in his eyes. "Nothing happened, if that's what you're wondering."

"Where did you sleep?"

"In his bed."

"Where did *he* sleep?"

She sighed, this time with frustration and anger. "*In his bed.*"

"You slept in the same bed together and nothing happened? I don't care how gay he says he is, you can't just—"

"We're just friends now. He was comforting me."

"I'm sure he was."

"My God, Mike, look at me." She stared into his eyes, naked, open, daring him to read her mind. "If I really cared so little about you, why would I come back here and do *this* with you?" Her glance took in the rumpled sheets and the pillows and the bed and their clothes hanging off the side of the mattress and the entire forty minutes they had just spent together. "Do you think I was lying just now when I said I love you?"

"No. But you said yourself you'd decided to leave me. And you changed your mind in the morning. I guess whatever happened in between then isn't technically cheating, is it?"

"We slept with our clothes on. We never even touched each other. He never even touched me."

"Jesus Christ, do you think I'm fucking stupid?"

"*I asked him not to.*"

Every paranoid cell in Mike's brain screamed at him not to believe her. And yet...when he looked into her eyes, he knew she wasn't lying. And what did it matter if she was? She was here now. He had her back. She wasn't leaving. And she loved him.

Never feel the need to resolve a fight. Just follow her lead.

She still stared at him, waiting for his response. He leaned toward her and kissed her gently on the lips. "I'm sorry," he said. "You know how paranoid I can get."

She returned the kiss. "I know." She stroked his cheek with the back of her hand. "If the situation was reversed, I guess I'd be suspicious too. It's okay."

He laughed. "I didn't know we'd have another argument again so damn soon."

She laughed as well. "I guess we just need to make up again then."

And they started in on each other again, and in the middle of it Mike said, "Let's just argue like this all day."

Never once did he mention the old man or the test reel or the house in the Hollywood Hills.

Ygor rushed up the elaborate stairs within the House of Frankenstein and approached the ornate double doors that led into the master bedroom in which Wolfgang and his beautiful wife Elsie now slept. Ygor paused outside the doors. Should he interrupt their dreams and introduce them to the nightmare he had just witnessed? A part of him wanted to go back to sleep and forget that any of this had happened. Everything had been going so well for him. But, as always, when things went well that meant tragedy lay waiting just around the corner.

Ygor pushed open the door ever so slowly. Sure enough, Wolfgang and Elsie were asleep. He crept toward the edge of the bed and touched Wolfgang on the shoulder.

Wolfgang shot up to a sitting position, as if ready to lash out even in his sleep. But then he saw that it was only Ygor.

"Wh—what's wrong?" he whispered. He glanced over at his wife. Though she stirred fitfully, she remained asleep.

"There's trouble...at the Temple," Ygor whispered. "You... have to come."

"*Now?*"

"Trust me."

Wolfgang stared at him skeptically. He sighed and said, "Very well." He slipped out of bed as quietly as possible, put on a robe, then followed Ygor into the hall.

Once the doors were locked behind them, Wolfgang said, "What is this all about?"

"I broke into the...Masonic...Temple tonight—"

"You did *what?*"

The look on Wolfgang's face was clear. He was now doubting himself. He was wondering if he should've brought this abnormal criminal mind...this *monster*...into his home.

"You...don't understand," Ygor said. "I *had* to. I had...a *dream*. The feeling...I experienced tonight. Too similar...to what I would feel...when our father...would drain me of energy. I knew... something...was wrong. I saw Banoub...in the inner Temple... worshipping...a statue...an unholy thing...a monster...a *real* monster."

"Are you sure this wasn't a nightmare?"

"You must...see it...for yourself. I can *show* you."

Wolfgang thought about it for a second, casting a nervous glance at the bedroom door. He was no doubt concerned about

Elsie. "Very well," he said, "just let me get into some proper clothes and we'll—"

The bedroom doors opened at that moment. Elsie stood in the doorway, clutching her robe to her throat. "Wolfgang, what in the world is going on out here?"

Wolfgang patted Elsie on the shoulder. "Don't worry, dear. There's been a problem down at the Lodge. We have to go down and take care of it."

"But it's so late...."

"It won't take long dear, I promise you. Now let me put you back into bed." Wolfgang turned to Ygor and said, "Wait right here."

The couple disappeared into the bedroom.

"I don't like this at all," Elsie said as Wolfgang covered her with the blanket.

"I'll only be gone for a few minutes."

"But what could be so important that—?"

Wolfgang sat down on the edge of the bed and patted his wife's hand. "Apparently there's been a break-in at the Lodge. We just have to go down and assess the damage."

"But why does Ygor have to go with you?"

"He's a brother now. It's as much his problem as mine."

"Wolfgang, you've been acting so strange ever since Ygor came to this house. You're not...conducting your experiments again, are you?"

Wolfgang laughed. "Of course not. Silly. Where would I perform them? I have no laboratory here in the house. I left all the necessary equipment behind in my father's castle. What wasn't wiped out by the flood was certainly destroyed in the fire. You have nothing to worry about."

"I suppose so."

"Go back to sleep, dear, and I'll be back within the hour." Wolfgang leaned over his wife, kissed her on the forehead, then dashed toward the door.

Elsie lay in bed for only a few moments, not even really trying to sleep. Something was wrong, something more than a break-in. She knew that now.

She rose to a sitting position and peered out the second story window that looked down upon the street below. She could see her husband and that...*creature*...walking through the snow toward the East. Soon the light smattering of snow swallowed even their silhouettes.

Elsie shot up out of bed and started putting on her clothes.

17.

"It's just too fantastic to believe!" Wolfgang said, drawing his coat close to his throat.

"So is…a dead man's brain…being put…into someone else's…body," said Ygor.

Wolfgang couldn't argue with that. But someone as respectable as Khalid Banoub dabbling in black magic? It was almost inconceivable to him.

Ygor led him around to the back of the Temple. "We should… enter…through the back…just in case."

Ygor reached into his pocket and pulled out two pencil-thin lock picks made of hand-finished clock spring steel. He slipped them into the lock and went to work.

"Where did you learn to do that?" Wolfgang asked.

"I've always…known," said Ygor. "I must have been…good at it…in my past life…whatever that was. It's not…something… I'm proud of."

"No, I should think not," Wolfgang said. He glanced from side to side, hoping a constable wouldn't stumble upon them. "But I guess it serves a purpose at the moment."

The tumbler snapped aside. Ygor pushed the door open and stepped into the kitchen, slipping the pick back into his pocket. Wolfgang shut the door behind them, then Ygor led the way across the linoleum floor.

"I've never been back here," Wolfgang whispered.

"This is…where…all…your…food…comes from."

"Of course I know that. I just never had a reason to…."

"Through here," Ygor said, leading Wolfgang out of the kitchen, down a short corridor, and into the main hall. Across the expansive room stood the double doors that would take them into the inner Temple.

"Where's Banoub?" Wolfgang whispered.

"Hopefully...he's not...in the inner Temple."

They padded across the tiled floor, winding their way through the gallery of Egyptian statues and artifacts, until they reached the double doors. Ygor pulled out his lock pick and did the deed again. Sister Marie had told him a long time ago to throw those things away. He never did, as they sometimes came in handy—not to commit crimes, but to right grievous wrongs—like the time he stole bread for Gertrude, that sweet little girl dying of malnutrition. She lived only a block away from Sister Marie's shelter, but since she had parents of her own Sister Marie could not bring her into her fold and help her. Ygor felt the crime he performed for her was justified. Nonetheless, he prayed for forgiveness each time he violated the law. He would do so again tonight, several times over, if he managed to survive Banoub's wrath.

Ygor led Wolfgang to the statue of Anubis inside the inner Temple. Banoub was nowhere around. Ygor grabbed Anubis' right fist and pulled. Immediately, the statue swiveled around on some kind of marble platform and was replaced by a much larger statue, the abomination he had seen before, the beast Banoub referred to as Anubis' familiar, the daemon that would lay waste to all of London if he and Wolfgang did nothing to stop it.

"I recognize this hideous phantasm," Wolfgang said. "I saw pictures of it in the ancient books of Masonic lore my father kept in his library. It's called Onbuljah, a mythological beast that comprises the darkest traits of three of the world's oldest religions: Semitic, Abyssinian, and Egyptian. It's all the devils of the world rolled into a single form."

"Banoub...wants to call it forth...to destroy the entire city... as an offering...to his god...Anubis."

"But Banoub is a man of science, not a devil worshipper!"

"In my...limited...experience...I see...little distinction... between the two."

Before Wolfgang could even attempt a response a woman's

frightened scream cut through the darkened Lodge, through their very hearts, like a blade of ice-cold steel.

The two brothers glanced at each other, then dashed across the hall toward the source of the scream.

He wasn't sure why he didn't tell Lucy. Perhaps because, in the heat of the argument, they had more important things to discuss. Perhaps because he was slightly embarrassed about believing the old man's tale. Perhaps because he didn't want her to be disappointed if it turned out to be a hoax. Perhaps he wanted to surprise her if it turned out to be true. Perhaps....

Perhaps he just wanted to experience it for himself.

The next night he borrowed Lucy's car and drove to the address scrawled on the piece of paper Kurt had handed him over Bela's grave. The house was indeed located up in the hills. Not far from the Hollywood Bowl, a small winding road transformed into Mulholland Drive. The dark, snaking path led up into the labyrinth of the Hollywood Hills, past mansions that grew grander and grander as the path became narrower and darker and more isolated. This was Mike's second time up here, but the first time by himself. It seemed to him as if anything could happen way up here. No one would come to your aid. The mansions were so far off the main road that the residents could probably hear nothing that happened on the road. That's the way they wanted it. He felt all alone up here. All alone.

At last he came to the address not far from the crest of Mulholland Drive. He pulled over to the side of the road. For a moment he sat there staring at the lights of Los Angeles spread out before him, down below at the bottom of the hill. All was quiet. For the thousandth time he pulled the envelope out of his pocket and rechecked the address. He glanced up at the numbers written on the massive black gate separating him from the driveway and the mansion beyond. Yes, this was it all right.

He restarted the car and wound his way up to a speaker mounted on a high brick wall. He pushed a button. A voice, perhaps an old man, responded immediately, "Yes, who is this?"

"Mike Fenton. I'm here to see Kurt."

"For what purpose?"

"Purpose? He asked me to come. I met him yesterday at the cemetery. In Culver City."

A brief silence. Then: "Just a moment, please."

The gates swung open by themselves as if pulled by a ghostly presence. Of course, the ghostly presence was called "electricity," but Mike preferred to think of this entire affair in supernatural terms. There was something so odd about all of this. A Gothic mystery unfolding....

Once Lucy's car was all the way through, the gate closed behind him. He parked the car in the driveway. Lucy's beat-up 1960s Mustang looked out of place next to the two convertibles parked in the driveway. Why did old men always own shiny red convertibles?

Mike walked up the palatial steps and was pleased to see a real honest-to-gosh butler opening the double doors for him. An old man, far older than Kurt. He was slightly bent over, perhaps arthritic.

"May I take your coat, sir?" the butler asked.

Mike waved him away. "No, thank you." It was cold in here anyway. Mike glanced around. It was a hell of pad, no doubt about it. High ceilings, a *Magnificent Ambersons* staircase that wound its way up into nowhere, paintings on the foyer walls that looked old and impressive though Mike recognized none of them.

The butler showed Mike to an inner room, a massive library, where Kurt stood beside a green velvet chair in which sat another man—a man Mike had never laid eyes on before.

"Good evening," said Kurt. "Welcome to my sanctum sanctorum." Kurt's German accent seemed to have thickened since the graveyard. Kurt delivered these lines with an over-the-top accent, making himself sound rather like Bela in *Dracula*. This, of course, would cast Mike in the role of Renfield. And Mike knew very well how Renfield ended up, both the character in the film as well as the tragic actor who had portrayed him: dead. The former by being tossed down a flight of stairs, the latter struck down by a heart attack on a Los Angeles bus while going to his day job in a manufacturing plant. Another sad Hollywood tale.

"This gentleman," Kurt said, gesturing toward the man sitting in the emerald green chair, "is named Gill. Lawrence Gill. I doubt you've heard of him, but he's famous in certain circles."

Mike walked toward the pair slowly, trying to take in all the books that surrounded him. Mike's dream had been to own a library like this.

Gill rose to his feet and reached out for Mike's hand. Gill's handshake was even more formidable than Kurt's. The man was big, almost seven feet tall. He had a roadmap of a face that belied not just character but experience and an intense love of the grape. His nose had that cherry-red shine of a man who prefers a liquid breakfast to bacon and eggs—prefers it over almost anything, in fact.

"It's a great pleasure to meet you," Mike said, trying to be as formal as possible to match the splendor of his surroundings.

"This fellow," Kurt said, gesturing toward Gill, "is the gentleman who gave me the test reel. Please, have a seat." Kurt took Mike by the arm and lowered him into a duplicate green chair that faced Gill's seat. Still, Kurt remained standing between them.

"Oh?" Mike said. "You gave this film to Kurt then?"

Gill shrugged. "It was part of a bargain."

"Okay," Mike said. "Well...if Kurt owns it now, then why...?" He wasn't sure how to phrase the question without being rude.

Gill said, "What business is it of mine, is that what you mean?" Gill spoke slowly and precisely, but no amount of elocution lessons could obscure the man's thick Midwestern accent.

Mike said, "Well...yeah, I guess."

Gill laughed. "Don't worry. I'm not going to get in the way of your transaction. That's not my purpose here. When Kurt contacted me this afternoon and told me what he planned to do...well, I can't stop him. That was part of the bargain. I advised him against this, I admit, but at this point in the game I doubt it will do any harm. But, you see, my main reason for coming here was to ask a favor of you."

Mike was getting more and more worried. "A favor?"

"Well, yes, you're a writer and I'm looking for a scribe. I'm *not* a writer. I'm nowhere near it. I've always been a man of action. I barely have the patience to write a damn letter."

Kurt smiled and nodded at Mike. "That's true, my boy, very true."

"Well...what would you want me to write?"

Gill turned toward Kurt and said, "I think I *will* have that Scotch now."

Kurt said nothing. He immediately turned and made the drink with great diligence—as if Kurt were *Gill's* butler.

Gill turned back toward Mike and said, "I have a theory."

All hope of this turning out to be a simple transaction had flown and/or crept out the door a while back. Mike was suspicious of anyone with a theory, particularly elderly men he didn't know.

"A theory?" Mike said.

"Why do you think Bela Lugosi was so good at portraying Dracula? Why does that performance stand out from the pack? You and I both know that the man was an accomplished actor in Hungary and on the stage in New York. He'd performed dozens of different sorts of roles: tragedies, comedies, supporting roles, starring roles, romantic parts, villainous parts, etc. But Dracula is what he will always be known for. Why?"

Mike shrugged. He suspected he was being asked a question to which Gill already had an answer. "Because...he was so memorable in it, he left an indelible impression in people's minds. I suppose."

Gill held up one beefy index finger in the air. "But how? How was Lugosi able to do that? As I said, I have a theory: Lugosi based his portrayal on the real Dracula."

Mike began biting the inside of his cheek, something he often did when he was anxious. "Dracula. You mean...what, Vlad the Impaler?"

A pained expression distorted Gill's face. He waved his massive hand in the air. "No, no. Vlad the Impaler existed, of course. The two men lived at the same time, but they're two distinct individuals. Vlad the Impaler was human. Dracula was not."

"Was not. Was not what?"

Gill spread his hands, as if to say, *What do you think?* "Oh, some legends are fairy tales, of course. But some are based in truth. Stoker's research led him to uncover an awful, hidden reality: There are indeed vampires in this world. Dracula was one of them. Bela Lugosi met him. Spent several weeks with him, studying him. Oh, now, let me assure you, Lugosi was a creative artist. He didn't merely copy Dracula's mannerisms and quirks. Not at all. Lugosi figured out how to convey the essence of Dracula's personality. In truth, Lugosi looked and acted and sounded nothing at all like the real Dracula."

Mike kept glancing over at Kurt to gauge the expression on the man's face. But Kurt wasn't laughing. He was simply staring at Gill as if the man were discussing the best place to go in Southern California to buy cheesecake or the upside of Reaganomics or the lowest priced gas station in town, something mundane and boring. Mike wondered if this were some kind of elaborate prank for his benefit. But why? Why would two rich old coots need to waste their time fucking with his head?

At last Mike heard himself saying, "And...you know this how?"

"I met Dracula myself." Gill took a sip of Scotch. Surprisingly, it was a rather dainty sip.

"Okay," Mike said. "And when did you meet, uh...Dracula?"

"Back in the 1940s. That's when I first tussled with the gentleman, if you want to call him that. It was in Europe. I was there to see an eccentric doctor who I thought might help me with a severe health problem. You see...well, you might not believe this. But Kurt here has shown me copies of your magazine and I believe you have an open mind and a healthy interest in the occult, the hidden side of reality. I particularly liked your Manly P. Hall article."

Mike cleared his throat, just to give himself a second to formulate a response. He was always open to compliments, but from a lunatic? Sure, why not? Mike was amazed that these two men had actually read the magazine. Kurt hadn't been bullshitting about that.

"Thank you," Mike said.

"You see," Gill said, "I'm a werewolf."

Mike pressed his lips together so tight he could feel the blood draining out of them. He realized he'd stopped breathing. He was in the middle of nowhere with a pair of total fucking loons. Who knew if they were dangerous or not? Who knew how many hapless Lugosi fans these two had lured up into the hills? No one would hear him scream in this fortified castle. He truly had become Renfield. He thought he could take both of them. After all, they were nothing more than old men. And yet…and yet Gill projected an aura of such strength and speed and raw power that Mike doubted he would even make it to the foyer if he had to run. The best thing to do in this situation, he thought, is just play along.

"A werewolf," Mike said. "Of course."

"You've read Manly P. Hall's work. You know such things are possible."

"I assumed Hall was being metaphorical when he talked about things like that."

"Not at all," Gill said. "Hall met Dracula as well. Bela introduced him."

Mike held up both palms. "Not too much at once, please, okay? Let's go back a few steps here. You visited a doctor to cure yourself of being a werewolf and that's when you met Dracula?"

"Yes. Dracula had arrived at the doctor's doorstep on the very same evening in order to seek a cure for his eternal curse of vampirism. But, of course, Dracula was just using that as an excuse to be invited into the house so he could have access to the doctor's beautiful nurse. The truth is, Dracula didn't want to be cured. He never did. Don't let anyone ever tell you otherwise."

Mike didn't care if these guys were lunatics or not. He couldn't stop himself from saying, "So…you do realize this is the plot of *House of Dracula*, the last big monster rally that Universal Studios made at the end of World War II? Right? You're aware of that?" How stupid did these two geezers think he was?

"Of course I know it," Gill said, "I gave them the idea."

"You did."

"Yes."

"That's funny, because in all my reading about Universal Studios I don't remember the name Lawrence Gill ever being mentioned...." Mike let the sentence trail off. He paused, remembering a passage from a book he'd read a long time ago. A book about the history of horror cinema. He *had* heard the name Lawrence Gill before. "Wait a minute," Mike whispered, almost to himself, "Lawrence Gill was the name that Curt Siodmak gave to the Wolf Man in his original draft of the screenplay. And in a later draft he changed it to Lawrence Talbot because the studio wanted the character to be the son of a Lord in Wales."

"That's right," Gill said. "Siodmak simply used my name in the script because I'm the one who fed him the original idea. I gave him all the necessary details. He changed it in the second draft so that no one would be able to trace those ideas back to me. It was very wise of him to do that. I was still working as a private investigator in London at that time. If anyone had known about my unusual curse...well, I would've been vulnerable to my enemies, of course."

"Of course," Mike said. "So, if I contact Curt Siodmak like, say, tomorrow—something I've been meaning to do for a long time anyway, for the magazine—you're saying that Siodmak will confirm everything you're saying?"

Lawrence nodded. "Why don't you just ask him now?" He gestured at Kurt with the half-empty glass of Scotch. The way the dim light played across the surface of the glass was almost hypnotic. Mike wondered, briefly, if he weren't in a trance at this very moment.

Mike stared at the old man's face. He stared hard. Yes. He'd seen a few photos of Siodmak over the years. *The Wolf Man* had been one of Mike's favorite movies when he was a kid. It could very well have been the second film in which he'd come across Bela Lugosi, who plays the old werewolf (appropriately named Bela) who bites Lawrence Talbot in the forests of Wales.

"Son of a bitch," Mike said. "You really *are* Siodmak, aren't you? It's...it's an honor to meet you, man." He found himself rising and shaking the gentleman's hand once again, as if this were the first time they'd spoken to one another.

Kurt returned the handshake. He just nodded and smiled.

As Mike sat back down, he asked, "Why'd you tell me your name started with a 'K'?"

"Because it always has. That's the name I was born with. I changed it to a 'C' just after Pearl Harbor in order to obscure its German origins. I didn't want prejudice to bar me from scriptwriting jobs in Hollywood."

"I bet it's even harder to get a job when you're a werewolf," Mike said and laughed nervously. He didn't know what to think or do now. Didn't Curt Siodmak live up north somewhere? Mike had never heard of him owning a mansion in the Hollywood Hills. *Okay, let's say this* is *Siodmak,* Mike thought. *He wouldn't be the first writer to lose his marbles after hitting the big 7-0. Just because this sick puppy is one of my boyhood heroes doesn't mean he's not crazy. On the contrary....*

"Actually, it was never difficult for me to find work," Gill said. "When I was a kid, I was a repairman. I worked with my hands, repairing telescopes for the Griffith Observatory when it was first built."

"They got that part right in the movie," Mike said. Suddenly, he wished Lucy was here taking notes.

"Well, yes, Kurt did at least. After I was bitten by the werewolf, I wandered the countryside from town to town, just trying to figure out what had happened to me. But eventually it turned out that my curse was actually an asset. I travelled to Tibet where I studied with the monks there. They taught me how to control the beast inside me through transcendental meditation. With my firsthand experience of the occult, it wasn't difficult to set up shop in London as a private investigator of supernatural matters. My wife and I worked in London for years. That's where we met Dracula for the second time."

"Your wife? Who was your wife?"

A genuine smile flashed across Gill's hardened face. "Nina. I met her in Europe, at the doctor's house I was telling you about. She was one of his nurses."

"The one Dracula was after?"

"No, no. The doctor had two different nurses. This is Nina." Gill reached into his pocket and pulled out a wallet. From inside the wallet he removed a faded, black and white photograph that was tattered around the edges. It looked like it had been taken back in the 1940s. In the photo stood a young woman on a street corner, probably in England based on the distinctive red phone booth beside her. She was young and vibrant with a beautiful smile. Her only drawback was that she was crippled.

Mike took the photo from Gill. "She's a hunchback," Mike heard himself saying before being able to stop himself. "I mean, she's beautiful and all, but...she's a hunchback."

"That's right," Gill said. "At first she didn't think anyone could love her because of that. I was able to overlook it. I fell in love with the person she was *inside*."

Mike was now rummaging through the garbage pile of cultural references in his mind. The last time he'd seen *House of Dracula* was when he was twelve or so. But it was all coming back to him now....

"There's a hunchback nurse in *House of Dracula*," Mike said, "isn't there?"

"Yes. As I said, Universal based all of those movies on the information I was feeding them, first through Kurt here and then through a series of other screenwriters."

"But...why? I mean, what would be the purpose of doing that? Was it for money?"

Both Gill and Kurt laughed at that one. "No, I never wanted any money," Gill said. "I told you, I was a very successful private investigator in London at that time. Neither Nina nor I needed the money. No, I agreed to work with the studio because of their previous association with the supernatural. From the very beginning the Laemmles, the family who owned Universal in the '20s and '30s, were well-versed in the occult. Carl Laemmle Jr. most of all. Like Manly Hall, his goal was to use the motion picture medium as a means of distributing truths about the hidden reality that surrounds us every day. That's why Junior had such a short reign at Universal. You can't get away with that stuff for very long. There are a lot of people—some of them not even human—who don't want the general public to be made aware of this hidden reality. In the early 1940s, through certain channels, some of the studio heads had heard about my exploits in London and approached me. I told them they could dramatize my experiences just as long as some of the profits would be diverted to finding a cure for Nina's affliction—not for Nina's sake, because she had gotten used to it by then, but for the sake of all the children who might be born with similar problems. The money generated by those films helped a great deal in that regard, though no text book on the history of medicine would ever mention it. All the proceeds were donated anonymously, of course. I made sure of that.

"But, to be honest, I had an ulterior motive for working with the studio. I wanted people to be informed about the truth of these matters in a way that wouldn't shock or upset them. In the form of fiction. Part of the main problem that faces humanity is their ignorance of the invisible forces that influence them. If they could be made aware of the existence of those forces—in a way that wouldn't shatter their faith and their daily lives, for example—then why not do so? Even if they were made aware of these truths only at a subconscious level, humanity would, overall, be better protected from these sinister forces than they were before the outbreak of World War II. How many Americans know that World War II was an occult war, initiated by bickering black magicians? Perhaps you know this, but not many others do, I can assure you."

"Uh...no, I wasn't aware of that," Mike said.

"See? And you're a writer, someone who's clearly more aware of these esoteric matters. This is the main reason I agreed to work with Universal to create these modern 'fairy tales.' They were a means of mass inoculation against psychic attacks from the Other Side. A means of psychic self-defense, I suppose one could say."

Though Mike thought this guy was completely off his nut, nonetheless he had the urge to preserve every word coming out of the gentleman's mouth. "Do...do either of you mind if I start taking notes?"

"By all means," Kurt said. "That's why Gill wanted to meet you. He'd like to repeat the process that Universal Studios initiated way back in the '20s. He wants to release even more information about his various misadventures in the realm of the occult world. But he doesn't want it released as non-fiction. No. He wants it to be presented as pure fiction."

"I...I don't understand," Mike said. "You're Curt friggin' Siodmak, a famous science fiction writer. You wrote *Donovan's Brain*, fachrissakes. Why don't *you* write it?"

Kurt just shook his head. He looked tired, very tired. "I've had enough of this son of a bitch." Gill laughed. "I've been listening to this man's stories since 1940. I'm retired. No, Gill needs someone young, with enthusiasm, who nonetheless has some knowledge of the occult realms."

"Yes," Gill said, "when Kurt showed me your Manly P. Hall article, I knew *you* were the one."

Mike was beginning to wish he'd left the Hall article out of the first issue. But then again...maybe this wasn't so bad after all. Maybe all of this *would* make a good article for the magazine...somehow....

Mike pulled out a pad of paper and a pen. He jotted down what he could remember of Gill's previous soliloquy, then said, "Okay. Continue."

Dracula and his consort stalked the rooftops of London, leaping from building to building as easily as a kite floats on the wind. They hadn't assumed any of their animal forms. Why bother? No human seemed to be around. They had almost forgotten all about feeding. It was so thrilling to play like children on this, their moonlight-infused playground. It felt like the whole city was theirs to do with as they pleased.

Aishe landed on the edge of a chimney atop a three-story building. She scratched excitedly at the brick when she caught the scent of a human female. Yes, perhaps they *would* feed tonight.

The silk sleeve of her sheer white gown pulled back as she extended her pale arm out as far as it could go and pointed a long fingernail at the new object of her desire. *"Master,"* she hissed, drawing the word out as long as possible.

A woman was walking the streets down below, all by herself.

Dracula crept up behind her, slipped his hands around her

hips, and embraced her. "Very good, my love," said Dracula. "Let's have fun with her for a while before we finish her," he said.

Dracula cocked his head to one side. "Odd that a young woman should be by herself this late at night. It's almost as if she *wants* to be attacked."

"Perhaps she does," Aishe said through an impossibly wide grin.

"Perhaps she does," Dracula whispered, "perhaps she does indeed."

"I'm tellin' you, Eric, these guys were freaks. With a capital 'PH.'"

"Now wait a second," Eric said. "Are you sure this was really *Curt Siodmak*?"

It was 9:30 the next morning. Mike had gone home after his nocturnal meeting with Kurt and Gill, caught a few hours of shuteye, slipped out of bed before dawn (long before Lucy would awaken), and took the bus over to Eric's store. He couldn't wait to discuss this whole crazy situation with Eric. He wasn't yet sure if he even wanted to tell Lucy about the meeting at all. He wasn't sure if he wanted to move forward with Gill's proposal or call the guys from the Pickle Factory to go over to that mansion and sweep up the two of them with big butterfly nets.

He hoped Eric's reaction would give him a hint about what to do.

Mike was following Eric around the store, gesturing frantically while Eric tried to get the store ready. It opened at 10:00 A.M. every morning, Tuesday through Sunday. Mike crossed his heart with his index finger and said, "I swear to God, I'd know him anywhere. I've seen the photographs. He was older, but it was him. No doubt about it."

"And this happened at a mansion up in the Hollywood Hills? I thought Siodmak lived up north somewhere."

"That's the first thing I thought too. Turns out the mansion wasn't Kurt's at all. It was Gill's mansion. Kurt was just staying there for the weekend."

"How can this Gill guy afford a mansion? What's he do for a living?"

"He claims he's a retired intelligence agent. He worked for the OSS and the CIA."

Eric laughed. "Wow, this gets better and better, doesn't it?"

"I know, I know, it's *crazy*. I should just rip up their phone numbers and forget about it."

"This could be interesting. If that really was Curt Siodmak, then this ties right into the subject matter of the magazine. I mean, this could be a great cover feature. Who cares if they're crazy or not? We're just interested in good copy, right?"

Mike shook his head. "Jesus. You've really slipped right into that publisher's mindset, haven't you?"

"What's wrong with making a buck?"

"If this man Gill is mentally ill, then it's not really ethical to make money off his ravings, is it? I mean, it's sort of...a form of exploitation, isn't it?"

Eric got a sour look on his face. "Where the heck did the high horse suddenly come from? Listen, look at it this way. You're a writer, correct?"

"That's what everyone keeps telling me."

"You want to keep people interested, don't you?"

"Sure, of course."

"Then just interview the guy. Let him talk in his own words and publish it in the next issue of the magazine. Hell, I'd pay to read that interview and I'm the publisher. This issue's gonna move, I'm telling you."

"No, no, that's the problem. He doesn't want me to interview him at all. What he wants is for me to write a novel, a piece of fiction, based on his weird adventures over the years."

"Well, why not? Maybe we could run it as a serial. You know, like the old-time pulps, just a few pages in each issue. Is he offering to pay you to do this little thing for him?"

"Not with money."

"What then?"

Mike placed his hands on Eric's shoulders, forcing him to stop his puttering around for a moment, and leaned in close. He whispered, "He wants...."

"...to give you the test reels you're so interested in," said Gill, "once the entire manuscript is finished."

Mike felt his jaw grow numb. "And I can do whatever I want with it?"

"Absolutely."

"I can sell copies through the magazine, incorporate the footage into a new documentary about Lugosi? You have no problems with that? Because Kurt said—"

"Forget what Kurt said. What does he know? It's been so many years, I doubt anyone will be harmed by the secrets revealed in these reels."

"And what secret is that?"

Gill downed the last of the Scotch. "Have you ever heard of a story called 'Pickman's Model' by H.P. Lovecraft?"

Mike nodded. Oddly enough, it was one of the few Lovecraft stories he'd ever read. He discovered it in an anthology of horror stories in his school library back in high school. "Yes, but it's been many years since I read it."

"It's all about an artist who paints very realistic looking portraits of ghouls. No one can figure out how he does it. At the end of the story, it turns out he's using real ghouls for models." Gill fell silent, then handed Kurt the empty glass. Gill didn't have to say anything. Kurt shuffled over to the mini-bar in the library and made him another drink.

"And...you're saying this applies to Lugosi?"

Gill nodded. "Just as Bela based his conception of Dracula on the real vampire, the make-up he devised for the Monster in Florey's *Frankenstein* was based on real life as well."

"Right." Mike wrote this down. "Bela met the Frankenstein Monster. In person."

"Well, he saw photographs of the real thing."

"When were these photographs taken?"

Kurt handed Gill his new drink. (Gill took it from him without even saying, "Thank you.")

"Back in the 1920s, I believe," Gill said. "That was before I got involved in this whole game."

"So...where's the Frankenstein Monster now?"

"His body or his brain?"

"Both."

"His body died in the 1940s in Carfax Abbey in London. I watched it dissolve into a formless mass of protoplasm. His brain, on the other hand, ended up in the body of Frankenstein's former assistant, Ygor. Ygor still lives to this day. He lives in Ibiza, an island off the coast of Spain."

"Ygor lives in Ibiza."

"That's right. He's a plastic surgeon now."

"And I suppose Lugosi based his conception of Ygor on the real dude as well?"

"Yes…but not as much as with Dracula and the Frankenstein Monster. Bela was a little more free to use his imagination when he created the Ygor character."

Mike wrote down the words "Ygor is a plastic surgeon in Ibiza," then glanced up at Kurt and smiled and said, "You sure you don't want to be the one to write this?"

Kurt shrugged. "It's all commonplace to me now. We need someone with a sense of wonder about the whole thing. To see all these strange events through fresh eyes."

"That's exactly what I need," Gill said. "You don't even have to believe what I'm saying. I just need your eyes."

"And I get the test reel at the end of this whole thing."

Gill nodded. "Scout's honor." He knocked back some more liquor. Was it whiskey this time? "I really was a Scout, you know."

"So, you saw the test reel then?" Eric asked.

"Well…not quite."

There was a knock at the window. A couple of people wanted to come inside. Mike and Eric glanced at the cheesy Marilyn Monroe clock hanging on the wall. It was fifteen minutes after 10:00.

"Oh…crap," Eric muttered. It was always odd to hear Eric curse. Eric walked over to the door to unlock it. "Sorry about that, folks," he said as the two disgruntled customers entered the store. The second they wandered off to look at the Psychotronic Section in the back, Eric approached Mike once more and whispered, "Why not?"

"He says he doesn't want me to see it until I write down everything that happened to him first. It's his insurance that I'll actually finish the project."

"That's bull ca-ca. You can't do all this work without even knowing if the footage exists. You need to demand to see at least a minute of it."

Mike nodded. "That makes sense. So, you believe this Gill character?"

"Of course not! But he's not the only nut I've met in Los Angeles who might have something valuable in his possession. You know what this could mean for the magazine if we got a hold of that footage? We could build a whole documentary around it, sell it through the magazine."

"Yeah, that's exactly what I was thinking."

Eric laughed. "Man, that would be fantastic if it really panned out this time. Can I go with you to see it?"

"They said they don't want to deal with anybody but me."

"What about Lucy? What does she think?"

"For now, just don't mention it to her at all."

"Why?"

"I don't want to get her hopes up. Besides, the whole thing's kinda nutty. I mean, how can I explain that I haven't finished the damn screenplay because I've been too busy writing the memoirs of a real-life werewolf?"

Eric and Mike just stared at each other for a few moments, then burst into laughter.

"Did you ask him to turn into a wolf?" Eric said.

"Of course!"

"And what did he say?"

"He said he might be willing to do it at some point in the future if I really demanded absolute proof, but that the entire process of shedding his human form is actually quite painful and might even be life-threatening given his advanced years."

Eric shrugged. "Why does that make sense to me?"

Nina Gill strolled down the street, wishing the attack would come sooner than later. She'd been at this act for hours now with no luck. Well, at least it gave her an excuse to warm her insides. Tonight was one of the coldest nights on record. Earlier she'd heard on the radio that the River Thames hadn't frozen over since 1814. That is, until *tonight*. Nina pulled a flask of rum out of her purse and took another sip. She hoped Larry wasn't "sipping" as much as she was. She didn't want him to be off-balance when the attack finally came, like that time in Indonesia when they had to bag that giant rat. Oh, but it didn't really matter. The case turned out fine in the end. They were still alive, weren't they? Alcohol made both of them think better. It had worked for them pretty well so far. Why change something that didn't need to be changed?

Nina stood still and glanced up at the rooftops. Suddenly, she felt as if she were being watched. Was it Larry? But Larry was supposed to be *behind* her.

She spotted a shadow flitting from rooftop to rooftop. Then a second one. They almost looked like…enormous bats?

The shadows disappeared.

She continued walking.

She put the flask away.

She reached into her purse and held onto the end of her wooden stake. In case she lost this one, she had another in her garter belt.

In her experience, vampires could be far faster than humans. The only way to survive a vampire attack was to *expect* it.

Her grip tightened, *tightened* around the base of the stake.

That's when she heard the scream.

18.

Elsie Frankenstein followed her husband and his strange companion through the snow. Even when they faded from sight, she kept walking. She knew the route to the Lodge. It wasn't too far from the house. Within walking distance.

She couldn't allow her husband to get drawn back into his old obsessions. They had left all the monsters behind in the village of Frankenstein almost eight years ago. She wanted nothing more than to leave them buried there beneath the rubble of his father's wretched laboratory. If this Ygor was filling his head full of his father's nonsense, dredging up all the old horrors again, she'd see to it that he was removed not just from the house but from the entire country. Her family wasn't without influence.

She couldn't bear it if Wolfgang endangered their son's life once more. She thought about Paul, at home safely in bed. She had ordered the nurse to watch him closely while she and her husband were out at the Lodge. She had tried to be as nonchalant as possible, not wanting the old woman to suspect that anything was wrong. Just one evil rumor escaping the estate and her husband's reputation might be in danger of crumbling again. When living under the shadow of the Frankenstein name, one had to be conscious of one's public image at all times.

While dealing with the horrors in the village of Frankenstein, Wolfgang had nearly suffered a complete mental collapse. She couldn't allow that to happen again. What would it do to Paul? What would it do to her? What would it do to their *name*?

So concerned was she about her husband's mental stability that she didn't give a single thought to the rash of killings that had swept the city lately. That is, not until she saw the man in the tuxedo and top hat materializing in front of her as if he were gathering his form from the mist itself.

He rose up out of the night, baring his bloody fangs, hissing like an animal, raising double-jointed fingers in the air that looked more like the talons one might find on an immense sewer rat. He charged her so quickly she didn't think she had time to flee, but she tried anyway.

She turned and screamed and ran right into a woman clothed in a sheer white gown whose fangs were even longer and bloodier than the thing behind her.

She screamed again.

19.

Banoub observed the two intruders from behind a statue of Bast. The cowan had brought along the gentleman who had sponsored him, Wolfgang Frankenstein. Frankenstein was an influential scientist and professor. He was famous, even infamous in some circles. His word bore weight. If he left here and talked about what he had seen, Banoub's entire plan could be in danger.

Banoub would have to kill them both now.

Just as he began to emerge from behind the statue, a scream cut through the hall from somewhere outside. Wolfgang and Ygor ran out of the inner Temple towards the main entrance. He watched them dash out to the street.

The situation had grown out of his control. There was nothing he could do now except cease waiting.

Perhaps it was destiny, the hands of the gods intervening, helping him along.

He couldn't afford to wait until the winter solstice.

He would summon Onbuljah now, *tonight*.

It would be far easier if the assembled brothers were here in his physical presence, but it wasn't necessary. When each of his initiates pledged themselves to him, he took a piece of their soul. They were permanently linked to him and his gods. He would draw upon that link now. It would take every ounce of concentration, every scrap of esoteric knowledge he had gathered over the course of five centuries in order to pull this off...but pull it off he would. He would have to. The luxury of waiting, the luxury of perfection, was no longer an option.

Khalid Banoub closed the doors to the inner Temple behind

him, pushed over an immense statue of Albert Pike (the right and honorable founder of Scottish Rite Freemasonry) onto its side directly in front of the entrance in order to prevent any further intruders, then dropped to his knees before Onbuljah and began to pray to all the gods of Egypt—even Isis herself—to lend him the strength to see this invocation through to its bloody conclusion.

Almost immediately Mike began the process of chronicling the life of Lawrence Gill, but not before demanding to see the actual reel of film. Kurt arranged to have the reel flown down to Los Angeles just to show Mike a few seconds of it. It was at this point that Mike realized how desperately Kurt did not want to write Gill's life story. He was ready to toss away a rare, one-of-a-kind piece of cinematic history just to shed himself of whatever obligation he felt he owed the old intelligence agent (if, indeed, that's what Gill was). Kurt decided to temporarily store the film in a vault underneath the mansion where Gill kept mementos from his past adventures. One day Gill and Kurt ushered Mike down a flight of winding steps that led him into this mysterious chamber. Once inside, Mike thought of it as a low-level Bat Cave. Most of the booty seemed to consist of documents of some kind. Gill called the documents "life insurance." Mike didn't inquire about that any further, as he got the distinct impression that the subject was off-limits. But there were even stranger things stored in here as well, including a coffin inscribed with the same Dracula Crest that one could see in *The House of Dracula* film from 1945.

"Is this what I think it is?" Mike asked. "An actual prop from *House of Dracula*?"

Gill laughed. "Well, I suppose you could say that. I allowed Universal to use it in the film. But it's far more than just a prop. That's Dracula's real coffin. I found it in Carfax Abbey...that was in the early '40s, I believe. Everything that happened in those movies actually occurred a few years before the release of the film. But sometimes only a year or so before. In those days it didn't take too long to make a film, not with the resources of a major studio behind you. Kurt might write a script in a few weeks. A couple of weeks later the sets are all ready. Four weeks later the entire film is in the can. And a month after that the completed film is being shown all around the country. Those were the days, back when a film was only sixty minutes long. Today they make three-hour films about...I don't know... horseshoeing in the eighteenth century." Gill sniffed with disgust. "I don't go to movies anymore. They've lost all of their magic. Who knows? Maybe it's just because I'm an old fart."

"I don't think so," Mike said, drawing a meandering trail in the dust that coated a waist-high shelf of old leather-bound books, "I agree with you. I can't stand modern movies. Well, most of them anyway."

"That's not to say the studios aren't still using the medium of motion pictures to disclose the essential truths of the universe."

"Is Universal still doing that?"

"Not to the same extent that they were in the 1940s and '50s when I was most actively involved with developing projects for them, but they keep their hand in. I still have contacts at the studio to this day. I've heard a rumor that a major disclosure movie is in the works, one that will blow the lid off some of the biggest secrets the Agency has kept under wraps for years."

"Really? What's it called? Who's directing it?"

"That I can't say. But if, at some point during the coming months, I recommend that you go see a particular new film, you'll have your answer. How about that?"

Mike nodded. "That's fair."

At the far end of the vault Kurt called out, "Stop lollygagging, you two! I don't have all day! I have work to do!"

Mike whispered to Gill, "What work does he have to do? I thought he was retired?"

Gill whispered, "He's working on his memoirs, the main reason he didn't have time to work on *my* memoirs. Can you believe it? As if his life story would be more interesting than mine. What's he going to say? 'On this day in 1941 I wrote this script. And then the next week I wrote this novel. And then I wrote a short story.' Writers shouldn't write autobiographies. They're always dull."

Mike laughed. "I've never read a writer's autobiography."

Gill slapped Mike on the back and laughed. "Good thinking! But don't tell Kurt I said so. I don't want to hurt his feelings."

Mike agreed, then the two of them approached Kurt who was busy threading the ancient film through a projector. Without ceremony, Kurt flicked it on and pointed the lens at the bare white wall at the back of the vault. A ghostly black frame appeared on the wall. Within that frame white words and numbers appeared. Mike whipped out his pad and pencil and jotted down everything he saw. The words read *Frankenstein Test Reel 1*, followed by a serial number. He jotted down the numbers, hoping they would help in the research he planned to do at Universal Studios. The words and numbers vanished to be replaced with what was clearly a Universal set. Any fan of the Universal monster films would recognize it as Sound Stage 12, where *Dracula* had been filmed. No actors stood on the set at all. It looked like a scene from a German Expressionist film from the 1920s: all cockeyed backdrops and lopsided walls and weird angular shadows. The set waited in silence for the arrival of its stars: Dr. Frankenstein and the Monster, Lugosi himself.

Then it was over. Kurt had flicked off the projector.

"Hey!" Mike said. "That's not enough! I want to see Lugosi as the Monster."

"You'll see it when you finish your work," Kurt said.

"That's only fair," Gill said. "We have to hold back something valuable, now don't we? We kept our end of the bargain by showing you this much. Now keep yours."

Mike sighed. "I suppose. Okay. When do you want to begin?"

"How about now?" Gill said. "We'll do it. Poolside."

Lawrence Gill was taking another nip from his flask of Captain Morgan when he heard the woman scream. He peeked out from around the corner of the alley and saw, thank God, that his precious Nina remained unmolested. The scream was coming from somewhere else.

Nina ran off toward the source of the scream. Gill cursed under his breath. The girl was as impetuous as ever. She had become so much more sure of herself ever since leaving her old life in Visaria. Not even imminent danger seemed to bother her any longer. Gill wasn't sure how much he liked that. Sometimes it was wonderful. At other times, like now, it was nerve wracking….

He returned the flask to his belt, then ran after her, his revolver cocked and ready.

He caught a glimpse of her dashing around a corner. Gill didn't like having her out of sight for so long. He stepped up his speed.

Around the corner, in front of the impressive marble steps that led up to the entrance of the biggest Masonic Temple in London, he saw Nina engaged in hand-to-hand combat with a female vampire dressed in a sheer white gown splattered with blood. Nina was down on one knee, trying as hard as she could to push the beast away from her while the vampire hissed and scratched at the air. Behind them, a man in a tuxedo and a top hat crouched over another woman who was trying to crawl away from her attacker. The man grabbed the back of her collar and threw her over onto her spine. The woman shrieked in horror again.

Gill had seen the nicely dressed assailant before, from behind, only for a second while the man was running out of Dr. Heidelmann's bedroom, but that was enough. Once one had laid eyes on him, even for a moment, one did not easily forget a creature like Dracula.

Gill fired the revolver twice into Dracula's back, hoping the silver bullets—miniature crosses carved into their surfaces—would do the trick. He got the bastard right below the shoulder blade. Dracula cried out in pain and spun around.

At that moment Nina managed to push the she-vampire away just long enough to pull the stake out of her garter belt and slash a deep arc into her attacker's belly. The she-vampire's eyes widened in shock and horror.

The double doors that led into the Masonic Temple burst open and two figures came running out. One was a tall, slender man with distinguished features and the other a short, disfigured man with a scraggly beard and a twisted neck. The disfigured man was much faster than the other and was already halfway down the stairs within moments. "Elsie!" the tall one shouted.

The woman on the ground glanced up and screamed, "Wolfgang! Oh God, help me!"

Dracula stood crouched in an attack stance, glancing ahead and to the side, wondering which danger was the most important to deal with first. *"Aishe!"* he shouted. "Come!"

The she-vampire backed away from the battle, but only reluctantly. She had murder in her eyes as she glared at Nina. She hissed once more, then spun around. The two figures dashed off down the street. Soon, Gill knew, they would be lost in the night and the snow.

Wolfgang dropped to his knees and slid to his woman's side. He held her and nestled her head on his lap. "Elsie," he whispered. "My God, are you all right?"

Elsie was too busy crying to respond.

"Can you get this woman to a hospital?" Gill asked.

"Yes, of course," Wolfgang said.

The disfigured one ran off down the street toward the fleeing creatures.

"Ygor!" Wolfgang cried. "Wait!"

"No, he's got the right idea," Gill said. He turned to Nina and said, "Stay here and help get this woman into an ambulance."

"But I want to—" Nina began to say.

Gill cut her off. "No time to argue. Just do it!"

Gill dashed off after Ygor, slipping more silver bullets into the empty chambers.

Mike wrote the first in a series of regular columns for *Ramboona* called *As Told To...: 20th Century Werewolf Part 1*. The first installment detailed his chance encounter with Gill. Mike made up a fictional scenario in which he bumped into Lawrence at the Scottish Rite Masonic Library in Long Beach. Mike reported he had been performing research for an upcoming article about Masonic symbolism in the Golden Age of cinema when a mysterious man approached him and offered to give him the story of a lifetime—the truth behind the classic Universal horror films for which Mike's readership held such an undying fascination. Mike explained that he couldn't reveal too many details, and had to present his secrets in the form of fiction. Of course, Mike knew that his entire readership would assume the introduction itself was pure fiction. No one would ever think for a moment that such outlandishness could actually be true.

Over the course of many months, the entire narrative unfolded: After being bitten by a werewolf in Wales in the 1930s, Gill made his way to Germany where he elicited the aid of a famous doctor to cure him of his disease. It was here that Gill had his first run-in with Count Dracula. Dracula survived their first battle and made his way to London with the Frankenstein Monster in tow. Gill and a hunchback nurse named Nina travelled to London to track down the fiends. It was there that they had met an ancient Egyptian mummy who had taken control of the largest Masonic Temple in London and planned to use it as a base of operations from which to destroy the world. The Egyptian Mummy was using Masonic rituals to steal the life energies of all his fellow lodge members. That energy was being used by the Mummy to summon an ancient heathen god from another dimension. Gill managed to stop the Mummy while also destroying the Frankenstein Monster and Count Dracula (at least temporarily).

Not long afterwards Gill and Nina opened a private detective agency in London that became quite famous in certain circles. In 1946 they were approached by the nascent Central Intelligence Agency to track down Dr. Mengele in South America where Gill had unfortunate run-ins with an Amazonian fish-man, an insane intelligence agent who had the ability to make himself invisible, the self-professed "daughter of Dracula," and the Count himself. Dracula was at last destroyed by the fish-man, Gill ate the invisible man, Mengele met an equally unfortunate end, and the daughter of Dracula committed suicide.

This operation was such a success, by Agency standards, that the CIA asked Gill and Nina to join their ranks. All throughout the Cold War the pair performed crucial intelligence operations around the world. In 1954, for example, in Arizona, they saved the world from an alien invasion when shape-shifting "xenomorphs" took control of a massive golem designed by an escaped Nazi scientist that Project Paperclip had smuggled into the U.S. military.

By the early 1960s, Gill and Nina decided to quit while

their luck was still holding. Unfortunately, Nina died of a heart attack not long after their retirement. Then, in November of 1963, Gill was approached by a young intelligence agent named Lee Harvey Oswald who warned him that someone was trying to assassinate the President. Gill and Oswald took a road trip to Dallas in order to prevent the assassination, only to come face-to-face with some of the meanest xenomorphs he'd ever encountered. Sadly, Gill and Oswald were unable to prevent the physical assassination of the President, but *were* able to help free his astral body from the prison of the Executive Office so that John F. Kennedy could continue to battle evil on the ethereal plane.

The response to this column was so strong that the readership of the magazine shot through the roof. The magazine went monthly. But Mike was so busy writing that he never had time to hang out with Lucy very much, not like before. And his headaches were getting worse. Much, much worse. He had begun popping Tylenol almost every day in order to get rid of the pain. He didn't want to go to a doctor about it, though. He hated doctors. He asked Gill about it one time. Gill advised him not to go. "What the hell did doctors do for my wife?" he asked. "The last place you want to go to be healthy is a hospital. If hospitals were so great, how come there's nothing but sick people in them?" Mike couldn't argue with logic like that. He didn't go.

Ygor didn't stop running until he saw the ruined remains of Carfax Abbey. He'd seen this building before. It had reminded him of his father's laboratory in the village of Frankenstein when it was in its most dilapidated state. He'd been intrigued and had wanted to explore the rotting interiors, but Wolfgang had talked him out of it.

Now here he stood in front of the Abbey again, watching two human-sized bats alight upon its rooftop. Swiftly, the two bats metamorphosed into human form again, crawled over the edge of the roof and down the wall like massive four-legged spiders, ultimately sliding through a thin space between two wooden boards nailed over a window without glass.

The man with the gun caught up with Ygor at that point and asked, "Did you lose them?"

"No," Ygor said, pointing up at the Abbey, "they went...in there."

The man cursed. "It would be foolish for us to confront them in their lair at night," he said, almost as if speaking to himself.

"Then you know...what these things...are?"

The man paused, as if reluctant to respond. "Perhaps I should introduce myself before telling you what I'm about to tell you." He held out his hand. "My name's Gill."

Despite his recent initiation, Ygor was still not used to people greeting him in such a formal manner. He shook Gill's hand, exactly as Sister Marie had taught him. "People...call me...Ygor."

"Ygor, you may not wish to believe this, but those creatures are vampires, undead beings that live off the blood of the living. You've probably been taught that such things are only mythological, figments of the peasant imagination. Not true. I know. I've *seen* them. Such things *do* exist! Are you willing to accept that?"

Ygor shrugged. "My friend...I've...seen...stranger."

Gill looked confused for a second. "Perhaps we can work with each other then. Most people have a hard time accepting such things."

"I think...we should confront them...when they're still weakened...from their wounds."

"You're as cautious as Nina. I might as well have brought her along. Okay, it's your neck." Gill knelt down and pulled a wooden stake out of a holster strapped to his ankle. He held the stake out to Ygor. "Here. Aim for the heart."

Ygor hefted the stake in his hand, as if testing its weight. He pointed at his own neck. "I lost...my neck...a long...time ago."

Gill seemed a little disturbed and chagrined. "Yeah, I guess so." He gripped the handle of his revolver tightly, as if to gain some confidence from it. "You ready, pal, or you want a drink first?"

Ygor shook his head. "I think...we should...just go."

Gill looked disappointed. "Yeah, I guess you're right."

Saying nothing more, the two men dashed toward the front entrance of Carfax Abbey.

20.

"What is it?" asked Old Ygor, waking up out of a dead sleep. "What's wrong?"

Still cursing, Dracula grabbed an empty beaker from his work table and tossed it across the room. It almost hit Krogh in the head, shattering against the stone wall. Krogh glanced up from the kitten he was gnawing on to see what was wrong with his master.

"What's *wrong*?" Dracula spun around and ripped off his shirt with his own talons, revealing the bloody wound in his shoulder.

Ygor seemed shocked. "I didn't know you could bleed."

"It's not *my* blood," said Dracula.

Aishe crawled into her coffin, trying to stop a massive amount of blood from leaking out of her stomach.

Ygor saw her and began to grow concerned. He rose from his makeshift bed. "I *knew* we were pushing our luck by coming to the city. We should've stayed where we were. We could've been *kings* with no effort at all!"

"Be silent!" Dracula said, dragging out an immense metal container from beneath his work table. Old Ygor had only carried it in the night before. "Once this is full with the liquefied form of the *Bavarian Formosa*, I'll need your assistance to carry it to the reservoir."

"What? *Tonight*?"

"Our plans have changed. We have enough now to affect a great majority of the city's populace, if not all of it. Enough to cause chaos. Enough to bring these pitiful creatures to their knees." Dracula chuckled. "Of course, they won't have any knees once we're through with them. Or any limbs at all."

"But what happened to the original plan? Why not wait until—?"

Dracula turned on him, almost frothing with anger. Blood bubbled through his ivory fangs. "Because Count Dracula must not be humiliated again! These creatures must be taught the error of their ways! *Tonight*! Come, Krogh! Fill this container while I tend to my wounds!"

Krogh just stared at him from his little spot in the corner. He tossed the half-eaten kitten away from him, as if it disgusted him all of a sudden.

"Krogh!" Dracula shouted. "I said *come here*!"

Krogh remained motionless.

21.

Inside Krogh's mind two voices vied for dominance. One was that of Dracula, always commanding, always dominant. The other was Krogh's own voice mingled with the voices of his loved ones at home. His wife and child. Where were they right now? Did they think he was dead?

Krogh felt the cat's blood on his tongue. Perhaps he *was* dead. If not, perhaps he *should* be dead.

Krogh tried to remain where he was, but it was so hard. Hard to resist.

He stood up, trying to hold onto that fleeting image of his wife and son.

They're going to destroy London with the spores, said the-voice-that-was-not-his-master. You know that. You've overheard their plans numerous times. You must stop them, Father. You must stop them.

Krogh approached Dracula in stop-start motions, like a defective automaton.

"Come...*here*," said Dracula again.

Krogh felt the memory of his son, his wife, drifting away once again. The blood on his tongue tasted more and more delightful with each step that took him closer to his master.

One day, late in November of 1988, Mike entered Eric's store with the typescript for the new issue tucked under his arm. He wanted Eric to proofread it before it went to press. He was feeling bad. Real bad. Sweat poured down his neck.

Eric seemed to think there was a problem the second Mike entered.

"Hey, you're not lookin' so good," Eric said. "You want to lie down in the back?"

"I don't know what's goin' on," Mike said. "It just hit me when I came through the door."

"Just *now*? Are you sure? You look kind of gray, like you've got no blood in you. Come on." Eric wrapped his arm around him and led him past a group of barely legal teenage boys hanging out in the Asian Erotica section. They were too engrossed in studying the VHS covers of *Beautiful Dead Body* and *Erotic Dream of Red Chamber* to notice the potential dead man in their midst.

Mike's fingers felt weak. The typescript fell out of his hands.

"Just leave it there for now," Eric grunted. The second he laid Mike out on the couch in the back office, Eric said, "Listen, you need to take some time off. You're working yourself ragged. You try to do too much. Let me take over the magazine for a while. Just rest for a few weeks, at least. Go see a doctor. You've been running this thing all by yourself for over a year now. It's just too much."

"What do you mean all by myself? Lucy's been helping me as much as she ever has. I don't know what I would do without her."

"What're you talking about? Did she...did she come back?"

"Come back?" Mike laughed. "What do you mean? She never left."

Eric pulled up a chair and sat next to Mike. "Mike...do you have a fever or something?"

"I don't know. Maybe. I feel sort of hot. Why?"

"Mike...Lucy left you over a year ago. Don't you remember? You pushed her up against the wall when you had that argument over you not finishing that screenplay. She said she was so pissed off about you getting violent with her that she never wanted to come back."

"What the fuck're you talking about? Lucy's at home reading the letters to the editor, just like she always does this time of day." Mike laughed, this time long and hard. "What're you doing, trying to fuck with my head? This some kind of joke?"

Eric had a worried look on his face. "Mike, listen, Lucy's living with Chad now. You know that. They're making a movie together. We had dinner with them the other night. You said you'd help Chad with the script. Remember?"

All humor was leaking out of the situation quickly. Mike rose to a sitting position. "I'd never help that son of a bitch with anything. He fucked Lucy behind my back that night we had the argument. I've never brought it up with Lucy. I've never asked her about it. But I know. I just hope they...." He began weeping violently. "Lucy...."

Eric wrapped his arms around Mike and hugged him. "God, Mike, we need to get you to the doctor."

Mike pushed him away. "Gill said not to go."

"Who?"

"Gill. You know...Lawrence *Gill*. Jesus Christ. From the articles!"

Eric just stared at him. "Listen, just sit right there while I make a phone call."

"I need to call Gill. He'll be able to help me. He has contacts in the intelligence world. They have cures for things like this. They have cures for everything, squirreled away in a warehouse somewhere. Just like in *Raiders of the Lost Ark*, that last scene. It's just a flu. Nothing to worry about." Mike erupted from the sofa and pushed Eric against a stack of VHS tapes.

Mike tore through the middle of the store and dashed out onto Hollywood Boulevard. Where was Lucy's car? Hadn't he used it to get here? Someone had hijacked him. Sons of bitches. You couldn't trust anyone in this town. No time to call the police. He'd catch a bus. He'd hitch his way over to Gill's mansion. Whatever he had to do.

By the time he reached the mansion it was night. He couldn't even remember how he'd gotten there. He felt horrible. In fact, he'd felt horrible for so long. He'd been trying to hide it from Lucy. He didn't want her to worry. She worried about him too much already....

Nina had just finished helping the grief-stricken Wolfgang into the back of the ambulance and was watching it speed away into the thickening fog when she heard vast rumbling sounds that seemed to erupt from somewhere beneath her. The ground shook. Did London suffer from earthquakes? she asked herself. She had no idea. She'd lived in Visaria her entire life. She felt the vibrations travel up through her feet, her spine, and directly into her brain. Her teeth rattled in her head as she fought to keep her balance.

She turned and saw the roof of the Masonic Temple explode as if a bomb had gone off somewhere within. Something strange emerged from the hole in the roof. Through the fog a trio of immense heads swayed. A toad. A bearded human. A cat. The toad croaked ominously, the human bellowed with Old-Testament-style anger, and the cat hissed in disgust. A grotesque parody of human life magnified to impossible proportions.

A tall, seemingly fragile man stepped out onto the steps of the Temple, raised his fists into the air, and shouted, "And thus, Anubis, your familiar Onbuljah has been invoked to raise havoc on Earth!" He pointed at Nina and said, "And *there* is your first victim!"

Nina wanted to run, but couldn't. She was too fascinated with the intricate horror of this weird demon. Two thoughts swirled in her brain: *We're going to need more than silver bullets for this one.* And: *I wish I had time for a drink.*

He staggered up the snaking driveway and slammed his fists into Gill's front door. He practically collapsed into Gill's arms. Even at Gill's advanced age, the man still had the ability to help Mike over to the couch in the living room. Gill's butler was nowhere to be seen.

"My God, what's wrong with you?" Gill asked. "You're sweating like a pig."

"I don't know," Gill whispered, "I don't know. I feel like I've got the flu or something. I think...I think I might be going crazy."

"Hell, kid, you're as sane as I am. Isn't he?" Gill turned around and spoke to someone standing in the corner of the room. Mike lifted his head up slowly and saw the butler standing there with an ominous expression on his face. The butler looked worried. Even frightened. Despite this, the man nodded silently in response to Gill's question.

"See?" Gill said. "Merkel is a good judge of character. You can believe him. Now tell me what's wrong. Maybe I can fix it."

Mike realized that he'd never known the butler's name until this very moment. Why would that be? It didn't make any sense. Had he known it and forgotten it?

"I've...I've got this terrible migraine. It feels like it's cutting into the middle of my brain. I'm seeing these...weird lights. It's...it's confusing."

"Maybe it's the brain tumor."

"What?"

"The tumor. In your brain. Remember what the doctor told you."

"The doctor? I haven't been to a doctor since I was a kid."

Krogh had just begun pouring the liquefied essence of *Bavaria Formosa* into the metal container when the gate to Dracula's crypt flung open to reveal two men, one of whom he recognized. It was Ygor...or rather, it was Ygor's *body*. But if Ygor was inside the Monster, who was inside Ygor? Was it possible that...?

Standing beside Ygor was a man Krogh had never seen before. He held a revolver in his hand and was aiming it at Dracula's chest. "So, we finally meet face-to-face, Count Dracula."

"Who are you?" Dracula shouted.

"I'm Lawrence Gill, and I hold the instrument of your destruction in my hand."

Dracula laughed, despite the fact that Krogh could see the terror in his eyes. "I'm afraid you hold nothing in your hand but a minor annoyance!" Dracula made his move against Gill.

Gill squeezed the trigger. A bullet burrowed into Dracula's chest. Dracula screamed. His flesh hissed and bubbled where the bullet hit. Dracula dropped to his knees.

"WHAT ARE YOU DOING WITH MY BODY?" The voice came from the corner of the room. Frankenstein's Monster lumbered out of the shadows toward Ygor and Gill.

Gill's eyes widened when he saw the fiend. "The Monster of Frankenstein!" Gill said. "So, we meet again!"

Gill fired at the Monster's head, but the bullet merely ricocheted and buried itself in the stone wall. Krogh knew that Gill was wasting his bullets on the Monster. He needed to resume his attack on Dracula while he was still wounded.

Aishe, the she-vampire, leaped out of her coffin and attacked Ygor. Ygor slashed at her neck with a wooden stake, missed, and cut a bloody arc into her forearm. She hissed in pain and backed away.

Krogh felt Dracula's influence waning. He felt himself grow dizzy. He dropped the container on the ground. He could hear his son's voice inside his head. "Help them, Father! Help them!" Krogh leaped in between Gill and the Monster.

"Focus on Dracula!" Krogh shouted. "I'll take care of the Monster!"

"You'll do *nothing*!" Dracula groaned, rising to his feet. He leaped through the air, talons outstretched. Gill spun away from the Monster and fired two bullets into Dracula's body just as the undead Count dematerialized into mist and reformed right behind Gill. Dracula grabbed Gill from behind and clawed at his chest, ripping open his coat and shirt.

Gill screamed.

The Monster bellowed, "I should've done this a long time ago!" He picked up Krogh, held him over his head, and carried him to the edge of the pit in the middle of the room. "Die, Krogh, *die*!" The Monster tightened his grip on Krogh's mechanical arm, ripped it out of its artificial socket, and tossed the flesh that remained over the edge of the pit.

Krogh fell, screaming.

Gill sighed and shook his head. "The pain started getting real bad right after you published the first chapter of *20th Century Werewolf.* Lucy forced you to go to the doctor. That's when he told you about the tumor. It'd been growing for so long, there was nothing to do about it. It was too big to extract. But he told you that it might have been influencing your thoughts for a great period of time without you knowing it. Remember? You were fascinated by that whole concept. Remember what you asked the doctor?"

"Yes." Mike smiled. "Yes, I do. I asked him, 'Are you saying that the tumor is *thinking*?'"

"And what did he say?"

"He said...he said, 'Yes, it is.'" Mike realized that tears had begun to stream down his cheeks.

Gill knelt down beside him and took his hand in his and said, "Kid, there's no reason to cry. This isn't a sad occasion. No, sir. This is the moment of your birth. You see, you don't fully understand what kind of role you're playing in this whole drama. That tumor enables you to see beyond what's apparently real and get at what's really real. Remember that movie I told you to review for the magazine?"

"Which one?"

"The new one from Universal. All about aliens taking over the Earth. They're shape shifters, able to blend in with other humans. In the movie, the main character, the hero, is able to distinguish between the humans and the aliens with what?"

"A...a pair of sunglasses. Gill, I'm sorry, I haven't written the review yet."

"It's okay." Gill's grip on Mike's hand tightened just slightly. "That's not important. What's important is that you saw the film and understood its message. God gave you this gift for a reason."

"Gift?"

"Your tumor, the divine presence in your head, it's your own personal pair of lenses. It enables you to see what the rest of us can't. Do you understand?"

Mike glanced over Gill's shoulder at the butler. The old man seemed even more frightened than before. He seemed....

Mike squinted his eyes and stared at him closely. The old man's harmless façade melted away to be replaced by something inhuman and horrible. A protoplasmic mass of viscous liquid with a single eye in the middle and long, spindly arms that bent in all the wrong places, impossibly, like the appendages of a nightmare. And it was staring at him. It was staring at him with naked hatred.

"Holy shit," Mike whispered. "What the fuck is it?"

Gill stood up and spun around. "Just as I thought. Where's the real Merkel?"

"The man's obviously delusional, sir," said the butler.

"Why don't we test that with a bullet through your eye?" Gill said and whipped a pistol out of his belt.

The butler ran out of the room, screaming. Gill pumped a bullet into Merkel's shoulder. Blood splattered against the original of Richard Dadd's *The Fairy Feller's Master-Stroke* hanging on the wall. "Damn it!" Gill said upon seeing the blood splatter on the painting. "That was Nina's favorite!"

The butler shed his human skin at last, a pillar of helix-shaped, jelly-like strings gushing up out the empty butler's attire and reforming itself into a massive battering ram that nearly took off Gill's head. Gill ducked to one side as the xenomorph crashed into the wall behind him. The entire room shook with the impact. If it had hit Gill's skull, he would've been crushed. That is, if Gill were human.

Mike watched Gill crouch down on the carpet and propel himself upwards like an acrobat. In mid-leap, hair shot up out of every pore in his flesh, silver fangs erupted from his mouth, and knife-like claws shot out of his fingertips.

The Werewolf landed in the center of the amorphous mass, punching a hole into Merkel's single eye with his hairy fist. A shriek like a thousand panthers dying at once emerged from the thing's wounded flesh. A clear, syrupy substance drained out of its massive pupil. The Werewolf didn't let up. He continued clawing away at the wispy tendrils that flayed at his hairy body like tiny whips.

Nina slowly backed away from the Temple and watched in shocked fascination as the man on the steps raised his skinny arms in the air and said to the three-headed beast, "And now, Anubis, in return for manifesting your familiar on Earth, Khalid Banoub demands that you give him what he deserves! Now, *now*, NOW!"

The beast, referred to by the shouting man as Onbuljah, wriggled its massive body out through the hole in the roof and scuttled over the ruined edges of the building. Its body was that of a grotesquely bloated black scorpion. The middle head of the trio, the human-looking one with the tangled black beard, glanced down at the shouting man with a look of enraged annoyance.

It bellowed in anger, then snapped its head down quickly and picked up the little man in its teeth.

The man screamed in terror and agony for Isis to save his soul as the bearded head chewed him to bits between yellowing teeth the size of several automobiles lined up in a row.

Then it turned to look at Nina.

Nina whipped out her crossbow, where it had been strapped to her back beneath her long winter coat, and aimed it at the demon. She let fly an arrow directly into its left eyeball. The toad croaked in pain and the cat hissed at her angrily. The bearded head screamed, bits of Khalid Banoub falling out of its mouth.

It scuttled toward her.

Nina ran, not knowing where on earth she could possibly go to escape the thing.

Mike struggled to his feet just as the xenomorph tossed Gill's body across the room like a bull bucking its rider. Mike espied the sword on the wall, the one that had belonged to Gill's dead father. He reached for the weapon, yanked it from the iron handles that held it aloft, and spun around just as the xenomorph tumbled across the carpet toward him like a massive amoeba. Its multitudinous tendrils slithered across the carpet, as if it had eyes in its wiry tentacles. How did it even know where he was? Mike thrust the blade into the xenomorph's single eye, wishing he could do the same to Chad. Chad? Why was he thinking about Chad?

Chad had done nothing but help him. In a way, it was because of Chad and his student film that Mike had met Lucy in the first place.

Chad had done him a favor. Such a huge favor. Lucy. Sharon. *Luna.*

Mike sank the sword deep down into the xenomorph's brain—if, indeed, it even possessed a brain. He aimed for the mass of gooey strangeness (whatever the hell it was) that trembled and quivered behind its ruined eye like a dissected frog attached to a web of active electrodes. A weird, low tone burst out of every pore in the xenomorph's formless body that sounded like this: *Ulla, ulla, ulla, ulla.* Wasn't that the sound H.G.

Wells used in *War of the Worlds* to denote the Martians' wailing death cries? Perhaps Wells had based his stories on the truth, just as Kurt Siodmak had done in the 1940s. What the hell was truth? What the hell was *fiction*?

"*Ulla, ulla, ulla, ulla,*" the thing said, spewing clear ichorous goo on the expensive shag carpet.

"We've got to get out of here," Gill said, grabbing Mike's elbow. "That cry will bring hundreds more within minutes. I've seen this before. Me and Oswald fought these fuckers back in '63."

"I know," Mike said. He just stood there staring at the nightmare melting before him. "You told me. I wrote it all down. The manuscript for your 1963 adventure is done. I was just about to give it to Eric. But...to tell you the truth, I didn't really believe you. I thought you were crazy. Hell, Eric always gave you more benefit of the doubt than I ever did. I was just using you. Exploiting your insanity to make good copy. I felt guilty about it, but then again, I didn't. I'm so sorry. You're not insane. Everyone else is insane."

"You just woke up. You've got the glasses on now. It's just like the movie."

"Just like the movie. I'll finish the review. That was the last thing I started writing for the magazine before I—"

"We don't have time to talk about this. We've got to go."

"Go? Where?"

"Someplace where that son of a bitch isn't screaming, 'Ulla, ulla, ulla, ulla.'"

"Screaming? I can barely hear it."

"But *they* can. Their hearing's not the same as ours. There's nothing human about them. You know that now. Don't you?"

Mike just nodded silently. Gill tugged at his arm, dragging him from the room while also pulling the sword from his hand. "Good work with the blade," Gill said. "The last person besides me to touch that sword was my dear, dead father."

On the way out the front door, Mike said, "You never told me how your father really died."

"Yes, I did. He died of a broken heart."

"But...but why? What happened?"

Gill pushed him into his Impala SS convertible. "Your memory's going, pal."

"It's these migraines." Mike reached up to massage his temples, despite the fact that such massages never succeeded in relieving his pain. What was that definition of insanity that Lucy had told him about? He'd quoted it in an article for *Ramboona*. "Insanity is doing the same thing over and over again, expecting different results."

Gill's tires screeched as he tore out of the long, winding driveway. "My father was devastated by my death. And the fact that he was the one who killed me."

"It's coming back now."

"You wrote all this down, Mike. You published it in your magazine. You got reams of letters praising the series."

"Yes. Yes, I know that. Why did he kill you?"

"I was about to murder the woman I loved at the time."

"And he killed you. And buried you. And you...."

"I rose from the dead. Because I'm cursed. I can't die. I can grow old and tired and bored and angry and depressed as all get out, but I can never die. That's the curse that Bela passed onto me."

"Bela? Bela Lugosi?"

"No. Bela the gypsy. The one who bit me."

"I always thought Siodmak named the gypsy after Bela Lugosi, since....since he knew they had already cast Lugosi for the film."

"No. The gypsy's name really was Bela."

"That's so strange."

"Not really." Gill disobeyed all posted speed limits as he wound his way down the narrow road that would take them away from these isolated hills and back into the heart of Los Angeles. Mike glanced out the window. Down below, he could see the freeway and the cars going about their business as if nothing was wrong. As if the entire world wasn't ending. As if it wasn't being invaded by monsters. Monsters that could take any form. Like a fatal tumor, growing within the body of society.

In the second that Dracula materialized in order to lash out with his talons, Gill spun around and pumped a bullet into the vampire's abdomen. Dracula shrieked like a skinned witch thrashing at the end of a gibbet.

Out of the corner of his eye, Gill saw Ygor holding his own against the she-vampire. The little guy was stronger than he looked, Gill had to give him that. The she-vampire tried to attack him with her claws and Ygor just hauled off and punched her in the jaw. She went flying backwards a few feet, landing against the side of her coffin with the sound of splitting wood. Ygor rushed her, his stake held high in the air.

At that moment, while Gill was distracted, the Frankenstein Monster grabbed Gill from behind and pinned his arms in place.

"This is the last time I will ever have to deal with you, little man!" said the Monster. He squeezed Gill's chest until he could do nothing else but drop the gun.

Dracula crept toward Gill. "And now…welcome to the ranks of the undead." His fangs seemed to grow larger as Dracula drew nearer and nearer.

A blinding white aura appeared in front of Mike's eyes. He screamed. The car pitched off to the left, nearly skidding off the road and down the side of the hill. Then the flashes went away just as quickly as they came and he saw a mass of xenomorphs dragging Gill out of the car.

"Gill!" he screamed. *"No!"*

Gill managed to pull away from them and landed on the hood of the car. He shot to his feet, sword in hand. "Get out of here!" he yelled. "Warn everybody!" He began hacking away at the creatures, dismembered gelatinous appendages flying in all directions. "Get out of here! These things are stepping up their plans, moving onto the next level!"

"What level?"

"Listen: *They're going to eat your brain!*"

"Please, Gill, get back inside!"

"We'd never make it together! Go! Don't let them spread their evil even more than they already have!"

"I don't want to be alone!" Mike said, tears streaming down

his face. "I've been alone for so long. But when I met you...when I met you, I finally felt complete. I love you. I love you so much. Please don't leave me. I'm so sorry. I'm so sorry I pushed you."

"Don't worry about me, kid! They can't kill me." With that, Gill leaped into the middle of the jelly-like mass. They spread over the old intelligence agent, subsumed him. Their intense hunger distracted them from Mike for a moment. And that was long enough.

Mike slid into the driver's seat and pulled away, trying not to look in the rearview mirror. He could hardly see through the tears and the residual white light. "I'm sorry," he kept whispering over and over again. "I'm so sorry I pushed you."

Vampires have always lived on souls. This thought entered Mike's head out of nowhere. Was that an original thought, or had he heard it before? Had Manly P. Hall told him that? Perhaps he'd read it one of Hall's voluminous books?

Is that what these aliens were? Is that what they had always been? Hall claimed that these astral beings, bodiless souls primitive people once called "vampires," could enter one's body, particularly in those belonging to people whose guard was down. People who didn't believe in the old superstitions. People who had no spiritual center. People who were focused only on themselves.

Where better for these beings to stage a major assault on the human race than in Los Angeles?

Perhaps all the supernatural beings depicted in those old Universal movies were based on legends that had been based on less mystical truths: the truth of the alien parasite. To think that something anti-human could invade one's brain, could make you do things you'd never dream of doing in your right mind. It was scary. It was beyond horror.

Who could he trust? Who hadn't already been infected?

He needed Lucy. Needed to warn her. Warn her about the coming apocalypse. He couldn't let Gill's noble sacrifice be in vain.

Krogh lay at the bottom of the pit, staring up at the pinpoint of light high above him. The curved, stone walls of the pit were as smooth as glass and glistened as if they were wet, made slick by the hordes of white spores that grew all along their subterranean surfaces.

There was no way he could climb that distance, even if his bones weren't broken. Besides, by that time the fight would long be over, the monsters having triumphed again.

Why did the monsters always seem to triumph in this world?

Don't give up, said the voice of his son. There must be a way. There's always a way.

"Always a way," Krogh muttered to himself, but how? How with a body full of shattered bones?

He reached out for the wall, trying to find a spot not covered by the spores. He'd seen what happened to flesh when injected with its liquefied concentrate. When the spores themselves touched one's body, the result wasn't quite as fatal but devastating nonetheless. They softened one's bones until....

Krogh's eyes widened. Yes, of course. His son had been right. There was a way.

It took all of the effort left in his crippled body to wriggle out of his clothes, grab a fistful of spores, and began smearing them all over his naked torso.

Mike arrived back at his apartment about thirty minutes later. There was an eviction notice on his door. He read it, confused. He'd been paying his rent on the first ever since he'd moved in with Lucy. There was no way he was behind. And yet the eviction notice was marked "SECOND NOTICE" in big bold letters where anyone roaming through the hall could see it.

He tore the notice off the door and crumpled it into a ball. He slammed the door behind him, knowing now that not even his landlady could be trusted. Had they infected *her*, too?

If so, there was no way to know if some of these xenomorphs weren't lurking around his building, trying to remove evidence from his apartment. He grabbed all the notes he'd taken during his interviews with Gill as well as the complete manuscript of *20th Century Werewolf*. The concluding chapters still needed to see print in *Ramboona*. If something should happen to him, then the truth needed to come out. This was the only copy of the

manuscript. He'd go over to Chad's house and give it to Lucy
for safekeeping.…

Chad's house? Why would Lucy be at Chad's place?

He glanced around the cluttered apartment, as if seeing it
for the first time. The place was disgusting. It was as if a clan of
slobs had been living here, rolling around in their own dirt. The
place hadn't been dusted or vacuumed in months. Paper plates
with half-eaten Chinese take-out sat in the middle of the carpet
and on the sofa cushions. What the fuck had Lucy done to the
place? She never would've let the place get like this. It had been
immaculate only the day before. Perhaps the xenomorphs had
been in the apartment. Were they trying to drive him crazy?

The migraines kicked in again. They got him good this
time. A knife to the center of his brain. He fell to his knees,
weeping from the overwhelming pain. He clutched at his own
skull, gritting his teeth, praying to God the pain would stop.

An electromagnetic pulse to the medulla oblongata,
perhaps? Gill had told him that the xenomorphs possessed
deadly psychic powers. Were they trying to kill him from a
distance? Well, they wouldn't succeed. They would not succeed.

He reached out for a dirt-encrusted wall, clawing at a five-
foot-long movie poster of It Conquered the World. The poster tore
down the middle as he pulled himself up to his feet. It felt as if
he were climbing a mountain.

He needed to reach Lucy, make sure she was safe.

What if Chad…? God, no. Would they go that far? Work
through Chad to get at their real target—Mike and his magazine?
Hell, what wouldn't they do? What couldn't they do?

Mike grabbed the last bills he had stored in Lucy's old
jewelry box, the one he'd bought for her birthday. It was one of
the few things she'd left behind when she moved out.

What?

He screamed and tossed the box across the room. It shattered
the third story window and went falling to the street below. He
threw open the door and ran down the stairs. He pushed past
his landlady on the way out and ran towards Gill's convertible.
The box lay shattered in a thousand pieces on the sidewalk
next to a drunken homeless man who was looking up at Mike's

window in confusion and fear. Tears came to Mike's eyes when he saw the shattered box. He had bought that for Lucy on her last birthday. It was one of her prize possessions. She used it every day. In fact, she'd thanked him for it again earlier that day. Thanked him for the thousandth time. She was like that. Lucy was just like that. So grateful for all the little things he did for her. Most women wouldn't notice these gestures or just take them for granted. Lucy took nothing for granted. She was perfect. The perfect woman.

Mike knelt down beside the broken box and sifted through the pieces, hoping to retrieve Lucy's precious jewelry. But there was nothing there. As if the box had been empty from the beginning. Impossible. The homeless man, had he already stolen the jewelry?

He stared at the old man with mounting rage. "Give it back to me."

"Give what back, man?"

Mike thrust his index finger at the concrete. "The jewelry that was in that damn box."

"Fuck you, man. That thing just fell down out of the sky and almost took my head off. There wasn't nothin' in it. Believe me, I looked. Now just fuck off, man. All I'm doin' is tryin' to catch me some shut-eye."

Mike said nothing. He walked back to Gill's convertible, reached under the seat, and pulled out the sword. He walked toward the homeless man with the sword outstretched.

The homeless man saw him coming and began crawling away on all fours. "Hey, hey, man, cool it, I ain't got no beef with you!" The man scrambled to his feet and ran off down the street.

"Give me back that jewelry!" Mike screamed.

The homeless man ran away from him, bobbing and weaving as he did so, almost running into a brick wall. He disappeared into an alley and was gone.

Son of a bitch, Mike thought. Even if the man wasn't a xenomorph, he certainly acted like one. The man was anti-human. He didn't deserve to live. He was just an empty vessel with no soul waiting to be taken over by the alien parasites.

Fuck him, Mike thought. I don't have time for this. I have to find Lucy. I won't tell her about the box, though. I don't think she'd be able to handle it.

He tossed the box into the passenger seat, leaped over the door, slid behind the steering wheel, hit the gas pedal, and pulled away from the curb with a high-pitched screech.

Vampires love to corrupt the innocent. This thought entered Mike's head out of nowhere. Was that an original thought, or had he heard it before? Had Manly P. Hall told him that? Perhaps he'd read it one of Hall's voluminous books?

Lucy was innocent. If she had been corrupted, it stood to reason that the person most responsible was little more than a xenomorph in disguise.

"Lucy?" Mike said as he found himself opening Chad's door. How the hell did he get here so fast? Where was Gill's car? One second, he was driving towards Chad's apartment, and the next....

Lucy and Chad sat at the kitchen table drinking coffee. How Lucy loved her coffee. Mike had never been able to stand the stuff. Mike glanced around the neat and tidy apartment and saw all of Lucy's familiar things filling up the place. Worse yet, they seemed so at home here. How had she moved all her stuff in so short a time?

"What's going on here?" Mike asked.

Lucy looked surprised and frightened...and guilt-ridden. "Mike? What the fuck're you doing here?"

Chad erupted from his seat. Trying to seem masculine for once. For a change. He'd been working out; Mike could see that. Trying to transform himself. Inside and out. For his parents' sake? "Hey, man, you can't just barge into my—!"

Mike ignored him. He glared at Lucy. She looked so beautiful, even now, in this moment of betrayal. "I want an explanation."

Lucy acted confused. "Explanation?"

"Are you cheating on me?" Mike said. "Is that what's going on here?"

"*Cheating* on you?" Chad said. He laughed in that high-pitched way of his. "Lucy's been living with me for over a year."

"No!" said the deformed man, holding Aishe's struggling body in place by her long black hair. He held the stake up to her neck. "If you don't let...Gill go...I'll take her whole head off!"

Dracula hesitated, backed away from Gill's neck.

"What do you care?" said the Monster. "You can always make another one—just as good, maybe even better!"

Dracula nodded. "For once, you've made an excellent point. Very well. You may have her head. I'll just take Gill's in exchange."

Dracula opened his mouth wide and was mere centimeters away from sinking them into Gill's flesh when the Monster roared in surprise and dropped Gill on the stone floor.

Dracula glanced upwards, puzzled. What appeared to be a pale, flesh-colored snake that dwarfed the largest python in the world had wrapped itself around the Monster's entire body.

The Monster tried his best to dislodge the thing. He tried to shake it off, tried to get a grip on the thing in order to rip it off. In his frantic attempts to remove the creature, the Monster spun around, and Dracula saw that the snake had the head of a human being. The face of Krogh. But it was slowly melting.

"Now!" screamed Krogh's dissolving head. "Die, Monster, die!"

The Monster bellowed in response, trying to beat Krogh with his fists. Krogh slithered out of the way just in time and the Monster ended up hitting himself instead. Dracula tried to concentrate, to assert some of his hypnotic control on Krogh, but before he could do so Krogh wrapped himself around the Monster's head, thinned out the posterior of his elastic body until it was only the size of a fist, and began to stuff himself down the Monster's throat. The Monster gurgled in pain as Krogh slowly drowned him in his own melting flesh.

"Die, die, DIE!" Krogh screamed.

It was, possibly, one of the strangest things Dracula had ever seen.

To his left, he heard the click of a revolver being cocked. He turned and saw that Gill had regained his weapon.

Dracula willed himself into mist as Gill fired his gun. The bullet passed right through him.

The Monster had collapsed onto his back. His gurgling death rattles seemed to grow ever more convulsive and violent as the last remnants of Krogh's head disappeared down his throat.

Dracula felt it was time to leave and reevaluate.

He drifted toward the exit as the deformed man shouted in pain. Aishe had sunk her teeth into his hand, forcing him to drop the wooden stake. Gill spun around but did not fire his weapon, no doubt for fear of hitting his friend instead.

Gill slipped the revolver into his belt, ran toward the crippled man, grabbed Aishe by her gown, and pulled her off his friend. It would be very difficult for Gill to hold onto her for long.

"Take the gun out of my belt!" Gill told the deformed man. "Go after Dracula!"

The deformed man nodded, reached out, and avoiding Aishe's wild swipes with her claws, managed to grab the gun from Gill's belt.

Dracula drifted outside, merging with the fog-laden night.

Mike glanced back and forth between the two of them, over and over again, trying to figure out what the hell they thought they were doing. "Is this some kind of sick joke?" Mike asked. He glared at Lucy. "You trying to drive me crazy?"

Lucy rose from her chair slowly and said in soft tones, "The other day I was talking to Eric and he told me you've been acting stranger and stranger lately. What is it? What's wrong? Are you sick or something? Is it the headaches again?"

"Headaches?" Mike reached upwards, closed his eyes, and tried to massage his scalp. "Yes…they're pretty bad. Pretty bad."

Chad said, "Lucy, I want this fucking asshole out of my apartment. Now."

"Just shut up for a second," Lucy said. She drew closer toward Mike. "I think you need to see a doctor, Mike. You need to—"

"I don't need to do anything!" Mike shouted, slamming his fists at the air. "You need to tell me why all your shit is over here at Chad's fucking apartment."

"That's it, this guy's nuts," Chad said. He moved toward Mike. "I'm gonna toss him out on his ass. I knew you were nothing but trouble the first time I laid eyes on you, you son of a bitch. Why don't you go home and finish your fuckin' screenplay?"

"No, please," Lucy said.

Chad ignored her. Chad reached out to grab Mike's shoulder. Mike wrenched it out of his grasp and backed away. For a moment—for a single second—he considered the possibility that he really was crazy. But no. No. That didn't make any sense. Too much of the past year would have to be completely rewritten to make that true. It was too complicated. The simplest solution to any mystery was usually the most logical. The simplest solution was that the xenomorphs were fucking with him. With him and everyone he knew. They were trying to wear him down. Beat on him and beat on him until he was too sick to tell anybody the truth. Until he was so sick that no one would even believe him when he finally *did* tell someone the truth.

The truth was not here in this apartment. He didn't know these people. This wasn't Lucy. These were simulacra. Fakes. Empty masks.

What had they done with Lucy?

Chad said, "Just keep backin' up and everything will be—"

Mike didn't let him finish the sentence. He shrieked and propelled himself onto Chad, pushing both of them back onto the carpet. Mike wrapped his hands around Chad's throat and squeezed, waiting for the gelatinous goo of the xenomorph inside to seep out like noxious syrup. The Chad-thing wasn't expecting it. He tried to break out of Mike's grasp using some fancy karate moves, but no amount of martial arts could be a defense against pure, indignant rage. He watched Chad's face turn redder and redder as the pretentious little director squirmed in Mike's grasp. Too bad he'd left the sword in the car....

"Mike, no, please stop!" Lucy screamed and tried to pull Mike off. The poor girl didn't know. She really thought Chad was human.

"This thing's not human," Mike said as he dug his thumbs into the soft center of the Chad-thing's throat. "It doesn't even need to breathe. I'll show you. I'll show you."

"Mike!" Lucy screamed in hysterics. She stopped trying to pull him off. Instead, she backed away and said. "Listen to me. You're not yourself. You're sick."

Mike just laughed. "*I'm* not myself?"

"Remember the grave? The day we saw the priest eating the donut?"

For some reason all the rage drained out of Mike's body. He released the Chad-thing's throat. "The day we met?"

"Yes. And you said, 'Is this even real? Are we dreaming this?' And I said, 'How can we ever know the answer to that question?' And you said, 'The only way to know is to flap your arms real hard. If you fly, you're dreaming. If not, you're awake.' And you flapped your arms. And you didn't fly."

Mike nodded. He glanced down at Chad gasping on the carpet. The man had bloody scratches on his throat from Mike's fingernails. Mike had never hurt anybody, at least no one human. It didn't make sense that this was Chad. Mike wasn't a violent man. He would never hurt anybody, no one living. That meant this Chad-thing wasn't alive. This was pure logic. Mike wasn't dreaming. He had no intention of flying. He just wanted his life back. He wanted the world to go back to what it was when he woke up this morning: orderly, sane, filled with hope for the future. He had so much more he wanted to write. Ever since he'd met Kurt and Gill, his world had turned upside down. He'd been so focused on his writing that he'd neglected Lucy.

"I'm so sorry," Mike said, the tears coming once more. "I haven't been paying attention to you. I've been working so hard on the magazine. And Gill...well, it's just a stressful situation, me being the only one who knows the whole story. I haven't even told you the whole story, not all of it."

"Story? What story? Who's Gill?"

"Gill. You know. The man I've been working with for the past year. *20th Century Werewolf.*"

"Your novel? The one you've been serializing in the magazine?"

"It's not a novel. It's based on real life. You know that. You've been helping me proofread the chapters as I write them."

"Mike, I haven't helped you on the magazine for months. It's just been you and Eric. I let you have my apartment and I moved in here. You were pissed off at first, but you...you got used to it real quick. Almost too quick. You said you wanted to remain friends. You, me, and Chad, we've gone out to dinner together. Just a couple of weeks ago. Remember? Lucy's El Adobe Café? Mike, I helped with the magazine for a while, then stopped because...because Chad asked me to stop, so I did. Out of respect for him. You were so pissed off; you haven't returned my phone calls since. You honestly don't remember any of this?"

Mike couldn't stop crying. He couldn't figure it out. Was this all an attempt to confuse him? And yet she seemed so sincere....

Part of him wanted to finish the job he started with the Chad-thing; the other part wanted to be sure. He had to be sure.

At this moment there was only one person in the entire world he could trust.

Eric grabbed him by the shoulders and said, "Mike...Mike... can you hear me?"

Mike glanced around. He was standing out on a street corner. He saw the familiar sight of Musso and Frank's just across the street. He was on Hollywood Boulevard, right outside Eric's store. How had he gotten here? Where was Gill's car?

"Where's the car?"

"What car?" Eric said.

"Gill's car. We were attacked in his home. They came in and forced us to run. We hightailed it in Gill's convertible. But they pulled him out. I don't know what happened to him."

"Gill?" Eric said. "Who the fuck is Gill?"

Mike so rarely heard Eric curse like that. It was a little shocking.

"What's wrong, Eric? Are you feeling okay?"

"Am I feeling okay? I was just about to open the store when I saw you wandering around out here. You look horrible. What happened to your hair?"

Mike reached up and ran his hand over a bald scalp. He had no hair on his head at all. Had he shaved it, or had it just fallen out?

"Mike...you look a little confused."

"Confused?" He glanced up at the sun. "What time is it?"

"It's just before ten a.m. You know when I open the store."

"Ten a.m.? What day is it?"

"Friday."

"Friday. Jesus. A whole day has passed since I saw Lucy. Is Lucy okay?"

"Lucy's fine. But I don't know about you. Listen, Chad called the cops on you, Mike. That wasn't a smart move. I knew you were upset about Lucy leaving you, but you seemed to be handling it fine. I never thought…Jesus, Mike, you need to turn yourself in. It's only going to get worse from here."

Mike laughed. "Worse? You don't even know how worse this can get. Don't you even hear what I'm telling you? They got Gill. They killed him. Everything he told me was true. It wasn't fiction at all."

"Mike, please tell me who Gill is."

Mike sighed in frustration. "You know who Gill is. We've only been working with the man for a year now. I called him Gill in the manuscript."

"Gill? The *character*? In *20th Century Werewolf*?"

"The manuscript. Oh my God. We've got to find Gill's car. My manuscript is still in there. I've gotta give it to you."

"Okay, calm down. I'll help you. Well…when I first spotted you, you were walking from that direction." Eric pointed west on Hollywood Boulevard. "Maybe you parked down there somewhere, on one of the side streets?"

"Yes, that's possible. Let's go." Mike sprinted down Hollywood Boulevard, Eric following close behind. They eventually found the convertible parked halfway on the sidewalk and halfway on the street on Las Palmas just off Hollywood Boulevard, not far from The Egyptian Theatre. The car looked like a wreck. The fender was gone and the trunk looked like it'd been back ended several hundred times since yesterday.

"Where'd you get this car?" Eric asked.

"I *told* you," Mike said. "It's Gill's. We were driving up in the Hollywood Hills near his mansion when we were attacked."

"Okay," Eric said. "Do you have the keys?"

Mike patted himself down, and was relieved to discover a ring of keys in his back pocket. He popped open the trunk, reached in, and pulled out two items: a 400-page manuscript held together with two rubber bands as well as Gill's sword.

"Thank God they didn't get the manuscript or the sword," Mike said.

Eric backed away from him a few steps. "Um...where'd you get *that*?" Eric pointed at the blade.

"It belonged to Gill's father. You should've seen Gill use this thing. It was impressive. He had it in his hand when they pulled him out of the car." Mike stopped and thought about that for a second. He distinctly remembered Gill having it in his hand when Mike hit the gas and sped off. So, how did it end up back in the car? So many things didn't add up....

"Who's they?" Eric asked.

"You'll know for sure when you read the rest of the manuscript," Mike said. "It's all here."

Eric held out his hand and said, "Why don't you give me the sword?"

"No. Take the manuscript." He handed it to Eric. "I'm holding onto the sword for now. I don't know if you can use this as well as I can. Just in case they attack." He glanced from side to side. "You'd be surprised at how fast these things can be. Let's go back to the store and barricade the door before it's too late."

"Okay, sure," Eric said and tucked the manuscript under his armpit. "Should we move the car?"

"There's no time. Let's get back to the store." Mike sprinted back the way they had come with Eric straggling several steps behind. "C'mon," Mike shouted over his shoulder. "Before one of 'em spots us."

"I have to tell you, Mike, you kind of stand out what with that sword in your hand and all. Even on Hollywood Boulevard."

"Perhaps," Mike said. "Perhaps. Good thinking. I'll have to find a weapon that's more easily concealed if I'm going to continue Gill's work."

In fact, Mike noticed that people were staring at both of them strangely. Even the gangster rappers milling around on the corner gave them a wide berth, a rare gesture in Los Angeles. Mike wondered how many of these people wandering around on Hollywood Boulevard at 10:22 in the morning were actually human.

Nina ran through the streets of London, the demon only a few yards behind her. She didn't even have time to turn around and fire off another shot. If she could just get him cornered somewhere…imprison him someplace where she could fire shot after shot until he was dead….

That's when she remembered what she'd heard on the radio earlier this morning.

She ran for the Thames.

A few doors down from Tinseltown Book & Poster, Mike said to Eric, "Okay, let's go through the back way just in case they booby trapped the front entrance."

"The back door could just as easily be booby trapped as the front," Eric said.

Mike thought about that for a moment. "You're right. Let's go through the front then. Use reverse psychology on them."

Eric slipped his key into the front door and swung it open. Mike pushed past him and entered the store with the sword held out before him as if he were a samurai. He didn't want any of the creatures to get the drop on him in case they were lying in wait.

Eric closed the door behind them. "Listen, Mike, there's no one here but us. Just put the sword down. I don't want you to accidentally hurt yourself."

"Shhh," Mike said. "Listen." Mike craned his neck and listened intently, trying to discern if anyone else lurked in the bowels of the store. It didn't seem so. They were alone. Safe. At last. Mike lowered the blade and allowed the tip to rest on the floor. The thing was so damn heavy. How did an old man like Gill wield the weapon with such grace?

Eric breathed a sigh of relief. He pulled up a stool. "Here, why don't you sit down, Mike?"

"I don't have time to sit." Jesus, he could feel another migraine coming on.

The strength of this she-vampire was enormous. Gill didn't know how long he could keep her fangs away from his throat.

Desperate measures might have to be taken.

Back in Visaria, Dr. Heidelmann had managed to discover a cure for Lawrence Gill's affliction. At first Gill had thought it to be foolproof and permanent. That is, until he grew curious and began researching the scientific principles behind it. Heidelmann had told him that his unwanted transformations were brought about because his metabolism was "like a steam engine without a balance wheel." If anything, this one pitiful simile tipped Gill off to Heidelmann's little scheme.

Since there was no real cure for Gill's condition, Heidelmann had attempted a placebo...and it had worked, by God, it had worked.

But after a few months, when Gill realized what Heidelmann had done, he'd also realized the incredible power of the human mind to overcome any affliction, including cancer and leukemia and polio...and lycanthropy.

Instead of reverting to his former state, Gill's realization had an effect that not even Dr. Heidelmann could have hoped for.

He could, when he really wanted, bring about his transformation through sheer force of will.

Which is what he did right now.

The expression on the she-vampire's face was one of extreme pleasure when Gill released her from his grip. He sank to his knees, sobbing in pain. Through his peripheral vision he watched her approaching his crumpled body, her talons outstretched. Then he looked up into her eyes and watched her expression dissolve into one of confusion and even fear.

Not even vampires fancy werewolves.

Gill leaped up off the floor and sank his fangs into the she-vampire's neck, rending her stomach open with his claws, tearing out the viscera as she shrieked as only the dead can shriek when they find themselves dying all over again. And for the last time.

Then Gill went to work on her neck.

"Okay, *I'll* sit then." Eric lowered himself to the stool, keeping one foot on the floor. "Listen... you need to do a couple of things in the next few minutes if you don't want to end up in jail for a very long time. You need to put the sword away, and you need to start thinking clearly. Okay? Just let me pick up the phone. They'll go easier on you if you—"

"Who do you want to call?"

"We need to get the police down here as soon as possible."

"The police. Why?"

"Didn't you say you were attacked? Don't you think you need to report that?"

Mike laughed and shook his head back and forth. "Eric, Eric, you just don't understand. You don't think these things wouldn't make themselves look like police officers? How do I know who to trust?"

"You can trust me, can't you?"

"Of course, but...but you don't understand the entire situation."

"Explain it to me, then."

"It's all in the manuscript. You've read the first half already, in the magazine, but not the second half. That's the good stuff. Particularly the chapter about 1963."

"I don't think I really have time to read it right now. Time is of the essence, Mike. Don't you agree?"

"Yeah, of course, but—"

"Why don't we call the police right now, and I'll read it while they're on their way over here? You see, they're looking for you right now. Because of what you did to Chad."

"Chad's not even human!" Mike screamed. "Don't you understand that? Are you even listening to me?"

"I'm listening."

"No, you're not." Mike fell to his knees. The pain hit him again, this time in his temples. He dropped the sword and dug his fingers into his scalp. "Vampires are real. People really can turn into monsters, Eric. I've seen it. Possession. Real, actual possession. Not fiction. Spirits from other worlds can take the form of humans. I've seen flesh melt in front of my face. What's making that ringing noise?"

"I don't hear anything."

The white spots returned. Amorphous blobs dancing in front of his vision. They reached out for him with pale, spindly arms. They stared at him with uncaring eyes. Each mass of protoplasm possessed only a single eye. Cyclops.

"Cyclops," Mike whispered. He could hear something moving toward him. Spear it in the eye, he thought.

He lifted the sword and lunged forward. He heard Eric screaming, "Stop!" Was Eric screaming at The Cyclops? Or was Eric himself The Cyclops? Why did he want him to call the cops so much? Was he in on it?

"Are you in on it?" Mike asked. "Are you one of them?"

"No," he heard Eric say. "Just stay back, please. You don't want to do this." Mike kept backing up. He'd gotten all turned around. Now his back was pressed up against the front door. The white lights abated for a second, just long enough for him to see Eric running towards the back room. Why was he running? Did he feel guilty about something? Mike would get the answer out of him if he had to....

Ygor scanned the mist with his eagle eyes (this body, despite its handicaps, had been a trained hunter before the original owner had abandoned it). The mist that had once been Dracula's body was discernible amidst the heavier fog. There was a slight reddish tint to it that prevented it from camouflaging itself completely from view.

Ygor aimed at the mist and fired Gill's revolver.

Never before had Ygor heard mist scream.

Apparently, Gill's special bullets still maintained some effect even when a vampire was immaterial. Ygor couldn't have been happier. He wouldn't be satisfied until there were no more monsters in the world, whether undead or not.

The mist reformed into Dracula's physical body about a block away from where Ygor stood. He saw the tails of Dracula's tuxedo disappear around the side of a building. Ygor ran in pursuit.

Ygor chased him past the remnants of what had once been

Khalid Banoub's grand Masonic Temple, over the ruins of multi-story buildings that had been smashed to bits by some unknown force of destruction, toward the banks of the River Thames.

He screamed and charged the door in the back. It slammed in his face. He heard it lock from the other side. "Let me in!" Mike screamed, attacking the door with the blade. "Let me in! Don't call the cops! If you're my friend, you won't call! If you're my friend...." No friend would urge him to call the enemy like that. Eric wasn't his friend. What was this *thing* in human form? Where was the real Eric? Was he already dead? Mike would do his best to save him by killing this creature that had taken his place.

The blade managed to cut a nice vertical hole in the door within a few minutes. He peeked through and could see Eric hiding behind his desk with the phone in his hand.

"Stay back," Eric said. "I've got a gun in here!"

"The real Eric never owned a gun!" Mike said. "That just proves it! You've gotta go, you cyclopean son of a bitch!" And then the white blobs returned, sending him to his knees again. He was almost out of breath. The pain in his skull felt like atomic fire, like the breath of Godzilla compressed to the size of a nickel within his brain.

He heard voices behind him: "Holy shit!

What the fuck?"

He spun around and saw two Asian teenage boys standing in the front entrance to the store. Mike recognized them. The pair who liked to hang out in the "erotic" section. "Run and get help!" Mike said. "I've got a monster trapped in this back room here."

"A monster?" one boy said. "What...kind of monster?"

The second boy grabbed the collar of the first one and tried to drag him away. "Don't start up a conversation! Let's just go get a cop!"

"No!" Mike said. "The cops are monsters too."

"Go!" the second boy said.

"I can't let you do that!" Mike screamed and chased after

them down the aisle. They could not be allowed to alert the xenomorphs. He didn't want to, didn't want to at all, but he'd have to do something drastic to prevent them from inadvertently destroying humanity.

Nina just barely dodged the razor-sharp point of one of the scorpion's legs and dashed out onto the frozen Thames. The demon was so intent on capturing Nina in its multiple jaws that it followed her right onto the frozen surface.

Nina backed away from it, loading another arrow into her crossbow. She watched the ice beginning to crack beneath its weight.

It paused, as if confused by the sound.

"C'mon!" Nina shouted. "Just a little closer!" She aimed the crossbow, fired, and hit the hissing cat-head in its left eye. It emitted a long, drawn-out scream, then bobbed limply on the shuddering body. She got it right in the brain.

The bearded head screamed something in a language Nina did not recognize. The scorpion body scuttled toward Nina a little further, the cracks spreading, spreading.

Nina loaded another arrow into the crossbow.

That's when Nina heard the sound of footsteps behind her. She turned and saw a man in a tuxedo running out onto the ice.

It was Dracula.

Somehow, he didn't seem that frightening anymore.

"I hope you brought a crossbow with you!" she shouted, spun around, and fired another arrow at the demon. The arrow hit the croaking toad right between the eyes.

Someone tackled him from behind. "Let me go!" Mike yelled. This was the first time he'd ever seen Eric work up a sweat. Mike swung at him with the sword, but Eric grabbed his wrist and squeezed, then slammed Mike's hand onto the edge of a bookshelf filled with discounted film books. *The Art of W.C. Fields* by William Everson fell off the shelf and slammed into Mike's head. Mike screamed in horror and frustration as his grip loosened and the sword went tumbling onto the floor. Eric looked up at the kids still huddled in the doorway and said, "Go get some help!" The kids hesitated. Then one of the kids reached out for Gill's sword, nabbed it, and both of the little tykes took off down Hollywood Boulevard. In that moment Eric was too distracted to prevent Mike from kicking him in the balls. Eric groaned and collapsed onto his side. Mike knew this store as well as Eric. He knew Eric kept a toolbox under the cash register. Mike grabbed the W.C. Fields book and tossed it at Eric's skull, leaped to his feet, then vaulted over the counter. Eric staggered after him, but not before Mike had a slotted screwdriver in his fist. "You're one of them," Mike said. "I know that now."

The white blobs returned to obscure his vision. Some kind of power possessed by these aliens.

"Listen to my voice," Eric said. "This is Eric. I don't know who you think I am—"

Gill had said that the cyclopean aliens were most vulnerable in the eye. Hadn't he said that?

"The eye has to go," Mike said and charged Eric. He pushed Eric up against a shelf containing a complete VHS collection of Bela Lugosi's Monogram Nine. *Invisible Ghost* fell off the shelf and hit Mike in the shoulder, but he ignored it. He lifted the screwdriver high into the air, then brought it down in a swift arc towards Eric's right eye. Right eye? His only eye? Mike could only see a single eye in the middle of Eric's forehead. Eric was melting at that second into a xenomorph. The xenomorph was screaming, "No, no, *please!*" The thing reached out and grabbed Mike's arms with its weird tentacles. But the tentacles weren't strong enough. The screwdriver stabbed Eric in the face and the neck, drawing blood. He couldn't quite jab the weapon into the alien's eye. So many tentacles in the way. He lifted the screwdriver into the air one last time, confident he had opened a clear path towards the offending pupil when the most crippling migraine of them all burst in the center of his skull, blowing Mike off his feet like a bomb hidden inside his body. He fell backwards against one of the horror shelves, *Hangover Square* and *House of Horrors* (in Beta) flying off the top shelf and hitting him in the right temple, making the pain even worse. The light was so blinding, he couldn't even see. The xenomorph had done something to him. He heard Eric scrambling to his feet, running away. He heard a door slam. The back room? Yes. He charged toward it, slamming his entire body against the door, stabbing the thin wood with the screwdriver. "I won't let you get away with it!" Mike screamed. "What did you do with Eric? What did you do with him?"

He reared back on one leg and slammed his foot against the doorknob, or where he thought the doorknob should be, until the door swung inward with a bang. The light began to recede. He saw Eric hiding behind his desk with a black rotary phone in his hand. His entire head and shirt were covered in blood. Red blood.

Xenomorphs didn't have red blood, did they?

Aliens disguised as cops tackled Mike around the waist and dragged him to the wooden floor. Fear filled Mike's brain. He screamed, pushed both cops off him, and rose to his feet, and tried to get at Eric again. Then the nightsticks came out. Mike's knees buckled. Something the size of a planet rammed into Mike's stomach. All the air left his body. But still he didn't go down. Five minutes of continuous pummeling from the cops' fists finally brought Mike to his knees again. And he dropped the screwdriver. And his jaw went one way and his consciousness went another. And the white light claimed him at last.

22.

The Werewolf ran through the streets of London far faster than Lawrence Gill could ever hope to do. He loped through the fog, sometimes on all fours, past crowds of grief-stricken bystanders whose homes had been destroyed by something huge.

Confused, the Werewolf followed Nina's scent to the edge of the Thames.

Then he became *really* confused.

When he saw Nina standing between a demon out of man's worst nightmares and the Lord of the Undead himself, the Werewolf reverted to his human form and dashed over to the edge of the frozen river where Ygor stood staring in shock at the three-headed demon.

"What *is* that thing?" Gill said to Ygor.

Ygor said, "I thought...*you* might know. It's called Onbuljah."

"I'm afraid I've never had the pleasure," Gill said. "But I know I'm not going to let it get Nina." Gill ripped the revolver from Ygor's hands. He aimed at the bearded head and pulled the trigger. Nothing happened.

Out of bullets.

Gill could only stare in frustration as the thing drew ever nearer to his beloved wife.

It all happened so suddenly. The cracks spread, the ice snapped, and everyone and everything went sinking into the Thames: Onbuljah, Dracula, and Nina.

"Nina!" Gill shouted.

He ran across the ice that was still intact and threw himself into the freezing water.

The demon thrashed around in anger, trying to escape the water. Nina latched onto the neck of the bearded head, aimed her crossbow at his forehead at point blank range, and fired. The arrow plunged directly into his brain. The scorpion's tail continued to thrash around in the water, but only out of reflex. The body sank to the bottom of the Thames, taking Nina down with it.

23.

Bela Lugosi was dressed like a mad scientist in a white lab coat with crazy looking goggles wrapped around his wizened face. Tesla coils sparked behind Lugosi like the flames of hells in a Goya etching. By his side stood a malformed assistant, some mutant hybrid of Tor Johnson and Dwight Frye. The assistant asked Lugosi if there was anything he could do to Mike while Lugosi readied his equipment.

"Yes," Lugosi said. "Play with him. Keep his mind off the proceedings."

Tor/Dwight nodded and moved toward Mike slowly. He gave Mike a glossy magazine with a beautiful woman on the cover. Perhaps it was *Reader's Digest* or *Parenting*. Tor/Dwight flipped the glossy pages to an article on page ninety-six about horror films and what modern moms should know about them. "I know you like these things," the hunchbacked giant mumbled.

Mike glanced at Lugosi. "Wh—what's he going to do to me?" Mike asked.

"He's just examining you," said Tor/Dwight. "It won't hurt a bit."

"Indeed, do not be alarmed, my friend," said Lugosi. "My name is Dr. Vornoff, and I couldn't help overhearing your concerns. Just relax and read a magazine. This examination won't hurt a bit. You needn't worry about us performing surgery on you any time soon. You see, the tumor is so large and so precariously positioned, that we couldn't possibly remove it without killing you in the process. So, I'm afraid you're stuck with your little friend inside your brain. You just have to get used to each other."

"Will it just keep getting bigger and bigger?" Mike asked.

"Hopefully not," Varnoff said. "Who's to say in this crazy world?"

"So…it's an alien. An alien taking over my brain. Slowly."

"So slowly you wouldn't even notice it at first. The technology of the beings who placed it in your head must be quite advanced indeed. Too bad no earthly science can combat it…yet. But, as you know, Earth is filled with very clever people. Scientists who look like tennis pros. And they're all working on your problem now. Who knows? At some point in the future, perhaps we separate you from your little friend. And you can both move on to live productive lives."

"And in the meantime?"

"In the meantime, you will stay here. And enjoy yourself."

"What about Lucy? Is she all right?"

"She's, as you say, all right."

"Can she come and see me?"

"If she wishes."

"And Eric?"

"He's been asking about you."

"And Gill? Is he…?"

"No one's heard from him lately. It's possible he's gone underground and is continuing the good fight against these evil creatures."

"So, you understand what we're up against?"

Vornoff clasped his long, wrinkled hands over his waist and nodded like a kindly grandfather. He sighed with world weariness. "I understand all."

And Tor/Dwight bent down and offered Mike a cookie. It was a Fig Newton.

24.

Wolfgang von Frankenstein, his wife Elsie, their thirteen-year-old son Paul, Ygor, Lawrence Gill, and his wife Nina all sat around the long table in the Gills' dining room.

They were laughing as Nina poured more wine.

"An incredible tale," Elsie said. "I wouldn't have believed it myself if I hadn't read it in the newspaper. Well, what little they decided to print."

"Even though you experienced it yourself?" Wolfgang asked.

"Nothing's real until it's in the newspaper, my dear," said Elsie. "You know that."

"What are your plans from here, Ygor?" Nina asked. "That *is* what you want to be called now, right?"

Ygor shrugged. "I've gotten…used to it. Why not?"

"Ygor is welcome to stay at our home as long as he wishes," Elsie said. She was a little tipsy. The Gills liked to store a lot of liquor in the house.

"That's very kind," Ygor said, "but…I wouldn't want to live off…the kindness of others. I want to make…my own way…in this world."

"Work for us," Lawrence Gill said.

"That's a wonderful idea," Nina said. "We need another operative. We can't handle all these caseloads by ourselves."

"But…do you really think I'm qualified?" Ygor asked.

"To investigate the supernatural and the uncanny?" Gill said. "Who could be *more* qualified?"

"When you…put it that way…I suppose…I can't refuse."

"Excellent!" Nina said. "I think this calls for another glass of wine!"

"Why not?" Gill said.

"What's your next case?" Wolfgang asked.

"The American government wants us to track down some kind of bloodthirsty murderer lurking in the jungles of the Amazon. Hopefully it's nothing but a legend."

"Let's drink to that!" Wolfgang said.

And they all laughed and clinked their glasses together and continued to drink long into the night.

25.

The aliens stashed him away in a tall tower in downtown Los Angeles. He wasn't allowed to go outside. There were other prisoners there. But, unlike Mike, these people seemed to be genuinely crazy. Of course, the aliens thought that their insanity would rub off on Mike. But Mike had a very strong will. That plan never succeeded. Sometimes, however, the loneliness threatened to push him over the edge. He felt like Nell Bowen from *Bedlam* (RKO, 1946), or Patrick McGoohan from *The Prisoner* (ITC, 1967-68).

He missed Eric.

He missed the bookstore.

He missed his apartment.

He missed the magazine.

He missed so much about the outside world.

Above all else, he missed Lucy. She never even came to visit him. He never received any visitors in the tower. Did his friends even know he was here?

…no visitors, that is, until one day a guard unlocked his soft white room and told him that an old friend had dropped by to see him.

Mike managed to rise to his feet, knowing it *must* be Lucy.

It wasn't.

Nonetheless, he was so happy to see a familiar face.

He was still alive. Mike tried to hug Gill, but he couldn't move his arms. They were restrained. The alien guards had punished him for trying to puncture one of their evil, cyclopean eyes.

"How…how did you manage to get in here?" Mike asked.

Gill patted him on the shoulder and told him to sit down. "Just rest for a bit. You've done enough for The Cause already." He leaned in close to Mike's ear and whispered, "Me and my friends are trying to bust you out of here. At the moment, me and the aliens have reached a truce. A mutual understanding. I have something they want, and they have something I want. Namely, you."

"What is it that they want from you?"

Gill waved away the question. "They want me. But don't worry. I've agreed to do something for them—something relatively minor—in exchange for being able to see you today. I knew your spirits must be very low indeed. And so, I brought you a present. You can't keep it, I'm afraid, but at least I can show it to you. I don't know if you'll ever be able to see these images again, so make sure you commit them to memory."

Helen Whemple, who in another life had been the Princess Mehet-uret, awoke in a rumpled queen-sized bed. Her husband Frank came into the bedroom holding a silver tray bearing eggs, bacon, grapefruit, toast, and tea. A copy of the morning newspaper lay on the tray as well.

"What a wonderful surprise," Helen said sleepily. "But set it down on the floor for a second. I want you to just lie here next to me."

"Your wish is my command," Frank said and crawled into bed with her.

"According to the paper," Frank said, "there was some kind of tragedy on the Thames last night. And the Masonic Temple was shattered to bits."

"Hm? Oh, really?" Helen said, yawning. "That's interesting... but not as interesting as you. Come here."

Frank and Helen leaned in for a kiss that lasted such a long time, while breakfast grew colder and colder.

Gill walked over to the door and called out for the guard through the tiny barred window. "Please bring it in now."

The alien guard pushed a small sixteen-millimeter projector into the room, then left Mike and Gill alone with it. From under his coat, Gill removed a reel of film and slipped it into the projector.

Mike said, "Is that—?"

Gill raised his finger to his lips. "Shh. You've earned this. Say nothing more." He flicked on the projector. White light shot out at the soft wall. But this light was quite different from the kind that assaulted him during his migraines. This was a comfortable white light, the kind that embraced you and made you feel like a child again. It made you feel as if you had returned home at long last.

A pale white hand, its double-jointed fingers clutching at the banks of the Thames like the legs of a spider, emerged from the cracked ice, clawing at the earth as the first rays of dawn began to burn away the fog that hung over London like an oppressive cobweb, or perhaps like the lid of an enormous coffin.

A lid that was now opening, slowly.

Gill sat beside him quietly, not saying a word. He didn't want to ruin the experience for Mike. This was a holy moment. This soft cell was a place of communion with God...or the gods. One of those gods was now being projected on the screen in luminous silver. A hideous golem, almost nine feet tall, stitched together from the castoff body parts of men who had once been great, or nearly-great, rose from a surgical table in a moment of pure expressionist terror. Black and white reality. And this moment, the moment Lugosi-as-Monster raised his shaking hands up towards the rays of a fading sun, was the ultimate representation of reality. It was nightmare given three dimensions. Hell made manifest on a creaky soundstage in Universal City in the fall of 1931. It was beauty. It was *Guernica* and *The Scream* and Goya's etchings all merged into one inexplicable micro-second.

He'd never seen Lugosi look more beautiful.

The miraculous sight dampened every migraine Mike had ever experienced.

The sound of the projector filled the tiny room, Mike's entire universe, as Gill faded away slowly. The old man's job was done, at least for the moment.

Tears streamed down onto Mike's restraints.
Shaking hands.
A fading sun.
Blackness.
The end of a test reel.

Until the gods chose to rewind the reel and begin once more.

ACKNOWLEDGEMENTS

I'd like to offer a tip of my gentleman's hat to the following people for their invaluable assistance in bringing this project to fruition: Eric Blair, Mike Copner, David Dodd, Chris Doyle, Joe & Karen Guffey, Melissa Guffey, Olivia Guffey, Randy Koppang, Patricia Lee Macomber, Catherine Bottolfson McCallum, Gary D. Rhodes, Craig Spector, and David Niall Wilson.

ABOUT THE AUTHOR

Robert Guffey is a lecturer in the Department of English at California State University – Long Beach. His most recent book is *Widow of the Amputation and Other Weird Crimes* (Eraserhead Press, 2021). 2019 marked the publication of *Bela Lugosi and the Monogram Nine*, coauthored with Gary D. Rhodes (Bear Manor Media). In 2017 came *Until the Last Dog Dies* (Night Shade/Skyhorse), a darkly satirical novel about a young stand-up comedian who must adapt as best he can to an apocalyptic virus that destroys only the humor centers of the brain. Guffey's previous books include the journalistic memoir *Chameleo: A Strange but True Story of Invisible Spies, Heroin Addiction, and Homeland Security* (OR Books, 2015), which *Flavorwire* called, "By many miles, the weirdest and funniest book of [the year]." A graduate of the famed Clarion Writers Workshop in Seattle, he has also written *Spies & Saucers* (PS Publishing, 2014), a collection of three novellas set in the 1950s. His first book of nonfiction, *Cryptoscatology: Conspiracy Theory as Art Form*, was published in 2012. He's written stories and articles for numerous magazines and anthologies, among them *The Believer, Black Cat Mystery Magazine, Black Dandy, The Evergreen Review, The Los Angeles Review of Books, The Mailer Review, Phantom Drift, Postscripts, Rosebud, Salon, The Third Alternative,* and *TOR.com. Bela Lugosi's Dead* is his second novel. His website is Cryptoscatology.com.

Curious about other Crossroad Press books?
Stop by our site:
http://store.crossroadpress.com
We offer quality writing
in digital, audio, and print formats.